Books by J. Lloyd Morgan

The Bariwon Chronicles
The Hidden Sun
The Waxing Moon
The Zealous Star

Bring Down the Rain

Wall of Faith

Going Down the Far Well

National Bestseller

The Mirror of the Soul
(Written in conjunction with Chris de Burgh)

The Night the Port-A-Potty Burned Down and Other Stories

The Howler King Trilogy
Darker the Shadow
Stronger the Barrier
Brighter the Light

Darker the Shadow

J. Lloyd Morgan

Pendr Publishing

To Pendr, for nudging me over the years to put his story into words

INTRODUCTION

When novelists are asked, "How do you write a book?" the answers will differ. Personally, my books are centered on the characters. When I sit down to write, I think to myself, "Ok, which character is this chapter about, and where did I leave off with him or her?" From there, I begin to write and see what happens. For me, that is the most enjoyable part of the writing process.

A friend who read an early draft of this book asked, "What will be the storyline of the next book in the series?" My answer? "I don't know. However, I can't wait to find out."

That isn't to say I don't have a general idea where my books are headed, but I've found the journey to be more interesting if the destination is somewhat of a mystery.

For this book, it got its start several years ago. A character, Pendr, developed in my mind while I wrote The Bariwon Chronicles. He was an interesting enough of a character to inspire the short story "The Howler King." I thought that story would be enough to appease Pendr, but this book indicates I was wrong.

While exploring more of Pendr's story, a whole new world of characters and settings opened up to me. I hope you enjoy getting to know these characters as I did.

Chapter 1

The day Wyjec understood death, he understood power.

The Masters of Sothcar had power because they controlled who lived and who died. They ate their fill while Wyjec and the other chardi survived on scraps and thick gruel. "Be thankful," the Masters had told the chardi. "We rescued you from certain death. All we ask in return is unquestioned devotion."

Wyjec knelt in a row with thirteen chardi, head to the ground, and palms flat against the cold, stone floor. The smell of unwashed bodies assaulted his nostrils. He and the rest of the chardi were not allowed to bathe. Water was life, and the Masters controlled the water. The stone walls of the palace sometimes gathered moisture, and Wyjec was not above licking what water he could while the Masters were otherwise engaged.

"We are indebted to the Masters. We owe the Masters all. We live to serve the Masters." Wyjec uttered the praises along with his fellow chardi to the men in front of him. The mantra would repeat until the Masters told them to stop. Only then would the chardi be allowed to eat. Only then would the chardi be allowed to live.

A Master, tall and heavy, walked to Wyjec. Deliberately, the Master placed his thick leather boot on Wyjec's hand, and then the large man shifted his weight, causing Wyjec's fingers to crack under the pressure. Still, Wyjec prayed vocally, reciting the words. Crying out would show unworthiness. Pain lanced up his arm, but he would not give in. At nearly twice his size, the Master could do what he wanted, and there was nothing Wyjec could do to stop him.

"We are indebted to the Masters. We owe the Masters all. We live to serve the Masters," Wyjec chanted again. The pain became almost too unbearable. Wyjec was no match for the Master, let alone the rest of them who stood and watched. *Protection*, he thought. *I need protection.*

There. A trickle in his mind, like tasting cool water on a hot day. It was small, but the trickle was present. Careful not to let it slip away, Wyjec focused on the pain from the Master crushing his fingers. The trickle seeped forward through his mind, down his neck, to his shoulder and arm, then his hand. The pain began to lessen, though Wyjec could still sense the pressure of the Master's foot.

Abruptly, the pain ceased. In its place, Wyjec's hand acted as if encased in a plate gauntlet, though it appeared no different to his eyes. At the same moment, his body became weakened—a feeling akin to having just climbed several flights of stairs. His heart did not beat any faster, yet every part of him felt tired. Still, the pain in his hand was gone. The trade-off of fatigue was worth it. He continued to chant, though his mind was not on the words he spoke. *What's this? What's stopping the pain?* He had an idea but dared not believe it to be true.

After a moment, the heavy-set Master removed his foot. "This chardi has proven his worth," he intoned. The Master moved to the chardi on Wyjec's left. He was of an age with Wyjec, not quite a man, yet too old to be a boy. They were friends, as much as possible in the Masters' palace. Once again, the Master stepped on the chardi's hand. Unlike Wyjec, this chardi cried out.

"Why do you cry out, chardi?" the Master demanded. "Is it you lack the strength to serve us? Are you so weak that even a little pain distracts you from your devotion?"

Wyjec continued to chant, along with the other chardi. It was dangerous to acknowledge the conflict. For a fleeting moment, he wondered if he could protect the other young man. *I don't understand how I helped myself. How can I help him?*

"Chardi!" the Master shouted to the rest of the kneeling figures. "You have an unworthy among you!"

Being labeled unworthy meant one thing: death.

None of the chardi moved to help the one labeled unworthy as the Masters dragged him to the front of the room. None of the chardi dared flinch when the unworthy was beheaded. None of the chardi dared hope. None of the chardi even believed in the *possibility* of hope.

None except Wyjec. *If the Masters cannot harm me, they hold no power over me.*

Chapter 2

Pendr stepped out from the darkened blacksmith's workshop and into the sunlight. There, down the dirt-packed road, he could see the king's bannermen. Nothcar's green standard, the symbol of an evergreen tree embroidered with silver thread, fluttered in the spring breeze.

"They're coming!" Pendr called out. "Father, come see!"

"One moment, my boy," Osbrik said from inside the smithy.

Word of the king's men visiting the town had arrived two days previous. Pendr's father had expressed his doubts of the news and had told his son not to hope for what might not be. However, the traveling merchant's word proved true.

Atop large stallions, knights rode with silver plate mail glimmering in the mid-day sun. Even their mounts wore armor trimmed in silver and green. They approached steadily, seeming to ignore the townspeople while at the same time observing everything.

The vanguard had reached the smithy by the time Osbrik emerged. Neither father nor son spoke as they watched the knights head toward the town center. Pendr counted fourteen knights in all, a lucky number. He hoped it was a good omen.

"C'mon then, my boy," Osbrik said. "Let's see what this is all about."

The town of Logs Pond was in a remote part of Nothcar, away from most main roads that led from the king's castle to other larger towns in the kingdom. While roughly eight hundred people lived in the town proper, at least twice that many lived on the farms around the area. Visits from the realm's protectors were uncommon. The last time Pendr recalled seeing knights was when he was twelve winters. Six winters had come and gone since then, but he still enjoyed revisiting the memories of seeing the gallant men mounted on war horses.

A group of townsfolk followed behind the knights, whispering excitedly to each other. Pendr and his father joined the throng.

"Why are they here?" Pendr asked.

Osbrik's face tightened. "Could be a number of things. We shall see."

Logs Pond's town center was oval shaped with a large fountain in the middle. The land roundabout was mainly forest, with red maples being the most predominate. The granite used in the construction of the fountain had to be shipped in from the mountains in the west. It was not easy, but Osbrik had explained to Pendr when he was younger that custom dictated that each town or village have a fountain at its center, though he was unclear why.

The knights rode around the fountain, and it seemed to Pendr that the lead knight was inspecting it. Appearing satisfied, the knights came to a stop in front of the largest building in town: the mayor's home.

Mayor Lonz was already standing on his porch which doubled as a platform for town meetings. He wore a green tunic embroidered with silver stitching—the tree symbol matching the knight's banners. Pendr had only seen him wear the outfit on the most prestigious of occasions. The mayor's long, white hair cascaded over his wide shoulders.

"Welcome to Logs Pond," Mayor Lonz boomed. "We are honored to have knights from the realm visit us. We offer our hospitality."

The town center now contained what Pendr guessed was nearly every person in the nearby area. He spotted his mother and three younger siblings on the other side, but there was no way to get to them without pushing people out of the way.

For a moment, none of the knights spoke; they remained still as statues. Slowly, the knight at the front lifted the visor of his helm. Pendr could only see him from the side, but it was enough to tell that the knight had a thick, dark mustache which connected with his trimmed beard.

"I am Fueron, Knight of Nothcar. We accept your welcome. We shan't be here long. We bring grim tidings from King Viskum."

"Oh?" Mayor Lonz asked, his face paling. "And what tidings are these?"

Fueron responded by turning his horse to face the crowd. The multitude stood quietly on, watching. The knight peered out at the townsfolk, his facial expression unreadable to Pendr.

"War," the knight said.

The crowd's reaction was palpable. Mothers held infants closer to their chests. The elderly looked at the ground and shook their heads. Pendr felt his father wrap a muscular arm around his shoulder.

"War?" Mayor Lonz asked. His face had turned nearly as white as his hair.

Fueron nodded. "For a generation, this town has enjoyed the hard-won peace achieved by King Viskum. Alas, it was not meant to endure. The southern part of the realm has come under attack, with the enemy capturing the town of Iredell. The king intends to respond with no small measure of force."

The grip on Pendr's shoulder tightened, though he wasn't sure why. Surely Logs Pond was far enough north to not be in danger. *Why is father fearful?* Pendr thought.

"What is it you require?" the mayor asked.

The lead knight turned back and faced the town's leader. "We need to see your book of records. King Viskum, in his wisdom, understands that we need towns like Logs Pond to continue to function and send supplies in support of the war. He thereby will only be conscripting young men and women between fourteen and nineteen winters."

Several people in the crowd gasped. Pendr felt his father sigh deeply. *Conscripting? What does that mean?* As a blacksmith's apprentice, Pendr's schooling focused mostly on the skills needed in the smithy.

Fueron continued, "We require a mid-day meal, care for our horses, and access to your records. We'll then be on our way. You will have four days in which to prepare at which point we will be back for the conscripts as well as other supplies which we require."

Mayor Lonz nodded gravely. "It shall be as you say." Lonz motioned to two young men in the crowd. "Tikan, Wescro, see to the horses." His focus returned to the knights. "Sirs, if you will follow me."

"C'mon, my boy," Osbrik said, pulling Pendr back from the crowd. "We have much to discuss."

"But Tik and Wes will need help with the horses," Pendr said.

His father continued to pull him back. "Your friends are quite capable of that task. Back to the smithy. No more questions until we get there."

Pendr glanced over his shoulder one last time to watch as the knights dismounted. They looked regal and powerful. The last time the knights had visited, Pendr had dreams of riding on a horse, adorned in plate mail armor, and going off to fight whatever foes dared threaten the kingdom. He had told his father about these dreams. His father chided him, calling it the foolishness of youth. The fantasies of becoming a knight faded with time. Pendr was destined to be a blacksmith, like his father—a fate he now readily accepted.

The crowd began to disperse. Mothers were crying, and their children were crying along with them, though Pendr believed the younger children were merely reacting in kind. *I don't understand.* Any threat was far from Logs Pond; it had to be. Maybe it had something to do with what the knight said about the young men and women … oh, what was the word again? Ah, yes, conscripting.

"Father, what does conscripting mean?" Pendr asked as they continued back to the smithy.

"I told you no more questions until we were back inside. I meant it then, and I mean it now."

Pendr was taken aback by his father's harsh response. As the town blacksmith, his father was the strongest man in town, and probably the region. He was also the tallest, though Pendr nearly matched his height. Even with his imposing physical appearance and skill as a blacksmith, Osbrik was known as much for his wisdom and composure. Pendr could not recall the last time his father had spoken harshly to him.

The blacksmith shop was only a few structures away from the town center. Next to it was the tanner's building, owned by Canod. He and Osbrik were good friends and had been as far back as Pendr could remember.

"Light guide us," Canod said as they passed. His blue eyes showed sadness, something else that was uncommon as Canod was always quick with witty comments.

"Light guide us," Pendr and Osbrik echoed.

Upon reaching the smithy, Osbrik motioned for Pendr to enter first. The glow from the forge was enough to illuminate the inside of the building. The embers needed tending, which Pendr did habitually. As he stoked the coals, his father closed the main door—something normally done only at the end of the day.

"Father, what is it? What has you so rattled?"

"You're being conscripted, my boy."

"I don't know that word, father. Conscripted." The word felt strange coming off his tongue.

"That's because it's a word I'd hoped you'd never hear. It means you're going to be a soldier. The king is pressing you into service."

A soldier? That was what he had dreamed about becoming when he was younger. Now, the idea lacked any appeal. "I don't understand. I'm an apprentice blacksmith, not a soldier. Can the king do that?"

Osbrik walked over and stared into the forge. "He's the king. He can do as he pleases."

This idea of being conscripted did not make any sense to Pendr. His whole life, the king was someone who lived in a faraway castle. Never had the ruler of the land directly impacted Pendr's life—certainly not to the point where Pendr had learned any skills aside from what the town needed. "But, I know nothing of combat or swordplay."

Without moving his eyes from the glowing embers, Osbrik said grimly, "You'll learn, my boy, or you'll die."

Chapter 3

Not one part of Wyjec felt free of pain. It was not unlike when he had felt the trickle in his mind and used it to protect his hand—his whole being felt weary. However, the toll on his body he felt at the moment was not for the same reason. He had been up before first light, worked the whole day with only a brief moment for a mid-day meal, and now the waning crescent moon illuminated the night sky. The Masters had been especially overbearing today. Floors scrubbed this morning had to be scrubbed again. More than one of the chardi had gotten splinters while attempting to smooth out the wooden benches and tables in the meeting hall. Even the chamber pots in the guestrooms were polished until they shined.

Wyjec spent a good part of his afternoon bringing up bucketful after bucketful of water to the higher levels of the palace. It was a cruel punishment as the chardi were not allowed to drink any water unless provided by the Masters. Each bucket had lines near the brims, the water filled to the line. If Wyjec arrived with water below the bucket's line, he would be punished—one lash per occurrence issued at the end of the night. He had not spilled even a drop.

"If you can endure the pain from the test of the trodden," the Master who gave him the task had said, "then certainly you are strong enough to be the water carrier."

It was not that Wyjec could endure the pain when the Master had stepped on his hand. Wyjec had blocked the boot from crushing his hand, still unsure how he had done so. His hand still hurt from when the Master stepped on it initially, which made carrying the water even more challenging. *What had protected me yesterday?* Whispers at the palace of the Masters told that the ability to create such a protection was rare enough.

If the gift were possible, certainly only the noblest and powerful would have it—not the common person, and certainly not a lowly chardi.

Before exhaustion sent Wyjec to the land of dreams the previous night, he had tried to touch the trickle in his mind again, but failed. Throughout the day, while he descended from the upper levels of the palace, he tried without success.

But he had felt it yesterday. He knew what he had done and could not deny it. He *would* not deny it. With the trickle came hope—a feeling as rare as the Masters showing mercy to the chardi.

On a wooden pallet which served as Wyjec's bed, he lay down slowly as not to make any sound. The rest of the chardi were asleep, and it was an unwritten law between the chardi to let each other rest when given a chance.

Upon stretching out his legs, Wyjec noticed a small tear in his leggings. He sighed. Before long, it would need to be sewn. The Masters dressed the chardi in simple clothing, but they were supposed to remain free from holes. Each chardi was taught basic sewing skills, though they were expected to do the work on their own time. Free time for a chardi was sporadic, which usually meant that the sewing would have to wait for the block allotted for sleeping. The hole would have to wait. *I'm simply too exhausted.*

Placing his hands behind his head to act as a pillow of sorts, Wyjec tried again to recreate the experience he had when the Master stood on his hand. After concentrating for several moments, he could sense the trickle. *There!* He tried to grasp it, but it was like trying to pick up a tomato seed with his bare fingers. *What is different now than before?* The pain had been intense in his hand, whereas now, he was sore all over. Nothing hurt significantly more than anything else aside from his trampled fingers, but that pain had faded over the course of the day. Too tired to try again that night, Wyjec surrendered to the land of dreams.

Pain. A sharp stabbing originated in Wyjec's left foot, and then raced up his leg. At first, he thought it was simply night cramps, an experience happening more often as he grew taller. But this was different.

10

Wyjec opened his eyes and looked down at his feet, bending his left leg at the knee to see if that would ease the agony. The sharpness of the pain diminished, though the bottom of his foot still ached. Sitting up, Wyjec felt the sole, and his hand came away slick with wetness. His eyes adjusted enough to the moonlight coming through the room's only window that he could see his fingers were red—blood red.

Vermin! It had to be. Looking beyond his leg to the end of the pallet, Wyjec's deduction proved to be true. Sitting on its hind legs was a vermin with long, sharp teeth glinting even in the dim light.

How did it get in here? The chardi took extra care to plug any holes, no matter how small, in their sleeping quarters. If they did not, vermin would come in and chew on the soles of their feet. Wearing shoes or socks to bed was not an option because the chardi were forced to go barefoot everywhere.

Scanning the room, Wyjec searched for the answer of how the vermin got in and found it. The door was slightly ajar. *But I closed it! I'm certain.* Perhaps he had been so tired that he forgot. No, he remembered closing it. All the chardi knew better. It had to be a Master—one of *them* opened it.

As the feeling of outrage built up inside Wyjec, he sensed the trickle in the center of his mind, this time, more powerful than before. Mentally, he reached for it and was able to grab a hold. His sore muscles loosened, their ache replaced with another form a fatigue, something deeper.

At that moment, the vermin skittered over to Wyjec's right foot. It went to bite. Wyjec cried out *No!* in his mind. The weariness in his body increased as he directed the protection to cover his feet. The vermin's teeth connected with his right foot, and though Wyjec felt the pressure, he felt no pain. The vermin squeaked loudly and jumped back. Its paws went to its teeth as if they were hurt.

I must have shielded myself again. The extra drain on his already exhausted body seemed to be connected to when he used the trickle. But it was not enough. If the vermin could not hurt Wyjec, it would probably attack another of the chardi. There were no weapons in the room; the chardi were forbidden to keep any. With that thought, Wyjec became angrier. When he did, something remarkable happened. Next to the trickle he sensed something else. It was like the trickle, but different, like how the color blue was different from the color red. It was an apt comparison, though he could not say why. Keeping a hold of the blue trickle, Wyjec reached for the newly discovered red. He grabbed it, and the sensation was powerful. Whereas holding the blue trickle felt like sipping a cool drink, and it drained his energy, the red trickle felt like pouring warm water over his whole body which energized him—it was an odd combination. His heart started beating faster in his chest.

In addition, Wyjec's vision shifted. He could see the red trickle flowing through each of the chardi around him, with various brightness, as well as the vermin at his feet. It was subtle, like dew on morning flowers, but the trickle was there, as well as something else. A deep amber glow emanated from the vermin toward Wyjec's right foot. *Intention.* Unsure how he knew, Wyjec realized the amber glow indicated the vermin's intent, its focus.

My foot is not your supper! Still gripping the red trickle tightly, Wyjec pushed with his mind against the amber glow. The glow shifted slightly to the left, and with it, the vermin's head swiveled a little. Wyjec pushed harder, this time using the stone wall as a destination.

The amber glow intensified between the vermin and the wall. In three quick bounds, the creature was to the wall, clawing at it with its hands and biting the stone with its teeth. Fascinated, Wyjec watched as the vermin continued, seemingly unaware of the damage it was doing to itself. Within moments, the vermin had worn itself out and had chipped its teeth to nubs.

Gingerly, as not to step on his tender left foot, Wyjec arose from the pallet and picked up the exhausted vermin by the tail. At that moment, something wondrous happened. Next to the trickles which Wyjec defined as red and blue, two *other* trickles became manifest—though both were weaker in comparison.

Still holding the nearly dead animal in his hand, Wyjec felt a connection between him and the vermin. It was like a thread, with each end tied to the very center of their beings. This connection, Wyjec realized, linked with the new trickles. They were different still. Whereas the two trickles experienced before were associated with the colors of blue and red, for these—this thread between him and the creature—the colors yellow and green ran parallel. Aside from the different hues, the green felt as if it ran from him to the vermin, while the yellow was the opposite—as it if emanated from the animal.

Instinctively, Wyjec plucked at the yellow element of the string. Three things happened at the same moment. First, the vermin's twitching lessened, as if it was dying. Second, Wyjec's left foot, the one gnawed upon, felt whole. Lastly, the other of the two new trickles, the green, disappeared. What remained was the sensation of three unique trickles: blue, red, and yellow.

For a moment, Wyjec stood there, trying to puzzle out what happened. *It's all so strange.* The vermin stopped moving. The yellow thread vanished, and Wyjec could no longer see any red glimmer in the beast. Soon, the realization that he still held the vermin in the middle of the sleeping quarters spurred him into action. The Masters would be cross if they found him in such a state. The chardi were not allowed to defend themselves.

He walked over to the room's only window, made from thick glass which distorted the images from the outside. The window opened on its axis, which Wyjec did by pressing against an edge of the pane. He then tossed the dead vermin out the window. He heard it splatter on the palace grounds below—several stories down.

With the threat gone, Wyjec's heart slowed, and in the process, he lost hold of the blue and red trickles. A sense of loss followed, but a feeling of elation replaced it. *Anger is the key to accessing the trickles.* With that singular thought, Wyjec made sure to close the door and window tightly.

He sat back on the pallet to inspect the damage to his foot. To his shock, where there had been a gash, pink skin now existed. *But how?* And then Wyjec realized that his hand, the one which the Master had stepped upon, no longer hurt as well. *The yellow trickle does something more*, Wyjec realized: *It heals.*

Chapter 4

Jaunty music filled the air, and drink flowed in Logs Pond's town center. Pendr sat on the edge of the granite fountain, sipping his spiced apple cider. He did not understand how people could be enjoying themselves. On the morrow, he, along with the other conscripts, would be leaving.

"What's this then?" a voice said to his left and behind him enough to be out of view. "Have you forgotten that this event is in our honor?"

Pendr knew the voice. It belonged to Tikan, a lifelong friend, and son of Logs Pond's stable master. Shorter by a head than Pendr, what Tikan lacked in strength, he made up in quickness.

"I'm not much in the mood," Pendr said. "We are, after all, headed to war." Instead of being excited by the prospect, as he dreamed he would be when he was younger, Pendr found himself leery of change.

"Sounds like the perfect reason to live as much as possible tonight," Tikan said. He raked his fingers through his sandy, straight hair. "I'll bet you a moon cycle's worth of suppers Danla will give you that kiss you've always wanted."

Pendr scoffed. "I've never said such a thing."

"You haven't had to," Tikan said as he jabbed Pendr in the ribs. "It's as plain as the leaves on the trees whenever you are near her."

Danla was the tanner's daughter, a winter younger than Pendr and Tikan. As children, Pendr and Danla would play together because their parents were good friends. Once hair began to sprout from Pendr's chin, his relationship with Danla shifted. She, too, changed, and he could not help but notice. Their parents would often tease that they would marry one day, and it was funny when they were little, but now…

"You're speaking nonsense, Tik. Remember, she's been conscripted as well," Pendr said. "I'd rather she'd remain here, safe."

"Bah, she'll be safe enough. It's not like she'll be in battle."

Pendr took another sip of his cider. His father explained that the young women were conscripted as cooks, apprentice healers, and general laborers to keep the camps running. A few women were used in battle, but Pendr did not want to think about *them*. It made him uneasy.

"She might not be fighting, but *we* will be," Pendr said. "Doesn't that scare you?"

Tikan laughed, though it contained a hint of nervousness. "We're going to be trained as bannermen and shield bearers. The knights, pikemen, and archers do the fighting."

"Bannermen and shield bearers are pikemen and archers in training. That's what my father says. And regardless of our assigned roles, if our camp is attacked, we'll need to defend ourselves."

"You certainly know how to take the enjoyment out of a celebration." Tikan patted him on the back. "I'm going to go find a pretty girl to dance with."

Pendr watched his friend weave his way through the crowd. As an only child, Tikan was the only one conscripted from his family. Pendr's other siblings, all girls, were too young. He could have had other brothers or sisters of age to be going with him, but his mother had lost two children not long after they were born. At the time, Pendr was too young to understand the anguish it caused his parents. He wondered if the grief then was worth the heartache they would feel now because those lost children would have been conscripted along with their oldest son.

For the next several moments, Pendr sipped his drink and stared at the stars. He had never left Logs Pond. *Will the stars look different where I'm going?* It was an unsettling thought. There was comfort in familiarity.

He spotted Danla on the other side of the crowd. She was standing next to two other girls of her age, Binca, and Michella. Danla's light, blonde hair was just long enough to touch her shoulders. Though he only saw her from the side, he knew it was her. Binca noticed Pendr watching and nudged Danla. She turned, and catching Pendr's eye, gave him a smile—not one of happiness, but a familiar smile between two people who had known each other a long time.

Maybe I should go ask her to dance. Unsure why, he felt a stronger fear at that notion than marching off to war. Pendr stood, nodded to Danla, and then turned to head for home.

The knights, true to their word, arrived soon after dawn. A total of eighty-seven young men and women had gathered in the town center, carrying what few possessions they were allowed to take on their backs.

Several of the conscripts had celebrated with stronger drink than cider the previous night. Now the scales were tipped the other way. Tikan shielded his eyes from the morning's rays, and several of the others were grumbling about how thick their heads had become.

Danla stood next to her friends. Her sturdy woolen dress was practical in material and style. It was just snug enough to show off her curves. Like most of the conscripts, she looked nervous but was not crying, unlike Binca and Michella.

At the front of the knights, mounted on his stallion and looking as regal as Pendr remembered, was Sir Fueron. With his visor raised, blue eyes scanned the crowd, and a hint of a smile peeked out under his mustache. "Good. You look prepared. I have every confidence you will make Logs Pond proud with your actions. Now, follow me."

And with that, the conscripts were on their way. Sir Fueron led the procession down the main road which stretched to the east, keeping an easy pace so those on foot could keep up. Pendr chose to follow almost directly behind the leader. The rest of the knights followed behind the conscripts, though Pendr was not sure why. *Maybe they are keeping an eye on us to make sure none will run away.* Residents of the town lined the road, waving and saying goodbye. Unlike the night before, there was no merrymaking. Pendr looked straight ahead. He had said his goodbyes this morning. His mother and sisters had cried while his father had given him a big hug and told him he loved him—something that his father rarely said, but had shown in other ways.

A few mothers rushed out to give their sons or daughters one last hug as they left the town. Pendr was glad his parents showed restraint. Soon enough, Logs Pond was left behind.

Tall, red maples, all grown tightly together, reached toward the morning sky on either side of the road. Because of how closely the trees grew, Pendr could see no more than a dozen paces into the forest on either side from where they walked. None of the conscripts spoke as they traveled. Perhaps the reason for the silence was due to the knights remaining quiet, or maybe no one wanted to bring attention upon themselves. Pendr did not know much about knights, aside from what he heard in stories. One trait common among knights was solemnity. It made sense to Pendr; after all, fighting to the death was not to be taken lightly.

Just before the sun reached its peak, Pendr heard commotion ahead. At first, he tensed but then noticed that Sir Fueron kept on as if there was nothing to fear. Upon getting closer to the sounds, Pendr could pick out voices and horses neighing. There was a bend in the road ahead, and once they turned it, Pendr understood why the lead knight was not concerned. Green and silver banners, rustling in the wind, flew above a large camp. Makeshift stables corralled horses on the outskirts with tents pitched toward the middle. The shelters varied in size, with the largest in the center.

A muscular man with blond hair rushed forward upon seeing them. "Sir Fueron!" he called out and offered a salute. "Welcome back."

Fueron dismounted in one fluid move and then handed the reins to the young man. "Ewan, what news?"

"The conscripts have arrived from Umstead and Brentwood, Sir," Ewan said. "We are still awaiting those from Willow Springs."

"Understood." Fueron peered around. "Has Sir Lokan found a suitable spot?"

"Yes, Sir," Ewan said. "To the south and west."

Fueron faced the group who had followed him from Logs Pond. "The males will train with Sir Lokan. They will follow me. The females will remain here. Shortly, Mistress Halima will come for you."

Pendr glanced over his shoulder. Among those behind him, he spotted Danla staring at him. He nodded at her, and she responded with an uneasy smile. He chided himself for not seeking her out last night. They were friends, after all. With the future uncertain, he realized it was not a matter of *when* he would see her again, but rather *if.* These thoughts weighed on him as he, along with the other young men from Logs Pond, began to follow Sir Fueron toward the next phase of his life—however long that might be.

Chapter 5

If any of the Masters found the dead vermin the next morning, they did not speak of it around Wyjec. Perhaps it was his imagination, but the Masters were acting differently—more pompous. It could be due to the visitors who were to arrive today. Any who visited the Masters' palace always cowed, even the captains of the army.

Wyjec placed the morning meal in front of one of the Masters, and the fat man sighed as if he had been waiting for an exorbitant amount of time. The chardi never knew the Masters' real names. Each of them demanded to be called "Master," though, in Wyjec's mind, he named this particular Master "Glutton." As the heaviest of the Masters, he ate more than the others. Wyjec learned that if Glutton was well fed, he tended to be less disagreeable.

"That will be all, chardi," Glutton said.

Wyjec bowed and backed away from the long table without speaking. His responsibilities this morning were to feed the Masters, and Glutton was the last of them. When the sun reached its highest point, Wyjec was to report to the Master he had dubbed "Cruel"—the one who had stepped on his hand a few days previous. That meant he had some free time, a luxury, one which would be taken away if any of the Masters spotted him resting or relaxing. Fortunately, Wyjec knew a place he could go.

The palace had seven levels, the bottom of which was the main hall where meals were eaten and where the Masters held their meetings. Where the first and second levels connected, a half-door opened to a small walkway that spanned over the main hall. It was used to access the large candle-lit chandeliers. The morning sunshine streaming through the colored, plate glass windows and light from the fires burning in the hearths was enough to illuminate the room, so the chandeliers remained unlit.

Careful not to make any noise, Wyjec climbed to the second floor, opened the half-door, and then crawled out onto the walkway. *Why are the Masters acting so differently?* It had to be the visitors coming today. The only people Wyjec had seen in the palace aside from the Masters were the captains of the army and those of the village bringing chardi. At any given time, between ten and twenty chardi served the masters, starting as young as five winters. None of the chardi had lived to see eighteen winters, at least none Wyjec had known.

Wyjec was one of the older chardi. He had seen sixteen winters, according to the Masters. Actually, with the beheading of the other chardi four days previous, Wyjec realized he *was* the oldest chardi—not a good position to hold. The older chardi were usually the ones the Masters sacrificed. With a sickening realization, Wyjec understood for the first time the reason there were no chardi who had seen at least eighteen winters. *Perhaps the Masters feared the chardi when they got older.*

If only Wyjec could control his ability to grasp and use the trickles: red, blue, and yellow, the Masters would fear *him*, and not the other way around. Anger seemed to be the key to tapping into the trickles, but could he make himself angry at will? His thoughts on how to make that happen were interrupted when he heard one of the Masters speak.

"King Viskum is a fool." Glutton burped loudly. "He will *not* respond in kind. Sending troops south would incite further conflict. He should recognize that Iredell is ours by right. We did not capture the town. We liberated it."

"*You* are the fool," another Master said. Wyjec recognized the voice. He was the smallest Masters with a bushy, white mustache that reminded Wyjec of whiskers. Naturally, Wyjec had dubbed him "Mouse."

"Viskum will certainly try to retake Iredell," Mouse continued. "It is a manner of honor. A king who cannot protect his kingdom will not remain on the throne for long."

"The captains will want reassurances," another Master said. This one was who Wyjec called Cruel. "I, for one, say any who question us should go on the front lines to oversee Iredell personally."

"Agreed," said several other voices at the same time. Wyjec imagined it was the rest of the seven masters, including Glutton.

"Phhh," Glutton said. "At the very least, the captains need to see a sacrifice."

"I will arrange it," Cruel said. "The captains will get their show of our power, and the chardi will learn their place once again."

"Which one will it be?" one of the Masters asked. Wyjec was not sure who had spoken.

"Wyjec," Cruel answered. "He is getting too old, too strong."

Me? No! I will not allow it! Wyjec felt his heart start to pound violently in his chest. With that came the awareness of the red and blue trickles. The red trickle seemed to call out to him, and Wyjec responded by grabbing a hold of it as hard as he could. When he did, he felt dominant; *he* was the one in control. Unlike using the blue trickle, Wyjec felt more alive when accessing the red. The yellow trickle was not present, though Wyjec could not say why. Unlike when he held the vermin, no threads appeared between Wyjec and the Masters. *Odd, but that is something for another day.*

No longer caring if the Masters might spot him on the walkway, Wyjec leaned over to view the men below him. As before, he could see the red trickles flowing through them, some stronger than others. For each of them, the amber glow was focused on the food and drink in front of them.

Each of the Masters went to take a mouthful of food now that they decided who would be sacrificed. As they brought the food to their mouths, Wyjec could see the amber glow shifted to their stomachs. *Their intention is to swallow the food.* Glutton was the first to try to swallow. *What if I were to change the focus of their intention as they ate?* He imagined he could get the Masters to spit out their food, but that would not be enough to stop them. He watched as each of the Masters ate, and each time the amber glow moved from their mouths, down their necks and chests and into their bellies. An idea came to Wyjec. *This could work!*

When Glutton took his next bite, Wyjec watched as the larger man began to swallow. As the food passed through the Master's neck, Wyjec pushed with the red trickle causing the amber glow to go neither up nor down, but to the sides. The result triggered the Master to begin to choke.

Before the rest of the Masters noticed, Wyjec did the same to two others. He would have done more, but he could only manipulate them one at a time. The remaining four Masters stood to help.

The one closest to Glutton reached out to help the fat man. Wyjec sensed his amber glow and redirected it toward one of the hearths where a fire blazed to ward off the chill of the morning. Another Master was directed to the large room's other hearth.

Three Masters were choking now—Glutton's face an ugly shade of purple. Two of the others had placed their heads in the fires. They were screaming in pain, yet they did not move away from the flames.

The last two remaining Masters remained in place, seemingly frightened into inaction.

"What is this?" Mouse shouted. He reached for a long, sharp knife used for cutting meat.

The other Master who remained, a bald man with a pockmarked face, also grabbed a knife. *They're trying to defend themselves.* Wyjec watched as each of the last two men's amber glows flitted around the room, searching for a target on which to use their knives.

Wyjec eagerly assisted their search by directing their amber glows toward each other. Again, he could only manipulate one at a time, but he managed to do both rather quickly. The last two Masters came together and began to stab each other wildly. Neither tried to defend themselves.

Screams of pain faded to whimpers and then to silence.

Fascinated, Wyjec watched as his tormenters died horrific deaths. He should feel vindicated, but there was something missing.

Part of him wanted more. *What am I missing? I just killed those who had tormented me. They were going to kill me!* What more could he want than this?

And then he understood. It was not enough to kill them; he wanted the Masters to know it was him, Wyjec, who brought them down. They had died, yes, but they did not know why or who had done it. It was a victory, but a hollow one.

Next time I kill someone, I will stand over them and see understanding in their dying eyes.

Chapter 6

Sir Lokan's hair thinned on top, but the back was long and pulled into a braid. The knight stood in front of the young men from Logs Pond, muscular arms folded and a scowl displayed prominently on his face.

"This is all?" he asked. "You aren't much to look at." His eyes scanned through the group, and Pendr thought they remained on him the longest.

None of Pendr's fellow town members spoke, not even Tikan, standing to Pendr's right, who rarely was at a loss for words.

Lokan began to walk back and forth in front of them, clasping his hands behind his back. The soldiers stood on the edge of a field that once had knee-high grass spread across it. Now, all the vegetation lay flat upon the ground, trampled, from what Pendr could tell. On the far side of the field were hundreds of young men. They stood in groups of roughly fourteen each, forming a circle. Inside the circles, some type of action was happening, but from where Pendr stood, he could not exactly see what the other young men were doing.

"For those of you who want to see your families again, you will take this training seriously. A casual soldier is a dead soldier," Sir Lokan said. "For the rest of the day, I'm going to separate you into groups of fourteen, hereafter to be known as a squad."

"What about our mid-day meal?" a voice called out.

Lokan stopped mid-stride and faced the young men from Logs Pond, his face stoic. "Those of you wise enough to have brought something with you may eat quickly while I create the groups. For those who didn't, you've learned your first lesson in preparedness."

In his tanned leather backpack, a gift from Danla's father, Pendr had some hard cheese, a bladder of water, and some jerked meat. No one had told him to pack the items; it seemed like common sense. While Sir Lokan walked to the other end of the group, Pendr unshouldered his backpack.

"Did you bring something?" Tikan asked Pendr just loudly enough for him to hear.

Pendr nodded in response. "You didn't?"

"I wasn't thinking very clearly this morning."

After unwrapping a corner of the cheese, Pendr broke off a couple of small chunks. He popped one in his mouth and handed the other to Tikan. While chewing, Pendr ripped off a couple of pieces of the meat.

"Next time, think ahead," Pendr told his friend as he handed him the food. "And don't have as much to drink the night before."

They had only enough time to finish the small meal when Lokan approached them. "Twelve, thirteen, fourteen." Lokan counted, pointing to the conscripts as he walked, ending with Tikan. "This squad will go over there." The knight pointed to a clear area toward the west. "As a squad, you will decide who will be your leader. It can be by common consent or a competition of your choosing. How you choose will tell me as much about your group as who is chosen."

Pendr headed to the area Lokan had indicated, realizing that everyone else was following him. Once they arrived, he looked around. He knew all of them, some better than others. Tikan, of course, was a friend, but so were Wescro, Ayab, and Rilam. Wescro worked with Tikan at the stables, though they were not directly related. Ayab and Rilam were brothers, Ayab being the oldest, who worked on a sheep farm with their father. Pendr had wondered on more than one occasion if Ayab and Rilam's family were drawn to sheep farming because they all had curly hair that mimicked sheep's wool. Rilam tended to be less serious than his older brother. For whatever reason, Rilam and Danla almost always got into a heated discussion whenever they were around each other. *Perhaps because Danla takes everything so seriously.*

And then there was Lunz, son of Mayor Lonz. Like his father, Lunz was wide-shouldered and had a reputation of always having to be right—even when it was obvious to Pendr that sometimes Lunz was in error.

It was Lunz who spoke first. "Why should there be a debate? It's clear to me that as the son of the mayor, I am the natural choice to be the leader."

Pendr noticed Tikan bristle at the statement. "Just because your father is in charge of the town doesn't mean you should be in charge here," Tikan said.

Lunz took a step towards Tikan, hands balled into fists. "Who then should be the leader? You, stable boy?"

"Yeah, why not? At least I don't sit inside all day. I know how to work." Tikan tensed up, looking like he was going to spring at Lunz if he got close enough.

The rest of the boys in the squad watched in anticipation. Pendr found the situation ridiculous. He stepped forward and stood between Lunz and Tikan. "Enough. We already have one war we're fighting. We don't need another."

Undaunted, Lunz kept coming toward Tikan. Sensing the situation beginning to escalate, Pendr intercepted Lunz, grabbing his fine cloth jerkin by his chest. "We won't fight amongst ourselves," Pendr said, not raising his voice.

Lunz used both of his hands to grab Pendr's wrist which held him into place. Though Pendr did not like to flaunt his strength, earned through hard work at the smithy, it was moments like these that it was useful.

"Back off, Lunz," a boy from the group called out.

"You're no match for Pendr," another said.

A third boy said, "Pendr should lead us."

With that statement, several others chimed in their agreement.

Surprised, Pendr wondered if he could do what they expected. Unlike Lunz, Pendr preferred to let his actions speak for him. *Do I have what it takes?*

"What do you say, Pendr?" Ayab asked.

Pendr considered it. Most of those in his squad were younger. They needed someone to help them through this difficult time. "I will do my best," he heard himself say.

Lunz mumbled something under his voice but did not outwardly disagree.

Later, when Sir Lokan approached the group, they all stood quietly in a circle. The knight appeared surprised. "Is it decided then?"

Pendr took a step forward. "Yes, Sir. I have been selected."

For the first time since they had met Sir Lokan, the knight smiled.

Chapter 7

The captains arrived at the Masters' palace at mid-day. Three in all, each dressed in dark plate mail with a crescent moon emblazed on their dark blue cloaks, stood in stunned silence. The Masters were dead; their bodies remained where they died. The three who choked to death lay next to the table. Two were several steps away, each sporting numerous knife wounds and laying in pools of blood. Though the fires in the hearths no longer burned, the charred heads of the last two Masters lay on pillows of ashes.

"What darkness is this?" one of the captains said. He was thicker than the other two, with three stars embroidered the shoulders of his cloak.

"It couldn't have been King Viskum," another of the captains said. His close-cropped golden hair contrasted against his uniform. "We would have known of forces this far into our territory."

"Then who?" the third captain asked, the youngest of the three and based on the single star on his shoulder, the lowest in rank.

"Me."

The three captains turned toward a darkened corner of the room. Wyjec stepped from the dark shadows and into the colored light created by the stained-glass windows.

"You? A chardi? You claim to have done this?"

Wyjec realized his appearance marked him as a chardi. The plain, roughspun tunic and breeches, along with his bare feet certainly did not inspire awe like the uniforms which the captains wore. *That's something I'll have to remedy in the future.*

"I do not claim it," Wyjec said. "I state it as fact."

"Nonsense," the captain with three stars said. "Such insolence from a chardi. Kishul, bring me his head."

The golden-haired man nodded as he unsheathed his long sword.

Instead of running, Wyjec felt a rush of anger surge through him. He considered his options. Both the red and blue trickles were at his use. The amber glow emanating from the approaching captain was centered solely on Wyjec, specifically his neck. Pushing the amber glow toward another captain may cause them to fight among themselves. But to what end? Wyjec did not want just the ability to kill; he wanted what the Masters had had: fear and respect that came with power.

What else will cause the captains to fear me? Kishul was almost to him now, lifting his blade. Instinctively, Wyjec took hold of the blue trickle, tighter than he had ever before. Instead of focusing only on his neck, he covered his whole body in protection. The draining effect on his physique nearly caused him to black out, but he fought against the darkness. He stood, unflinching as Kishul swung the blade at his neck.

The sword connected solidly—and bounced away leaving not even the slightest of marks. Wyjec felt the pressure of the blow. It was enough to make him stagger to the side two steps, though his shielding absorbed much of the force. A blow like that should have removed his head from his shoulders.

Kishul stared at his sword in disbelief, and then at Wyjec. "Captain Avadi! He wields the *myelur.*"

Myelur was not a word Wyjec had heard before, yet the sound of it pleased his ears. There was strength in the word as if it encapsulated how he felt when he touched the trickle. No. Not trickle. He was touching the *myelur.* Unsure how he knew, Wyjec realized that *myelur* was the proper word given to what he had sensed as trickles.

While being able to block the attack with the blue *myelur* was impressive, Wyjec needed to show them he was even more powerful. He seized the red *myelur,* and then directing his attention to Kishul's hand, caused the captain to drop his sword.

"What are you doing?" the eldest captain, the one called Avadi, asked Kishul.

"I did not do that of my own will," Kishul said.

Wyjec stood as tall as he could. "That's right. I made him drop it."

Backing away slowly, Kishul said, "Forgive me, chardi. I did not know."

"Not chardi. No longer chardi. My name is Wyjec." He took a step closer to the captains. "But you will call me Master."

Chapter 8

An arrow nicked Pendr's arm, just enough to leave a mark on his leather armor then it continued on, barely deflected from its path. A grunt sounded behind Pendr, followed by a cry of disbelief.

"We're under attack!" a voice called out from his right.

Pendr turned, and his eyes locked with Wescro. The young man who had come with Pendr from Logs Pond wrapped his hands around the arrow shaft that had pierced his leather cuirass, just below and to the right of his breastbone.

"Get down!" someone else shouted.

Precious little was available for cover. Pendr's squad sat on felled trees which doubled as benches. Only heartbeats previous, Sir Lokan had been instructing the eight squads of their responsibilities during the impending battle. The knight claimed the enemy was unaware of their presence, though the arrow embedded in Wescro told another story.

More arrows sliced through the early morning air, finding targets as often as not. Pendr motioned for his squad to lay prone behind the fallen trees. *We're not ready. We aren't supposed to be in the battle. We're reserves, tasked with running messages and supplies.*

Getting as close to the ground as he could, Pendr came face to face with Tikan.

"What is this madness?" Tikan asked. "The fighting is supposed to be several leagues down river from here."

An arrow slammed into the ground so close that Tikan could have leaned forward slightly and touched it with his nose.

Over the cries of surprise and pain, Sir Lokan's voice cut through the chaos. "To those trees. Quickly!"

Lifting his head, Pendr looked to see where the knight pointed.

He caught sight of Sir Lokan just as their leader took an arrow in the neck, below his plated helm. If the newly armored conscripts were not panicked enough before, seeing their leader receive a fatal wound eliminated any form of discipline learned over the last moon cycle.

Young men popped up, some scattering toward the river, away from the incoming arrows. More often than not, arrows found them before they could find shelter.

"Tikan, we're dead if we stay here," Pendr said. "Follow me."

Pendr stood, then turned toward the thicket where Sir Lokan had pointed before he was shot down. An arrow slashed across Pendr's thigh, cutting through the leather armor and the skin beneath. Once again, the arrow had not hit solidly enough to do any serious damage.

"Follow Pendr!" Tikan called out as they raced for the trees.

Fighting the urge to look how many friendly soldiers were still alive, Pendr kept his focus on the towering arbors in front of him. To the south: their attackers had taken a position in that part of the forest. It gave them cover while still allowing them a full view of the area Sir Lokan had used as a staging point.

The trees ahead of Pendr ascended a small hill away from the river. It curved to the northeast, which would put a natural barrier between the archers and young soldiers who followed Pendr. By fortune or fate, he reached the hill without being struck again. Huddling down behind a large red maple, Pendr spared a glance from where he had run. A string of young men lay dead or injured in a line behind him—one of which was Tikan. An arrow had caught him in the temple—most certainly a fatal blow. *Tikan's dead? But I just spoke to him!*

Pendr blinked, and then blinked again. He needed to focus. There would be time to grieve later. All was not lost. Ayab was still on his feet, as were Lunz, and a couple of other young men whom Pendr did not know by name but recognized from other squads and their standard green tunics.

"Here!" Pendr called out.

Each of the young men still coming in his direction appeared to gain an extra burst of speed, perhaps from the hope that safety was close. As each of them reached Pendr, he motioned for them to go deeper into the trees and around the hill. Once all five were safe, Pendr looked back one more time to the field. Rilam, Ayab's brother, was crawling toward them, an arrow in his shoulder and thigh. *He's too far. I can't help him.*

"Rilam!" Ayab cried out. "Pendr! We have to get my brother!"

Ayab had crouched behind a tree, down and to the right of Pendr.

The arrows flying in the air were not as thick as before. Maybe the archers were running low. Or maybe it was because they were running out of targets. Either way, Pendr consider the risk of trying to retrieve Rilam. *I'm a blacksmith, not a soldier. I did nothing to those killing us. They have no right!*

At that moment, Pendr felt something stir in his mind. It was cool, like when a drop of sweat would run down his back while working at the smithy. The sensation was a bit draining, yet the energy gained from the escape gave him enough resolve to make a dash for Rilam.

Four steps from the safety of the trees, the arrows returned again in earnest, apparently from spotting a new target. The odd weariness washed stronger over Pendr, but he kept his eyes on Rilam, vowing to get him to safety. Again, it seemed his luck was holding up as Pendr reached the younger man without any of the foes' arrows finding their mark.

"Hang on," Pendr told Rilam as he picked him up and slung him over one shoulder.

Arrows soared around him, some piercing the ground in front of Pendr as he raced back to the trees. Ayab watched him from the forest, his face displaying shock. Once they were out of sight of the archers, Pendr put Rilam down carefully.

"How—how did you do that?" Ayab asked.

Pendr looked himself over. The only marks were from the arrows that nicked him before. He had not gained any new wounds when saving Rilam. He felt tired, more so than just from the run and carrying Rilam, though he could not say why. "Perhaps the archers were getting tired."

"That's not it," Ayab said. "I saw arrows strike you."

Pendr once again looked over his body. No, he had not taken any new hits. "You must be mistaken."

"I'm not! I saw it clearly. Several arrows hit you, but then something strange happened."

What is Ayab talking about? "What do you mean?"

The curly-haired young man's eyes were wide with disbelief. "The arrows bounced right off you."

Chapter 9

Captain Avadi knelt with one hand flat against the stone floor and the other touching his forehead lightly in respect. For a long moment, he stayed in that position. The stained-glass windows in the main hall of the palace remained dark, covered with thick, black drapes. Tapers, lit by the dozen, lined the floor and offered the room its only light. The smell of burning wax lingered in the air, overpowering any other aromas.

The setting helped Wyjec see the red *myelur* in his visitors easier. He had practiced seeing the red *myelur* on the remaining chardi whom he had treated much kinder than their previous Masters. The chardi took care of all of Wyjec's basic needs, and in return, they could live in the palace with food to eat, water to drink, and shelter to keep them from harm.

Over the last moon cycle, Wyjec had developed the ability to see the red *myelur* in others without becoming angry. Though, without strong emotions, he still could not manipulate the amber glows nor grasp the blue *myelur*. The yellow *myelur* had not manifested itself since Wyjec's encounter with the vermin. *I wonder why that is?*

With sensing the red *myelur* came the amber glow, an indication of intention. At the moment, from Wyjec's position in the room's only chair, Captain Avadi's amber glow was directed inwardly, a sign that Wyjec took that the man was trying not to do anything but show respect. *Just as it should be.*

"Arise," Wyjec commanded.

Captain Avadi stood, dusting off the three stars embroidered on his left shoulder as he rose. Wyjec wondered if the action was a subtle reminder that Avadi was the highest-ranking captain of the Masters' forces. *No, not the Masters' forces. Mine.*

"My plan was successful," Avadi said. "We ranged west, around King

Viskum's vanguard, and hit their supply lines. Our archers killed hundreds of bannermen and shield bearers. Their knights and squires doubled back from their march toward Iredell, allowing us to send reinforcements to the town."

The respect in Avadi's voice delighted Wyjec. As a chardi, Wyjec had never been spoken to with such reverence—it had been mainly contempt, with occasions of tolerance. Next to Wyjec's chair was a maple table. A pewter cup full of water rested on it. Since overthrowing the previous Masters, Wyjec had made water available to the rest of the chardi upon request, as long as they continued to cook the meals and maintain the palace.

Before responding to the captain, Wyjec took a long sip of water and relished the sensation of the liquid filling his mouth. It was such a simple thing, easy to take for granted until denied. Wyjec vowed to enjoy each drink.

After swallowing, Wyjec said, "I know little of schemes of war, Captain Avadi. But I do understand that there are two types of people in this world: those who have power, and those who do not. By taking and holding Iredell, we are showing power. Yet, as you have told me, King Viskum wants that power back. Do we have the forces to keep the town?"

The question changed Avadi's demeanor. His confident expression faded. "Master, if I may speak plainly?"

"Granted."

"Ours is not a large land. We are still recovering from the last war with Nothcar. Our losses were devastating. By the last count required from the prior Masters, the whole of our population is just shy of thirty thousand. Of those, we can press maybe ten thousand into a fighting force, with an extra two thousand in support roles. The rest are too young, too old, or are needed to keep the lands producing. King Viskum controls at least thrice our number, if not more. His lands surround us to the north and west, and the wildmen rule the southern and eastern wetlands."

"You are telling me that the old Masters started a fight we cannot hope to win," Wyjec concluded.

"I counseled them against taking Iredell. We do not have the forces to win such a war."

This news intrigued Wyjec. *Is it possible the previous Masters made a mistake?* "What can we do to keep Iredell?"

"It's possible that after our last surprise attack, the successful one against the bannermen and shield bearers, that King Viskum will see taking back Iredell as a price too high."

"And of what you know about the king, do you believe this?" Wyjec asked.

Avadi laced his fingers together and bowed his head. "No. I do not think he will give up. Once he regroups and tries again, Iredell will be taken."

Wyjec took another sip of water. Ever since the captains discovered that he could wield the red and blue *myelur*, they had let him take the Masters' place as the leader of the land. From what Wyjec could gather, it had been three generations since someone displayed the abilities of both the red and the blue *myelur*. *And they have yet to learn about my ability with the yellow!* As Wyjec had come to know, the last man to use both the red and the blue *myelur* in this part of the world was named Domtain, founder of the Masters. Domtain had overthrown the king of Sothcar and placed himself and his friends as the ruling body. When a Master died, another was chosen from the populous—that was until Wyjec killed them all. With the Masters dead, a void of power was created, one that Wyjec readily filled.

"Captain Avadi, I understand that your visits are to keep up illusions. You still control the army and the power that comes with it. Yet, by coming to me, you also create a reason to cause your men to do things they might not do else wise. In some ways, I'm not much more than a stone statue that some cultures worship; the ones the Masters would mock during meals."

"No, not at—"

"I may have been chardi, but I grew up around the Masters. I learned how to speak from them. I learned how to think by listening carefully to what they said, though that was not their intention. Unlike the old Masters, I will not remain invisible in the palace. And with the *myelur*, I have power."

Avadi looked uneasy. "There is no need. I will ensure we hold Iredell."

"But you said we had not the forces to do so."

"With respect, a single man who can wield the *myelur*, even both the blue and red, cannot make the difference in such a battle."

Wyjec set the pewter cup on the table. "You forget, I killed the Masters. *All* of them. I am more powerful than you take me for."

"Of course, Master," Avadi said. "I know little about the *myelur* and what it can do. Please, forgive me."

Watching the captain, a leader of men, grovel before him gave Wyjec pleasure not experienced before. He reveled in it. "You are forgiven. Now, go. Make the preparations for our trip to Iredell."

Chapter 10

Pendr stared into the night sky. The stars did not look any differently here than in Logs Pond, but he was not comforted by their familiarity. He was not sure how far he was from his hometown. If he was truly honest with himself, he did not know where he was, exactly. It was one of many reasons he felt unsettled.

He had been in such a rush to escape that he had not taken the time to dwell on what Ayab had claimed—that arrows had bounced off him. He had not felt anything hit him, but his attention was focused on getting Rilam to safety. At times when he had been focusing on his blacksmithing, he would burn himself time and again, and not realize it until later when he saw the burns. Maybe, the same thing happened here. But there were not any marks on his armor aside from the ones he remembered. Aside from a brief inspection of his gear, he had not given it much thought—he did not have time until now.

Along with the other six young men who had followed him away from where the squads had been massacred, he had found refuge under a tall tree which had toppled and leaned against a steep hill, creating a shelter after a fashion. Pendr would have preferred a cave, but humans were not the only ones who found lodging in caves. He and the young men with him were in no shape to fight off the wolves which populated the area.

They had headed northwest away from the field by the river in an attempt to get away from their attackers. The going had been slow with Rilam unable to walk. The younger, curly-haired boy from Logs Pond complained about the pain. The arrows Rilam had taken did not cause a lot of bleeding, a blessing to be sure, but they did hamper his movements. Pendr ended up carrying him, thankful that his time in the smithy had given him the strength to do so—still, he felt as weary now as he had ever felt in his life. During their flight, Pendr's group had not encountered the enemy, but neither did they find friendly soldiers.

"What do we do now?" a voice from the depths of their shelter asked. It was one of the young men from the other squads.

"We rest and see what rations we have with us," Pendr said. "Forgive me. Those from the other squads, I don't know your names."

"Rheq," one of them said. "From Umstead." His voice held an odd accent, like the sounds of the words were pushed together.

"Eladrel," said the other young man, who seemed to be of an age with Pendr. "From Brentwood."

Whereas Rheq was younger and wiry, Eladrel was tall and lanky. While it was possible that Rheq avoided the arrows due to his small size, the same could not be said for Eladrel. It appeared that this young man from Brentwood also had luck on his side. Pendr made quick introductions of Lunz, Ayab, and Rilam—the others from Logs Pond.

"Pendr's our squad leader," Ayab said. His brother, Rilam, stopped complaining. Instead, he curled up in a ball, whimpering quietly.

"You'll have to be ours as well. My squad's leader was one of the first to fall," Eladrel said.

Pendr considered the soldiers in front of him. They were young, especially Rilam. "Eladrel, will you take Rilam back under the tree and try to make him more comfortable?" Pendr asked.

"I'll see what I can do," Eladrel said. Gently, he picked Rilam up and went further into the shelter provided by the fallen tree.

"What do we do now?" Ayab asked.

"I say we make a fire," Lunz said. "I have some flint in my pack, and there is plenty of dry wood around."

The mayor's son had reluctantly accepted Pendr as the squad leader … to a point. Lunz's idea for a fire was appealing. The coolness of the spring evening was settling in, but Pendr felt there were bigger things to consider.

"A fire could act as a beacon to our enemies," Pendr said. "I don't dare risk it."

"We didn't see any sign of them since we left the field," Lunz countered. "We don't even know for sure if they are following us."

"We don't know that they *aren't* tracking us, either," Ayab pointed out. "I'm with Pendr. We don't need to draw attention to ourselves."

"That's settled then," Pendr said.

"I don't agree," Lunz said.

"You don't have to," Ayab said. "Now close your lips and open your ears, Lunz."

Pendr did not like seeing conflict between Lunz and the others, but at least the other young men understood that Pendr had responsibility over the squad. "Everyone remove your backpacks and let's see what supplies we have."

"I dropped mine while escaping," Rheq said. He did not sound apologetic. It was stated as a fact.

"It's understandable," Pendr said. "We were running for our lives."

For the next several moments, the backpacks were emptied and sorted. Eladrel came out to join the rest of them and offered his pack for inspection. The result was better than Pendr had hoped. There was enough food to last for several days, and the small streams and ponds in the forest would provide any water they required. Each of the members of the squad had been given a short sword as standard equipment, worn in a sheath attached to their belts. They were mainly defensive weapons, not much more than glorified knives. There were also bandages and ointments to treat Rilam's wounds.

During the process of sorting out the supplies, Pendr had a moment to reflect on what had happened. The first person who came to his mind was Danla. She had not been in the same camp as Pendr, so as far as he knew, she was safe. *Or maybe her camp was attacked as well.* No. He could not dwell on thoughts like that. What he needed to do at the moment was focus on what he could control.

"So, what now?" Lunz asked. "We aren't trained for battle, at least not enough to take on seasoned soldiers. And since we've been running haphazardly through the forest, we're lost. We have as good of a chance running into enemy soldiers as friendly ones."

"Based on what?" Ayab asked. Bits of leaves stuck to his curly hair, most likely from when they made their way quickly through the underbrush. "We're still in Nothcar. We haven't ventured far enough south to be in enemy lands."

"Listen, you woolen head," Lunz said, jabbing a finger toward Ayab. "Haven't you been paying attention? We were on the king's land when we were attacked. The borders may have shifted. We could be surrounded by the enemy. We should have headed to the river instead of the forest. From there, I could have found our way home."

"Home?" Rheq asked snidely. "Which home? Yours? In Logs Puddle?"

"Logs *Pond*," Lunz said through gritted teeth.

"Home for a soldier is where he sleeps that night," Eladrel said. Like Pendr, Eladrel was tall, but when he offered to carry Rilam, Pendr was unsure. He was leery at first to accept the help, mainly because Pendr did not know the other younger man well enough to trust him or if he had the strength to do it. Soon enough, Eladrel's easy manner and willingness to help won Pendr over.

"Eladrel makes a good point. We're still soldiers," Pendr said.

"You all may want to believe that," Lunz said, "but I am smart enough to know it is a hopeless cause. We're better off back in our hometowns."

"Who's the woolen head, now?" Rheq asked. Though he was younger and small, Rheq talked like he was not intimidated by the older boys. "Don't you know what the king does to deserters?" He made a slashing motion across his throat.

"That's *if* the king is still alive," Ayab said quietly.

Everyone turned to face the sheepherder. "Do you know something we don't?" Eladrel asked quickly, though not confrontationally.

Ayab didn't meet any of their eyes when he said, "You all saw how our fellow conscripts were slaughtered. Even a seasoned knight like Sir Lokan didn't last long. And that was only *part* of the enemy we faced."

"It would have been different if more knights were there," Ayab said.

"How can you know that?" Lunz countered.

Ayab frowned in response.

"That's right," Lunz said. "You don't know. You all are—"

"Enough," Pendr said.

Lunz whipped his head toward Pendr. "Who are you to tell—"

"Enough," Pendr said again, this time with a harder edge in his voice. He did not like to be so forceful, but there were times when it seemed that was the only way to get Lunz to listen. "I was chosen as squad leader, and that hasn't changed." He faced Eladrel for reassurance. "We *are* soldiers. We need to act that way."

The rest of the group remained quiet, even Lunz, though he shifted uneasily. Pendr preferred not being the center of attention, perhaps because of his large stature, people noticed him whether he wanted it or not. At the same time, he took responsibility, of any sort, seriously. He considered the options and tried to prioritize them. He came up with a basic plan.

"First, we need to help Rilam. Does anyone here have experience treating wounds?"

"I have some skills," Eladrel said, though he did not elaborate.

"I see," Pendr said, after a moment. "Eladrel, please tend to Rilam. Ayab, go with him."

The young man from Brentwood nodded, gathered the bandages and ointment, and went back further under the fallen tree to where they had placed their wounded companion. Ayab followed.

Pendr rubbed his chin as he thought of the next step. "We need to get a sense of where we are—or at the very least, a direction we can head. Heading north is the most logical conclusion since that will take us away from our enemy's homeland."

"That's obvious," Lunz said.

"It's also foolishness," Rheq said. "Have you learned nothing?"

Lunz balled his fists. "I'm growing weary of your tongue, little boy."

"Fine," Rheq said. "Go north. You'll be dead before the end of the quarter-moon."

Before Lunz could inflame the situation more, Pendr interceded. "Rheq, what do you mean?"

"Remember, I'm from Umstead," Rheq said. "It's close to the border. My family lives with the constant threat of invasion. A tactic used in war is to divide and conquer. The enemy who hit us flanked our main force and hit our supply lines—namely us. If they're smart, they'll continue north, into the heart of the king's land and attack the villages and towns which supply the army."

Pendr let out a deep breath. What Rheq stated made sense. Yet, that did not help with what they should do next. Staying here, under the fallen tree was not a long-term option. Most likely the soldiers who had attacked had also seen them escape into the forest. Though they had tried to double back and cross streams, Pendr knew it would not be hard to track them.

"So, if we can't go north, and going south isn't an option, that leaves east and west," Pendr said.

"East is where we were attacked," Lunz said. "That means we go west."

"No, we should go east," Rheq said, sounding very sure of himself.

"Why?" Pendr and Lunz asked at the same time.

Rheq leaned forward. "Because it is the *last* thing our enemy expects."

Chapter 11

Iredell was five nights' travel from the palace, meaning Wyjec's company would have to stop to camp during the trip. Captains Avadi and Kishul, along with one thousand men and servants, accompanied Wyjec.

Everyone in the company was on horseback, wearing the land's symbol—a crescent moon on a dark blue background. The knights who wore plate mail displayed the standard on their cloaks, whereas the pikemen in quilted tunics had the pattern sewn into their armor. At first, Wyjec was unsure he could manage to ride on a horse. It was not a skill he needed as a chardi. From the deeper parts of his mind, areas he had not visited in many winters, he recalled riding a horse before he was sent to serve in the palace. With those memories came feelings of fondness. Animals had surrounded him as a child—dogs, cats, horses, sheep, chickens. A farm, he must have lived on a farm. Was his family still there? If so, why had they given him up? The Masters punished anyone who spoke of their lives before coming to the palace—over time, Wyjec stopped thinking anything about his early childhood. He would have to think more about those early seasons of his life at a different time. For now, he needed to be aware of his current environment. He had power, and he knew there would be others that would try to take it from him.

Before leaving the palace which Wyjec had claimed as his own, he grasped the blue *myelur* and surrounded himself with a protective layer— a shielding unseen by normal eyes—which covered his dark leather riding outfit. The experience drained him, but not as much as in the past. It seemed the more he used the blue *myelur*, the less of a toll it took. *Or perhaps I'm growing in strength.* That notion excited Wyjec.

He was already powerful, but he realized that he might become even more so.

They left before the sun rose, at Wyjec's insistence. He used the darkness to continue to help him see the red *myelur* more easily and with it the golden amber revealing people's intention. If any planned to do him harm, Wyjec would be able to see it first.

Upon reaching the horses, Captain Avadi showed Wyjec to the mare which he would be riding. Like the vermin Wyjec had faced before, the red *myelur* flowed through the animal, as it did for all living creatures. That meant Wyjec could control his ride by manipulating her intentions.

Wyjec mounted the horse, and in doing so, from his peripheral vision noticed a flicker of amber from Captain Kishul. It was fleeting, just a glimmer, but the amber glow originated from the captain's sword arm and focused on Wyjec's neck. *A warning.* Wyjec made no indication that he noticed. *Let him try. He will make a good example.*

For most of the first day, no one spoke to Wyjec as he followed behind Captain Avadi. While Wyjec would have preferred it was from respect, he understood it was most likely fear. *The weak fear power, as I once did. And now, I have the power.*

It was near sunset when Avadi motioned for the company to stop by a sloping, grassy field. Forest covered most of the area, with meadows appearing sporadically. The field Avadi chose looked big enough for the thousand people with whom they traveled. Captain Avadi trotted forward, toward the middle of the field. He motioned for two knights to flank him on either side. During this commotion, Wyjec heard Kishul remove his sword from its scabbard. At the same moment, Kishul kicked his horse into motion toward Wyjec.

With the blue *myelur* already protecting him from physical harm, Wyjec decided instead to make a special example from Kishul's foolhardy actions. Ignoring the man, Wyjec seized the red *myelur* and focused on Kishul's horse. Pushing with his mind, Wyjec forced the horse to come to a stop and remove Kishul from his back.

The steed bucked ferociously, unhorsing Kishul. The captain fell to the ground, face first, losing his sword upon impact. Another push from Wyjec's mind and the large, armored horse turned his attention to

47

stomping on Kishul. Wyjec watched in satisfaction as the huge animal crushed Kishul's body to a bloody pulp in front of onlookers. Another push through the red *myelur* and the horse came to rest as if nothing happened. With the use of the red *myelur,* Wyjec felt power flow through him—he felt energized, dominant.

Wyjec looked up at the soldiers still mounted who watched the scene with horrific expressions. "Does anyone else want to try to kill me?" he asked, speaking with open hostility.

No one moved, nor did Wyjec sense any threat from them. In reality, none of them met his piercing gaze. *Good. They know their place.*

"Master," came Captain Avadi's voice from behind Wyjec. "I had no idea Kishul would attack you. I've sworn myself to your service, and to break my vow would mean that I have no right being the captain of your forces."

Wyjec peered over his shoulder. The amber glow radiating from Avadi pulsed toward the captain's heart. *Interesting.* Perhaps intention toward one's own heart was an indication of sincerity. If that was so, it was another tool that Wyjec could use to keep his power.

"I believe you, Captain," Wyjec said. "Now, have camp set up before it gets dark."

"As you say, Master." Avadi saluted by pounding his right fist to his left shoulder—a symbol of respect.

In short order, the camp was established. A large, canvas tent stood at the center. Covering it was an oiled leather tarp to keep out any rain which may fall during the night. Wyjec was pleased to see the tent was large enough to fit a quilted, down mattress placed on a wooden pallet. Avadi had done well when he organized the supplies for the trip. The man understood what Wyjec had been taught by the Masters: "When you serve those in power, do more than they expect, lest you feel their wrath."

The scents of roasted mutton soon filled the campsite, causing Wyjec's mouth to water. Since taking control of the palace, he had been able to eat and drink as much as he wanted, yet he was still quite sinewy.

It would take time to build up a proper weight—and he had discovered that mutton was one of his favorites. Avadi once again had been paying attention.

Before dinner could be served, sounds of surprise and muffled shouts came from the far side of the camp. Armoring himself in a blue *myelur* covering, Wyjec stepped from his tent to investigate.

A middle-aged soldier, adorned in chainmail and a conical plate helm, raced toward his tent. Upon seeing Wyjec, he fell to one knee.

"Master," he said, his tone showing reverence. "Word from our scouts outside of Iredell: The enemy is once again approaching in vast numbers."

"How soon before they arrive?" Wyjec asked.

"Six nights, perhaps seven. But, Master, the force is too large. We won't be able to hold Iredell."

Wyjec grinned. "Oh? Tell the men we will be victorious. *I* will be there before the enemy can attack."

Chapter 12

Pendr used his left hand to shield his eyes from the morning's rays. After more discussion the previous night, it was agreed that the survivors Pendr led would head east, meaning they would be walking toward the rising sun.

They had taken turns keeping guard while the others rested. Pendr volunteered to go first, even though he had been bone-weary. When he finally slept, he had done so deeply and awoke more refreshed than he would have thought possible.

More remarkable was Rilam's recovery. His wounds were bound, yet even that would not explain how quickly he was able to recover from the arrows. Pendr knew he should be grateful that his group would be able to move faster, though he found he was uneasy for a reason he could not place. Rilam had even stopped complaining.

"We go east for how long? What are we even looking for?" Lunz asked after they had traveled for most of the morning.

Rheq, walking directly behind the mayor's son, answered before Pendr could. "Shelter. Provisions. And hopefully more survivors."

"Who put you in charge, little man?" Lunz asked over his shoulder.

Rheq responded by kicking Lunz's left foot, causing the mayor's son to trip. Lunz was able to stop his fall by grabbing onto a tree branch, but he was off balance enough that he could not respond with force.

"What's wrong with you?" Lunz asked as he steadied his feet.

Rheq crouched, shifting from side to side. "That's the last time you will say anything about my size. I am quicker than you and more experienced in combat. My people have to be. And I'm not in charge. Pendr is. I'm offering tactical advice. He's smart enough to listen. What are you doing to help the group aside from questioning everything?"

"You will *not* speak to me that way," Lunz said, reaching to unsheathe his short sword.

Before Lunz could brandish his weapon, Pendr grabbed Lunz by the back of his neck, his strong fingers squeezing tightly.

"Stop it!" Pendr said, speaking once again in a strong voice that surprised even himself. Rarely did he raise his voice in frustration, but the situation was dangerous enough without in-fighting. "Lunz, do not draw your sword. Rheq, take the lead."

The rest of the young men watched quietly, none appearing to want involvement in the conflict. For a moment, Lunz did not move, but then eventually he dropped his hand away from his weapon.

"That's why Pendr's in charge," Rheq said as he walked passed Lunz to take his place at the front of the line.

From that moment until mid-afternoon, the small group followed Rheq as he wove a path through the forest, stopping time and again to allow Rilam to rest and letting all of them eat small portions of the rations. Based on Pendr's previous experiences in the forest, which were few, he could not tell how far they had traveled. The noises of small animals and birds, mixed with the chirping of insects, gave the impression there was nothing to fear. Still, Pendr forced himself to stay vigilant. There had been no warning when their camp fell under attack, and he doubted he would be aware of enemies until they made their presence known.

The arbors began to thin, allowing Pendr to see further into the forest than before. Shafts of sunlight cut through the canopy, illuminating patches of the leaf covered ground. Ahead and to the left stood a copse of trees, thicker than those around them. Rheq shifted his direction to enter the heavily wooded area.

The walk gave Pendr time to think, and though he tried to avoid the subject, his mind once again returned to Ayab's claim of arrows bouncing off him. There were a few reasons this could have happened. First, Ayab could have been mistaken. There was no proof, and in the heat of battle, not all was as clear as it seemed. Second, the arrows may have glanced off Pendr and only appeared to have bounced away. But even glancing blows would leave a mark. The third option, which Pendr would rather not believe, was that it was something more. He had, after all, felt an odd sensation—like cool water coursing through him, yet draining him of his energy at the same time. Could it be the *myelur*? No. That was not possible. What Pendr knew of the *myelur* was that it passed from parent to child. Neither of his parents had the gift, so he could not possess it. *Unless they kept it a secret.* Pendr quickly dismissed such thoughts. His parents would not lie to him.

Upon entering the copse, the going became tougher. Thick tree roots hidden under a dense layer of decomposing leaves caused each of the group to trip at least once—all of them except Rheq, who was very sure-footed. The air became mustier, thicker. Breathing took more effort.

"I think we need a break," Lunz called out. "It's been a while."

Pendr could not think of a reason to disagree, aside that it was Lunz who made the suggestion. As the leader, it was Pendr's decision. He paused and inspected the group behind him. They looked weary. Yes, a break would be welcomed.

"Agreed," Pendr said. He turned back to tell Rheq to stop, but the younger man was no longer there. "Rheq!" Pendr called out.

There was no response.

Something's not right. Pendr crouched and motioned for the other boys to do so as well.

"What? What's going on?" Lunz asked, louder than Pendr would have preferred.

"Rheq's gone." Pendr drew his short sword.

The rest of the young men readied their weapons as well, aside from Lunz.

"I told you we shouldn't have trusted him," Lunz said. "He brought us to this spot because it would be easier to lose us here. He's probably headed back to his home—and laughing at us for being so stupid as to follow him."

"Quiet down," Rilam said harshly. The injured young man had not said much since being shot. Pendr was not sure who was more surprised about Rilam speaking out, Lunz, himself, or the other two boys: Ayab and Eladrel.

"*Now* look who decides to speak up," Lunz said. "Had you not been hit while we were trying to escape, we could have made better time. You lost any say when——"

Lunz's next words never left his throat. A spear, its thick wooden shaft stained dark and adorned with feathers, sprouted from his chest, embedded right above his breastbone. Confusion flitted over Lunz's face. He tried to speak, though only deep-red spittle escaped his mouth.

Ayab got to his feet in an attempt to help Lunz but promptly fell face-first to the ground. Two arrows were in his back, one of which caught him in the spine.

Out of the corner of Pendr's eye, he saw movement between the trees. *Another ambush!* Rheq must have led them to this trap. Once again, a cool sensation seemed to spring from the center of Pendr's mind. With it came the odd weariness. It was the same feeling experienced when he had saved Rilam from the battlefield.

"We surrender!" Rilam shouted. He threw his short sword into the underbrush. "Just stop! I beg you! We surrender!"

By now, Eladrel laid prone, though Pendr noticed he still held a tight grip on his sword. Already on his knees, Pendr considered his options. They were few. He did not know what would happen if the enemy captured them, but the dead bodies of Lunz and Ayab made it clear what results to expect if they tried to fight.

"Your hands!" a voice shouted from the wood. "Let's see them!"

Rilam immediately stood, empty hands raised. Pendr glanced at Eladrel. The other man reluctantly dropped his sword and got to his knees, displaying that his hands, too, were empty.

"You! The big one! Your turn!" the voice said.

Pendr realized that his choices were to die now, or perhaps live to fight another day. He chose the latter by letting go of his sword and lifting his hands.

"Smart, very smart," the voice said.

From the wood came four men wearing dark blue tunics with a crescent moon emblazed on their chests. Two held bows, arrows still nocked. The third held a spear, like the one which ended Lunz's life.

"By order of Master Wyjec," the spear-wielding man said, "I declare you prisoners of war."

Chapter 13

Wyjec peered over what would be the battlefield. From his position in the guard tower, which loomed over Iredell, he could see clearly in the direction where King Viskum's troops were approaching—at least according to the latest scouting reports. Captain Avadi stood next to Wyjec, unmoving aside from a few hairs fluttering in the breeze.

"By mid-day, correct?" Wyjec said.

"If the scouts' reports prove to be true." Avadi pointed toward the road which led from Iredell's main gate to the dense forest which lay beyond. "The trees will prevent any full-on assault. They have to come by way of the road."

"And the archers?"

"The trees are far enough away that the archers cannot take shelter while firing upon the city. No doubt that is why the forest was cleared away from the town at its current distance."

Running in either direction was the town's stone walls. At three times the height of a man, it offered protection from a wide-spread attack. His archers lined the tops of the wall, with hundreds of pikemen and townsfolk pressed into the militia waiting in the courtyard behind the city gate. It was only for show, however. Wyjec had a plan which would certainly inspire those who would witness today's events.

Wyjec walked three steps to the other side of the tower. Those gathered below, those pressed into service, would be able to see and hear him from this vantage point.

"People of Iredell and subjects of my land," Wyjec called out. "We see no sign of the enemy as of yet. Take this time to rest, to sup, and most of all, prepare the words you will choose to describe our victory this day!"

The men cried out in support. Some smacked each other on the back, motioning to Wyjec and smiling. Others offered a respectful salute. Wyjec paid close attention to those whose amber glows focused toward their hearts. There were only a few. *They are those who I will make my leaders.*

"A wise move," Avadi said, siding up next to Wyjec. "As the saying goes, 'hunger adds a second enemy in battle.'"

"And thirst? Is that yet another foe?" Wyjec asked.

Avadi nodded. "Fatigue adds a fourth. Your men will be well rested compared to those who march on the town."

"Then our enemy has many foes this day." Wyjec leaned against the stone wall and watched as women and children came out from the houses and shops to serve those armed for battle.

Baked bread and roasted meat not only filled the bellies of the men, but the aromas also filled the air. In the crowd, two men were playing a jaunty tune—one on a lute, the other a recorder. The scene almost felt more like a celebration than a preparation for battle. *And why not?* Wyjec had promised them victory, and victory he would provide.

Two serving girls, not much younger than Wyjec, brought up spiced sausages, buttered bread, sliced pears, and cool water. Both of the young women kept their gazes lowered, as a sign of respect, though Wyjec could see that both would sneak glances at him when they thought he was not looking. *Let them look. Let them tell all they encounter how they served me the day I conquered Viskum's army.*

Mid-day came and left, yet no sign of the enemy appeared. By late afternoon, many of Wyjec's army were dozing, playing dice, or laughing at jokes swapped back and forth.

"Where is the enemy?" Wyjec asked Avadi.

His second-in-command shrugged almost imperceptibly. "War is more often a guessing game than not. Many things could have happened. Most likely, Viskum's troops could have spotted one of the scouts and elected to slow their approach."

"Scouts or no, they know we would be watching for them this close to Iredell."

Avadi gazed at Wyjec, bringing a hand up to his mouth. His eyes searched piercingly.

"What is it then?" Wyjec asked. "Something wrong?"

"Forgive me," Avadi said. He took a more formal stance. "You continue to surprise me. I would not expect someone raised as a chardi to have such drive and insight."

This was not the first time Wyjec had heard someone question his background. One night while traveling to Iredell, the guards outside his tent were speaking in hushed tones, but Wyjec was able to sneak close to hear what they were saying—a skill learned as a chardi. One guard claimed that Wyjec was one of the previous Masters, trained by them to lead their people to a new glorious future. The other guard expressed his doubts but had seen what had happened to Captain Kishul when he had tried to attack Wyjec. That event caused enough fear to keep the other guards in line. In truth, the Masters had trained Wyjec—though not by intent. Wyjec learned to listen, to watch the Masters' actions. Yes, they were excellent teachers.

To respond to Avadi, Wyjec said, "I am more than I appear, and will become more than I am now."

The older man took the statement and appeared to ponder it. Wyjec noticed the captain's amber glow flow inwards, toward his heart, and brighter than before. *His respect grows deeper.*

"There!" a guard from another tower called out. "The enemy approaches!"

Wyjec and Avadi went to the outer edge of the watchtower. In the road that split the tree line, a single bannerman on horseback trotted toward Iredell. A large green and silver flag ruffled in the breeze. The man showed no sign of fear. *That will soon change.*

When the bannerman came closer, Wyjec could see the red *myelur* flow through him. An amber glow showed fifty or so paces from the castle's main gate. *That's where he'll stop. He's here to talk, nothing else.*

The sound of bowstrings pulled taut indicated that Iredell's archers were at the ready. Twenty men with longbows lined the wall, and at the moment, each had their focus on their singular foe.

"Tell the archers to stand down," Wyjec commanded Avadi.

His captain complied. The archers did as instructed, though many shared confused expressions.

"He's here to ask for terms," Wyjec said.

Avadi leaned over the wall a little, hands resting on the edge. "What terms could they hope for? We will not give up Iredell. They should know that."

The captain made a good point. It would take a huge army with massive weapons of war to take the town. Trebuchets could cause some damage, but Wyjec doubted the enemy would use large machines which could fling fiery projectiles. The damage to Iredell would be significant, and King Viskum would lose a valuable fortress in the process. No, the bannerman would want something else.

"It will be interesting to hear what he says," Wyjec agreed.

They did not have to wait long. Once the bannerman arrived at the spot where Wyjec had foreseen, he indeed stopped. Without any formal greeting, the man holding the green and silver banner called out. "In the name of King Viskum, I declare Iredell under siege. No supplies will be allowed to enter or leave the town. The king's men have taken control of all the roads roundabout. We do not wish the women or the young to starve, so we will allow them to flee before nightfall. They will be allowed safe passage. The only way to avoid the siege is to surrender Iredell now. King Viskum will grant amnesty to the soldiers, but the leaders will meet the king's justice. These are the only terms you will be given."

For a drawn-out moment, no one spoke. Wyjec was not sure if the people inside the town heard the words, but he was sure the archers on the wall had. Word would spread throughout the town in short order. If Wyjec did not answer forcefully, the battle could be lost before it even began. Fortunately, he had considered such a scenario and had already formulated a plan.

"I categorically reject your terms," Wyjec said as loudly as he could. "Instead, return to the men with you. Tell them they will be treated well if they lay down their arms and join me. If they do not, they will face the same fate as your horse."

The bannerman shifted uneasily in his saddle. It would be easy for Wyjec to tell his archers to shoot the horse, but that would not invoke the type of fear needed for men to switch sides. *A show of force is needed.*

Wyjec sharpened his focus on the horse's red *myelur*. Surrounding the base of Iredell's walls were large, sharpened wooden pikes, the ends buried at an angle to ward off a full-on assault. As with the situation with Captain Kishul, Wyjec first caused the horse to buck the bannerman from his saddle. However, instead of forcing the beast to turn on the man, Wyjec instead pushed the amber glow on the wooden pikes. Within a heartbeat, the horse rushed toward the town. It let out a cry of pain when it impaled itself, yet Wyjec continued pushing with the amber glow, the forceful intention, until the horse cried out no more.

From his back, the bannerman watched in horror. Once the horse ceased living, the king's man stood, and then began to back away.

"You have until the sun dips below the tree line in the west to surrender," Wyjec shouted. "But the longer you make me wait, the less pleased I will become."

Chapter 14

"Have you ever heard of a Master named Wyjec?" Eladrel asked in a voice just loud enough for Pendr and Rilam to hear.

Instead of answering verbally, and possibly catching the attention of their captors, Pendr shook his head. It was one of the few places of his body that he *could* move. After he, Eladrel, and Rilam had been taken captive, they were marched south for the rest of the day to a camp. Fifty or so men, dressed in blue with crescent moons displayed on their banners, had set up tents next to a slow-moving stream.

Pendr and his companions, at least those who were still alive, were tied securely to broad oak trees with thick hemp rope as the sun was setting. Lunz and Ayab's bodies were left to rot where the enemy killed them. *No, not rot. The wolves will get them first.* The thought should have bothered Pendr more, but from what he had experienced the last few days, the most present feeling was that of numbness.

"I've heard of the Masters before," Pendr answered. He, too, kept his voice low. "A few winters back a merchant came to Logs Pond. He told of how Masters ruled Sothcar, but he never mentioned any of their names."

"It seems this Master, this Wyjec, is their leader," Eladrel said.

"That's enough!" a voice called out from the camp. One of the spear-wielding men stood from his place by their campfire and approached where they were tied. Looming over Eladrel, the man said, "You will be talking enough tomorrow when we find out what you know. But for tonight, you *will* remain silent!" To emphasize the point, the enemy soldier used the blunt end of his spear and smacked Eladrel across the face. Blood oozed from a cut on Eladrel's cheek.

Facing Pendr and Rilam, the enemy asked, "Understand?"

Whereas Rilam nodded vigorously, Pendr avoided the man's gaze and bowed his head. Seeming satisfied, the spear-wielding man went back to the camp.

Darkness soon set in once the sun dipped behind the tree line. Pendr's stomach growled, a noise he could not prevent. Fortunately, it was not loud enough to get the guards' attention. Once the enemy soldiers began falling asleep, Pendr tested the strength of the rope that bound him to the tree. Four, thick cords wrapped around his chest. Even with the strength earned working in the forge, Pendr knew there was no way he could free himself.

A nearly-new moon, hanging in the sky among wispy clouds, soon bathed the campsite in faint bluish-silvery light. As Pendr expected, the enemy kept a guard on duty. The man walked around the camp, not following any type of pattern—at least not one which Pendr could discover. *Even if he was following a pattern, so what?* There was nothing Pendr could do. Or could he?

Memories of the cool sensation in Pendr's mind, followed by fatigue, once again bubbled to the surface. *Is it possible? Can I wield the* myelur? Perhaps this power was something Pendr could use. While he could recall the experience, he had no idea how to access the *myelur*. At different times during his life, he would try to remember a word or phrase, and could almost get it, but for whatever reason, it remained just out of reach. That feeling was not unlike what he was experiencing now.

The guard had said that tomorrow Pendr and his friends would tell them what they knew. With how casually they had killed Lunz and Ayab, torture was a realistic possibility. Perhaps during that moment, Pendr could access the power to protect himself. If so, he would need his rest.

Closing his eyes, Pendr tried to relax. Unsure why, the image of the last time he saw Danla came to his mind. Her waning smile reminded Pendr of a person saying goodbye for the last time while trying to be brave. *I should have asked her to dance.*

How long after that moment Pendr had fallen asleep, he could not say. Though within a short period, which could be deceiving when the land of dreams is concerned, Pendr felt the ropes loosen from around his chest. Prying one eye open, the darkness surprised him, though the moon had traveled to the other side of the night sky. He did not think the enemy would be up before dawn. Fighting to focus his eyes on the campsite, Pendr realized that the soldiers who served Master Wyjec were still asleep. Scanning around the area, Pendr could not see the soldier who was on patrol. *What's happening?* Slowly, as not to make noise, Pendr leaned forward and was able to pull himself away from the tree.

"Shhh!" a voice whispered from behind him. The sound was too fast and quiet for Pendr to recognize it.

Eladrel and Rilam were still tied to their respective trees and seemed to be sleeping. Within his peripheral vision, Pendr noticed a small shape silently move behind Eladrel's tree. The form was dark and moved quickly. *Who knows we are here?*

Pendr realized he was not even sure where *here* was. It was possible that King Viskum's men were in the area. If that was the case, why would they not attack the sleeping camp? Eladrel slumped forward with his bonds cut. The same whisper to be quiet came again from their liberator, and Eladrel appeared to heed the direction.

Shortly, Rilam was freed as well. He moaned a bit when he woke, but not enough to catch the attention of the men in camp. Once again, Pendr looked for the enemy who should be on guard duty, but he could not see him.

The person who freed them remained quiet. He remained shadowed behind a tree, but Pendr could still see him motioning for them to follow.

The three captives exchanged looks before agreeing with an unspoken understanding to leave with the person who released them. As quietly as they could, Pendr and his companions followed the shadowed form away from the camp. There was something familiar with the way the man moved, though Pendr could not quite nail it down.

After traveling a significant distance from the enemy camp, the figure stopped. The sun began to rise, giving a little more light, but not enough for Pendr to identify their liberator, hidden in a dark cloak with a hood pulled over his head. Slowly, he turned around and lowered the hood. Pendr could think of only one person who could have known where they were and could have saved them.

He was wrong.

Chapter 15

Wyjec frowned while watching the sun rise above the treetops. "They didn't come," he said, just above a whisper. "Why didn't they come?"

His second-in-command, Captain Avadi, did not respond. The older man had not left Wyjec's side all night, but at this moment, he offered no counsel.

It did not make sense. Wyjec had shown the enemy what he could do. That alone should have had them coming to Iredell before the previous sunset, begging to join his forces. But the road from the town's main gates to the forest remained quiet. Perhaps the messenger King Viskum had sent lacked the intelligence to explain what had transpired when Wyjec killed his horse. Or perhaps no one believed him, and therefore, they decided to continue with the siege. *Yes, that must be it. People doubt what they have not seen with their own eyes.*

"Avadi, what if they fail to follow my instructions and try to put Iredell under siege?"

Though the captain stood up straight, weariness shone in his eyes. "Siege tactics are effective, Master. We will run out of food while they can supply their troops with whatever is needed. But there is more than that."

Wyjec knew about the food concern, but the way Avadi uttered the last phrase caused him alarm. "What else?"

"Them, Master," Avadi said, pointing to the armed men within the town's walls. "For the majority of them, this is their home. Yes, we have the troops we brought with us, but we are outnumbered. Chances are they would mutiny before food became a serious concern."

"Mutiny? After what I have shown them of my power? They wouldn't dare!"

The lines on Avadi's well-worn face deepened. "Hunger and thirst can lead a man to do many things, Master."

Wyjec began to retort, but then stopped. It was not long ago that he, Wyjec, was a chardi. He often went more than a day without food or water, based on what the Masters allowed. In the end, Wyjec had done just as Avadi suggested the townspeople could, and most probably *would*, do.

But what of the *myelur*? Could Wyjec force them all to do his will? At that moment, understanding came: a moment of clarity which Wyjec had not experienced before. The red *myelur* flowed through all living creatures and with it the amber glow which tied to the individual's focus, or intention. Yet, not all creatures were the same. Animals—like horses and vermin—were easy to manipulate. People were much harder; their sense of will was stronger. When Wyjec killed the Masters, it was one at a time, quickly, yes, but he did not direct the amber glow on two of them at once. There had been seven Masters. The town contained thousands.

"What are our options?" Wyjec asked.

The surprise Avadi displayed was something uncharacteristic of the man. Wyjec understood why. Rarely had Wyjec shown uncertainty—uncertainty was a sign of weakness, but right now, Wyjec needed the experienced captain's advice.

Avadi only paused a moment before answering, "Our scouts should be back soon. If the town is truly under siege, they should know. While we wait, we could let the men rest in proper beds until word arrives. Keep several lookouts and archers on the tower in rotating shifts. The town walls will hold off any assault until we could rouse the rest of the troops."

Wyjec nodded. "See to it that happens. But first, if the town is truly under siege, what can we do?"

"Truthfully, that is not a battle we can win, Master."

Since Wyjec had killed the Masters who had treated him so poorly, he had felt like nothing could be out of his reach. He did not care for the idea that he could lose. *Certainly, there is something I can do!*

"See to the men, and get some rest yourself, Avadi. We will speak again when the scouts return."

His captain saluted. "As you say, Master."

As almost an afterthought, Wyjec peered at Avadi's red *myelur* as the older man walked away. It was fleeting, but for a moment, Wyjec thought Avadi's amber glow no longer focused on his heart—something which Wyjec took as a sign of wavering devotion.

I'm tired. I must have misread him. Instead of leaving the watch tower, Wyjec sat down on the gray stone. The coolness of the aged material seeped through his clothes. Drawing upon the blue *myelur*, he covered his body in a thin layer to keep off the morning chill. He closed his eyes, trying to think of what his next step may be. In the process, he fell into a deep sleep.

The sun had reached its zenith when Wyjec opened his eyes once again. He was still sitting in the tower. A young soldier, dressed in chainmail with a blue, padded tunic ornamented with a crescent moon, stood over him.

"Master, good. You're awake," the soldier said. He sounded relieved.

"What has happened? Have the scouts returned?" Wyjec asked as he stood. The brief rest had done wonders. His whole body felt reinvigorated.

"They returned some time ago, Master."

"And no one woke me?" Wyjec felt anger begin to build inside him. What happened in Iredell next was dependent upon the information the scouts provided.

"Begging your pardon, Master," the soldier said, obviously frightened, "we tried. You would not wake. We even tried to shake you, gently of course, but there was no response."

The claim concerned Wyjec. *Had I slept so deeply that I was unaware of my surroundings?* If that was so, he was vulnerable when asleep. However, when the vermin gnawed on his foot back when he was a chardi, that experience had woken him. *What has changed? Ah, I hadn't shielded myself before sleeping in the palace.*

Not willing to show feebleness in front of the soldier, Wyjec responded, "I am awake now. What is the report?"

The soldier licked his lips. "Perhaps Captain Avadi should update you, Master."

"I am asking *you*." Wyjec put an edge on his voice to make certain this was not a request.

Lowering his eyes, the soldier said, "The scouts have confirmed that King Viskum's forces have placed Iredell under siege."

Chapter 16

"Danla?" Pendr asked to the young woman who had freed him, Eladrel, and Rilam.

She smiled at him, her white teeth as pretty as he remembered.

"How did—"

She shushed him by putting a finger to his lips. "First, let's get you safe. Then I'll explain."

Danla led Pendr, Eladrel, and Rilam through the woods, appearing to know exactly where she was going.

Bewilderment was one of the many emotions Pendr felt as they traveled. In the last few days, he had been attacked, seen friends (both new and old) die, had been captured, and then freed by the person he least expected. Underlying everything was the lingering uneasiness about the *myelur* he may or may not be able to wield.

They traveled until the sun shone overhead through the thick forest. Hunger and fatigue caused Pendr to ache, but the drive to escape was greater. Neither Eladrel nor Rilam spoke much while they traveled, though Rilam would grumble time and again about being hungry. Pendr imagined they must be tired as well. Eladrel was especially sluggish in his movements. Though, ever since the night Pendr first met him after they escaped from the slaughter, Eladrel had been slow when he moved. *Perhaps that's just his way.*

At last, they came upon a camp. Green and silver banners fluttered in the morning breeze above several canvas tents. A campfire built in the middle had several spits over it, roasting and cooking the mid-day meal—rabbit by the looks of it.

"That smells delicious," Eladrel said. He placed a hand on his stomach.

Danla looked over her shoulder. "You're probably near to starving. We'll feed you as soon as possible. First, we must see Mistress Halima."

Pendr had never heard of her before, and from his companions' expressions, neither had they—though he doubted Rilam would have known her. His life on the sheep farm kept the boy fairly isolated in an already remote part of the kingdom.

When Danla spoke Mistress Halima's name, she did so with a certain reverence. Upon walking through the camp, Pendr noticed that all of those he could see were women—about ten to twelve of them. They looked at Pendr and his companions, varied emotions on their faces. *Why aren't there men here?* It was one more question he added to the rest.

No guards were posted outside of the biggest tent in camp, the location which Danla headed. The tent flaps were open, tied off to each side with thick, hemp rope. Pendr could see a lantern upon a table inside the tent, but not much more than that.

Before entering the tent, Danla said, "I can't fully comprehend what each of you has been through. It may sound odd, but I have as many questions as you. Mistress Halima will be able to explain. At least that's my hope."

Pendr wanted to pull Danla aside, to tell her ... he was not sure what he wanted to tell her. He never thought he would see her again, and when he felt as if they would be apart forever, pangs of regret came to him. *But regrets of what? What* do *I feel for her?*

"Come now," Danla said and entered the tent.

Rilam followed first, then Eladrel. Though there was no noticeable change in temperature inside the tent, a cool sensation washed over Pendr as he entered—one that reminded him of the sense he felt when he rushed to save Rilam.

Eladrel stepped aside allowing Pendr to get his first good look at who he assumed was Mistress Halima. When he first heard her name, he imagined a tall, regal figure of a woman. Instead, she was diminutive in stature. At first glance, she looked like she might be a child, but the long, silver hair which reached her waist countered that notion.

Halima smiled at each of them, her eyes nearly as silver in color as her hair. "Ah, wonderful. It worked. Well done, Initiate Danla."

Initiate? What is that? Some sort of title? Pendr had heard the word before but was unsure of its meaning.

"It did, Mistress. Would you like the charm back?" Danla reached around her neck. She wore a necklace, of sorts. Hanging from the end of the silver chain, which hid under her thick, brown blouse, was a green stone, roughly the size of an acorn. Perhaps it was Pendr's imagination, but he thought the stone glowed faintly.

"Yes. I need to study it to verify why you were able to find them."

Danla removed the necklace, pulling it up and over her head, and handed it to Halima.

"I'm sorry to interrupt," Eladrel said. His tone was that of respect. "I don't understand. Who are you? How did you find us? What is going on with the rest—"

Mistress Halima hushed him by holding up her hand. "Certainly you have questions. We have our own, such as how you were separated from the rest of the troops and were captured." She did not speak in an accusatory manner, at least not from Pendr's perception. "I've yet to eat our mid-day meal, and I'm sure all of you are hungry as well. Please, let us go outside to eat. We can answer the questions lingering around us. Danla, please see that they are attended to. I will join you shortly."

Pendr caught Danla's eye, enough to convey his concern. She smiled reassuringly, and then said, "Follow me."

The cool sensation once again washed over Pendr as he left the tent. It was not unpleasant, just ... odd.

Felled trees surrounded the campfire. They had been dragged from the nearby forest as a place to sit. A few women, most of an age with Danla, were already sitting and eating. In short order, Pendr, Eladrel, and Rilam were given portions of rabbit stew and tankards of water. While the food was delicious, Pendr found he hungered more for answers.

None of the women in the camp spoke as they ate, and they appeared tense, even Danla. An uncomfortable silence surrounded the campfire.

It was not until Mistress Halima exited her tent that the women visibly relaxed.

"My young initiates," the older woman said upon reaching the campfire. "Thank you for preparing this meal. As you can see, Danla was the first to return of those we sent out. It is as we hoped. She was able to find some of those who were missing." She turned her attention to Pendr, Eladrel, and Rilam. "Now, please tell us what you've experienced."

The other two young men faced Pendr, indicating they wanted him to do the talking. It made sense; he was still their leader, after a fashion. "Yes, of course," Pendr said. "After we arrived in camp, we were assigned…" For the next several moments, he told the basics of what had transpired. Unsure why, even to himself, he elected to leave out any mention of possible powers which he experienced. Each time he told of some of the young men from Logs Pond dying, he noticed Danla's shocked reaction. By the time he finished, she was crying softly to herself. Pendr could not blame her—these were young men with whom she had grown up.

"And that is when Danla found you? Correct?" Mistress Halima asked when Pendr finished.

Pendr nodded.

"And you say she freed you?"

"She did, though I didn't know it was her until we were away from our captors. It was a very brave action."

Halima walked over to where Danla sat and rested a hand on her shoulder. "Aye, she is brave."

"Now please," Pendr said, "tell us. How did she find us? Why did you send her? Where are the rest of the—"

Again, Halima stopped the conversation by holding up her hand. "I will answer your questions, the best I can. But first, I must warn you. You may find what I am going to tell you hard to believe."

Chapter 17

Wyjec felt helpless for the first time since he initially grabbed the blue *myelur*, back when one of the Masters had stepped on his hand. Since then, he had discovered he could do more with the power. With that, his confidence grew, yet now, that feeling of supremacy had dimmed, not unlike how light fades with the setting sun.

During the course of the afternoon, Wyjec had remained in his watchtower and considered his options. With the town of Iredell under siege, he was trapped. But it was not just him—Wyjec's soldiers were imprisoned amongst the town's denizens.

Less than a season previous, the people of Iredell were subjects to King Viskum. When Wyjec's former Masters seized the town, the townspeople had offered little resistance. Thinking back to one of the many dinners where Wyjec had served the Masters, he recalled a conversation about the town's capture.

"They were not expecting an invasion," Glutton had said. "Our troops entered the town under the guise of merchants and travelers. The battle was quick and decisive. Iredell had little in the way of weapons or armor."

What was true back then was much the same now. Those of Iredell pressed into service used crude weapons—pitchforks, wooden clubs, swords constructed from cheap metal. Their armor was not much better: mainly thickly padded tunics and leather caps. However, what they lacked in weapons of war, they made up for in numbers. Wyjec's troops were outnumbered over five-to-one when considering those who called Iredell home.

Captain Avadi had not returned to the tower, nor had Wyjec sent for him. *Why is that? Am I afraid to admit I was wrong? Showing weakness to the captain would only lead to—* Wyjec did not get to complete the thought. Something hit him, hard. The blow struck just underneath his rib cage. It had been strong enough to make him stumble two steps to his left. Confusion was the first emotion: he was the only one in the tower. A quick glance to his side replaced the confusion with clarity. An arrow protruded from his body. At that moment, the yellow *myelur*, something he had not felt since killing the vermin back in the palace, pulsed forcefully in his mind. However, this time, no thread from him to anything, or anyone, was noticeable. No enemy soldiers were visible. Who had shot him? It was puzzling, yes, but there were more pressing matters at the moment.

Foolishness! Wyjec had released the blue *myelur* after he had woken that morning and with it, the protection it offered. Believing the tower offered enough defense, Wyjec thought it best not to overuse the blue *myelur*. Although grasping the power did not drain him like at first, it still slowly sapped energy from his body. He wanted to be able to use the power when needed. Now was exactly one of those moments.

Quickly reaching for the blue *myelur*, Wyjec encased his body in an invisible shield—and just in time. Several more arrows struck him heartbeats later. *My men are firing at me!* These potentially fatal darts bounced off him, yet the archers continued to fire. *Why? They cannot hurt me now!* Part of his mind also recognized he did not feel any pain from the wound. Perhaps the blue *myelur* was blocking the pain as well. However, the arrow would need to come out, and soon. The yellow *myelur* still pulsated brightly in his mind, but without any living thing close to him, he could not use it.

From the two front watch towers, archers—dressed in blue with crescent moons on their chests—continued to fire. There were four soliders in each tower. It did not make sense. Surely those firing at him could see it was futile. Anger bubbled up from deep within Wyjec. He had shown the men the cost of betrayal before. It seemed some men never learned.

Focusing on one of the archers in the west tower, Wyjec isolated the amber glow flowing from the man. Not surprisingly, it was focused on Wyjec. Glancing over his shoulder, Wyjec located an archer from the east tower. With minimal effort, he pushed the glow from the western archer toward one of the eastern soldiers. As expected, the next arrow loosed from the subject flew passed Wyjec and connected solidly into the breastbone of the other man.

Instead of the remaining archers stopping, they increased their efforts. *This is madness! What do they hope to achieve?* Wyjec turned back toward the west, and in doing so, bumped the arrow in his side against the half wall of the watchtower. Though the shielding protected him from pain, Wyjec felt the tip from the arrow move inside his body. It was an unsettling sensation—unlike anything he had felt before. The yellow *myelur* flared again. The arrow in his side was too strong of a sensation to ignore.

He reached down to pull out the arrow when he noticed movement from the stairway which led to the tower. At that moment, realization struck. The archers knew they could not hurt him once he called on the power within him, but that was not their goal. They were a distraction.

Several large men, each wearing solid metal breastplates, raced up the stairs. They wielded no swords. Instead, they held large shields with the emblem of a crescent moon emblazoned upon them. These were the fighters which accompanied Wyjec to Iredell. *Betrayal!*

Wyjec tried to locate the amber glow from the lead man, but the soldier came on too quickly. Unable to do much of anything else, Wyjec reached for the blue *myelur* to draw upon as much protection as possible.

When the lead soldier crashed into Wyjec, he was startled when he felt the blow. It did not hurt, yet he could sense the pressure of the shield as it rammed into him. This was followed by a second blow, then another. With each subsequent attack, Wyjec was forced backward— toward the tower wall.

Understanding came to Wyjec when a final push forced him over the edge of the tower. The fall was quick, and Wyjec landed squarely on one of the large wooden pikes which surrounded the wall of the town.

The pike did not impale him, but the impact was enough to draw the breath from Wyjec's lungs. Wyjec's body bounced from one pike to another before landing with a loud *thump* on the ground. Momentarily losing the ability to breathe had happened to him before, back when he had been a chardi. Still, panic came with the incapacity to draw air into his body. Once again, the yellow *myelur* dominated all of his other senses.

Men cheered from the top of the town's walls. "He's down!" Wyjec heard someone cry out.

"Is he dead?" A voice asked. It was a voice Wyjec recognized: Captain Avadi.

"Unknown. Though no one could survive that fall."

Lying motionless, Wyjec waited for his breath to return. When it finally did, the yellow *myelur* faded a little, though it remained strong. He remained motionless. There was nothing they could do to hurt him physically—he still wielded the blue *myelur*. However, he ached more than he thought possible. The betrayal hurt as much as anything he could recall.

I need to get away. Tilting his head slightly, Wyjec looked toward the tree line to the west of the town. Seeking out with the red *myelur*, Wyjec found an area in the forest void of human occupants. Somewhere in the forest, the enemy lay in wait. And the enemy was also behind him, in the town. As a point of fact, Wyjec had no allies. *I am alone.*

With that solemn understanding, Wyjec got to his feet. Cries of surprise from the top of the town's walls followed, but Wyjec paid them no mind. The damage was done. For now, all he wanted to do was get away. Still holding onto the blue *myelur*, Wyjec stood. Though he did not feel pain from the arrow in his side, his body reacted oddly when he tried to walk toward the dense forest in front of him. Ignoring the taunts and threats from those on the wall, Wyjec shuffled-stepped to what he hoped would be the safety of the trees.

Chapter 18

For a moment, no one around the campfire spoke. Pendr noticed that Eladrel sat up taller than he had recently. Rilam kept his eyes to the ground, while Danla and the other women in the camp all focused on Mistress Halima.

"Why would we find what you are about to tell hard to believe?" Eladrel asked. Even his voice sounded stronger than before to Pendr.

The diminutive leader of the camp folded her hands over her lap. "Because we are going to talk frankly about things which will make you uncomfortable. When people hear things that they don't like, they tend to doubt them. However, for you to be successful, you must conquer your natural reactions."

The women around the fire—a dozen or so—nodded. Danla reached over and touched Pendr lightly on the arm. "Just listen before you make any judgments."

No one knew Pendr in this group like Danla. *For her to speak up, she must believe I'll be the one to doubt.*

"Danla was able to find you because one of your group can wield the *myelur*," Mistress Halima said.

"*Myelur?*" Rilam asked, speaking for the first time since they entered the camp. "What's that?"

Pendr had heard the word before—only in whispers. The leaders in Logs Pond had made it clear it was a word which was not to be spoken, let alone discussed, though they had not said why.

"The *myelur* is a power, of sorts," Halima said. "Every living thing contains all aspects of the *myelur*, though only a select few have the ability to manipulate it."

"I don't understand," Rilam said. "If what you say is true, why haven't

I heard of this before?"

Rilam had grown up in the same area as Pendr, though Rilam's family were sheep farmers and lived on the outskirts of Logs Pond. Because Pendr lived and worked in the heart of the town, he suspected he had heard more than his friend when it came to the things of the world.

"As I have said," Halima responded, "people often fear what they find strange or hard to understand. Many would rather not talk about it at all."

"Pendr? Eladrel? Have you heard of this … this …" Rilam struggled to say the word which was new to him.

"*Myelur*," Danla prompted.

"I've heard the word before," Pendr said slowly, "though only in hushed tones."

Rilam's eyes grew wide. "Oh? And you, Eladrel?"

The tall, thin man did not respond verbally. Instead, he nodded his head solemnly.

"So, then, what does it do?" Rilam asked.

Halima stared into each of the young men's eyes before she continued. "Wise elders study their whole lives to answer that very question. It is complex, yet simple."

"That's not very helpful," Rilam said.

Danla huffed. "Clamp your lips and open your ears, Rilam. Give Mistress Halima a chance to explain."

"Why? What does this have to do with anything we've experienced?" Rilam asked. Danla and Rilam knew each other quite well from growing up in the same area, and for whatever reason, the two of them always seemed to grate on each other, at least from what Pendr had observed. A spat now, between them, would only complicate matters.

Halima intervened before Pendr could. "Based on what Pendr told us about your experiences over the last few days, without the help of the *myelur* you'd most likely be dead, young man. You were shot with arrows, were you not?"

"Yes, but—"

"But, here you are, a short time later, and you show no ill effects from the wounds," Halima pointed out.

"I ... I don't remember much after Pendr pulled me from the battlefield until the following morning," Rilam said. "I can't say what happened."

Pendr made the connection. "I remember. Eladrel treated your wounds. Your recovery was miraculous."

Everyone around the cooking fire turned their attention to Eladrel. He kept his shoulders squared, though his gaze remained on the fire.

"Eladrel, did you use the *myelur* to heal Rilam?" Halima asked.

"That's a safe guess," he said.

For the first time since Pendr had met Halima, he thought he saw her tense up.

"This next question is very important," Halima said. "*How* did you heal him?"

Only the sound of the snapping and hissing of the fire filled the air after the question. Danla's hands gripped her brown skirt hard enough to make her fingers turn white. Though Pendr did not know why, much depended on Eladrel's answer.

"My mother is a healer," Eladrel said. "She taught me. She showed me how to tap into my inner power to heal—to let it flow from me to the person I intended to make whole."

Healer? Logs Pond had a healer, but she was unable to do what Eladrel had done to mend Rilam's wounds.

Halima visibly relaxed upon hearing Eladrel's words. "Were you able to rest enough after the healing?" she asked.

Eladrel shook his head. "I got some rest, yes—as much as possible when being hunted by men who want to kill you."

"Oh, you poor dear," Halima said. "You must have been exhausted."

Glancing at Rilam, Eladrel said, "Complaining about it wouldn't have changed anything. I couldn't very well take a nap in the middle of a war."

"That's true." Halima addressed Danla. "Eladrel is the reason you were able to find them. Because you share the same gift, the gemstone was able to guide you to him—like a candle in the darkness."

Wait! What? Danla has the gift? The girl Pendr had known his whole life, the girl who was more than a sister to him, she could use this *myelur*? *Why hasn't she told me?*

"So, this *myelur* can heal people?" Rilam asked.

Halima smiled. "That, and much more."

Chapter 19

Wyjec sat down, his back resting against a red maple. Normally he would be able to feel the rough texture of the bark, but with the blue *myelur* still encasing him, all he could sense was its solidness. He had walked far enough into the forest that he could no longer hear the sounds from Iredell. The people of the town taunted him as he left them behind, each word a dagger to his ears.

I had it. I had power. And I lost it. When he was a chardi, Wyjec had never known power or respect shown toward him. During his youth, he thought his life could not be more miserable. He was wrong. Having known power, and now no longer having it was worse. Much worse. *I didn't know what I truly had until I lost it.*

Almost an afterthought was the arrow still in his side. The blue *myelur* still shielded him from the pain, but Wyjec could not continue to walk around with an arrow protruding from his body. Regardless of his next move, the arrow would have to come out.

Wyjec took in a deep breath, grabbed hold of the arrow's shaft and pulled. It moved a little, but not enough to be free. He tried again and made a little more progress, but still it remained. *I don't have the strength to pull it out.*

For a drawn-out moment, he simply sat there. The sun's light had to fight its way through the layering of leaves overhead, creating a greenish aura around the area. Birds and insects chirped away as if they did not have a care in the world. *Oh, to be a simple creature.* They did not have to worry about betrayal and the pain it caused.

To his left, Wyjec heard a rustling in the bushes. It was fleeting, stopping almost as soon as it started. With the dimness of the forest to aid him, Wyjec focused his attention on where the sound had emanated. Glimpses of the red *myelur* shone through the gaps of the foliage.

Something alive, something *big*, watched him from just out of sight. *Is it a soldier or something else?* Wyjec thought of what he knew about the forest. It was not much. With the exception of a few images of his early childhood and the events of the last few days, life in the Master's palace had been all he had known.

Wyjec shifted his legs to face whatever it was which remained hidden. A growl, deep and throaty, rumbled from the creature's concealed area.

That's not a vermin! A jolt of fear rushed through Wyjec. Then, to his right, another growl—this one even deeper and more menacing. Only moving his head, Wyjec searched for the source of the other sound. His gaze locked onto the eyes of the beast. Wyjec had not seen its like before.

It had a large snout, with two large canines visibly protruding from an upper set of teeth. Its fur was black, streaked with gray. But it was the eyes, the *golden* eyes, which were the most intimidating. They displayed a sharpness not found in simpler creatures, like vermin. *Wolf. It has to be.*

Wyjec had heard of the wolves who lived in the forests. They were to be feared, of that he was sure. The second wolf, the one Wyjec faced, moved forward, revealing its presence. It appeared to be younger. Smaller, certainly, as well as more brown in color.

They can't hurt me. I still wield the blue myelur. Neither of the wolves knew that, Wyjec realized, as they lunged toward him.

The smaller wolf crashed into Wyjec's left side. The blow snapped the arrow, leaving the head still inside Wyjec's body. The bigger wolf attempted to clamp its jaws on Wyjec's right arm, and surprise appeared in the wolf's eyes as its teeth failed to tear into flesh.

"Enough!" Wyjec shouted. Sensing the larger wolf's red *myelur*, and the amber glow which accompanied it, he pushed with his mind to redirect its will toward the smaller wolf.

Immediately, the older, stronger wolf attacked. It leaped at the younger wolf's throat and snapped its teeth into the soft gullet.

Blood sprayed across the ground, along with the surprised whimper of the soon-to-be-dead wolf. A twist and a push from the larger wolf whipped the dying animal to land on top of one of Wyjec's legs. The yellow *myelur* flared, but Wyjec could not focus on it.

Wyjec's heart beat faster in his chest as he pushed with the red *myelur*, forcing the dominant wolf to focus its attention upwards—causing the beast to leap skyward again and again. Setting his hand down on the ground to move away from the wolves' battle, Wyjec encountered something odd. Wetness met his fingertips, and a quick glance revealed the dampness was red—blood red—and it was not from the wolves.

Blood pumped out of Wyjec's side where the arrow had snapped off. Energy began to drain from Wyjec along with the life fluid. Holding on to both the red and the blue *myelur* was becoming too much. Quickly weighing his options, Wyjec decided to release the blue *myelur*, rationalizing that as long as he controlled the red, he could keep the wolves off of him.

Dropping the shielding caused a different problem, however, as Wyjec soon understood. Without the protection came the pain of the wound in his side. Lances of agony raced through Wyjec's body, causing his sight to dim. *No! I can't let this happen!* Panic once again invaded when he realized that if he were to lose consciousness, he would lose control of the red *myelur*, and therefore, nothing would stop the larger wolf from turning on him.

There! Piercing the haze of his fading vision, Wyjec saw it: the yellow thread between him and the nearly dead wolf which still lay on his legs. Remembering the vermin he fought in the castle, Wyjec mentally pulled on the yellow thread as hard as he could.

Instant relief from the pain in his side was the first sensation. And there was something more. Energy flowed along the thread from the injured wolf to Wyjec, healing him and restoring his strength. Most curious of all was the feeling in his side. From the wound, Wyjec could see the head of the arrow being expelled from his body, until it finally was cleared and plopped to the ground. The restoration power of the yellow *myelur* also countered any pain he should have been feeling.

Before Wyjec felt completely whole, the yellow thread snapped. He reached for it again, but it was no longer there. At the same moment, he realized that the red *myelur* no longer flowed in the wolf on his legs. *It's dead. That must be why I can't pull any more energy from it.*

For a moment, Wyjec became distracted as he considered the implications of what the yellow *myelur* truly did. His control of the larger wolf ceased, and it turned its attention back toward Wyjec. Fangs bared, it moved to attack.

Almost instinctively, Wyjec located the beast's red *myelur* and seized the amber glow. Instead of redirecting it toward any particular object, he pushed it toward the wolf's own heart. That action meant loyalty, at least as far as Wyjec could understand.

At once, the wolf calmed. Instead of pressing the attack against Wyjec, it instead stepped back. Slowly, it lowered its head and grabbed hold of the dead wolf's tail and pulled the corpse off Wyjec's legs. Once completed, the wolf sat at Wyjec's feet not quite touching him, ears relaxed, and head resting on the ground.

From Wyjec's perception, the wolf was showing respect. The amount of effort to hold the wolf in check was minimal, barely causing Wyjec's heart to beat faster than normal. A moment of inspiration hit. *Men are too stubborn, too unpredictable to control. But not simpler creatures, like wolves.*

Wyjec now knew what his next move would be.

Chapter 20

Pendr's head still swam in questions about Danla's ability to use the *myelur*. She was right; he did not like the idea based on his initial judgment. But Eladrel also had the power, and without it, Rilam would most likely be dead. *I shouldn't rush to judgment.*

The three young men and the dozen young women let Halima's last declaration sink in before any of them spoke. "The *myelur* can do more than heal," she had said.

No one had spoken after her statement. The sun shone brightly in the sky, reminding Pendr how long he been without feeling safe. Also, being awake most of the night, and then eating a large mid-day meal was making Pendr drowsy. Sleeping during the hottest time of the day always hurt Pendr more than it helped, but he was not sure how much more he could take. Despite his uneasy feelings on the matter, Pendr wanted to know more about the *myelur*.

"Can it act as protection?" Rilam asked, seeming as anxious to know as Pendr. "The *myelur*, that is?"

Halima smiled and nodded. "Yes, it can."

Rilam then turned to Pendr and looked him up and down. Avoiding eye contact with his friend, Pendr asked, "How? How can it protect?"

"First, you must understand the basics of the *myelur*," Halima said. "The easiest way to do so is to relate it to something you can understand." The elderly lady pointed to the sky. "What color is that?"

"Blue," Rilam said.

Next, Halima waved to the trees around her. "And the color of the leaves on the trees?"

"Green," Pendr said, speaking before Rilam could make a comment which could come across as disrespectful.

"And the embers of the fire?" Halima asked.

"Red," Rilam and Pendr said at the same time.

Halima nodded. "Just as each of these colors is different, so is it with the distinct aspects of the *myelur*. Point of fact, those who can wield one of these traits often tell that the power they sense has an aura of one of those colors. Each of these has an ancient name, which in truth, are hard to pronounce, so instead, they are referred to as a color."

So far, Pendr was following. He imagined the *myelur* was like a sword. The weapon consisted of a blade, a guard, a grip, and a pommel—each unique—but part of a greater whole.

"Is it only those three?" Rilam asked."

Once again, Halima tensed. "No … there is also one which is known as yellow, though that is dangerous and not to be used."

"Why?" Rilam pressed.

"You are not ready to understand that yet," Halima said. "Even if I were to tell you now, it would not make sense."

Rilam rubbed his temples. "So far, not much of this is making sense."

The statement was odd to Pendr. No, he did not know much of the *myelur*, but neither was he lost.

"Keep listening, Rilam," Danla said. "It takes some time."

Rilam folded his arms and leaned back, away from the fire.

"As I stated," Halima continued, "the *myelur* can be broken down into red, blue, and green. Green is the aspect which allows healing in the proper way. A person who can wield the green shares some of their life force with an injured person. Those who perform this often describe it as seeing a thread between them and the person who is receiving the help."

"How far can this thread reach?" Pendr asked. "After all, there were soldiers, friends of mine, who died when we were attacked. Why didn't Eladrel heal them so they could make it to safety?"

Eladrel spoke next. "It doesn't work that way, I fear. I must be touching the other person for the thread to appear. It also takes a lot of concentration, and I am still learning. That's why I didn't heal Rilam until I had time to clear my head."

"More practiced healers, those who can access and use the green *myelur*, can use their gift in the heat of battle," Halima said. "It takes time to develop the skill, sometimes many winters, depending on the person."

Pendr looked at the young women of the camp. Each of them wore a green embroidered stripe around the arms of their robes.

"And these with you here," Pendr said, motioning to the females, "they possess the gift to wield the green *myelur*?"

Halima smiled. "Very astute of you. Yes, these young ladies are all healers in training, known as initiates. For some unknown reason, the ability to use the green *myelur* is more common in women, though there are men, like Eladrel, who can also wield it."

How long had Danla known? Why would she keep it a secret? As if reading his mind, Danla said, "Pendr, I had no idea I could do this. After we had arrived at camp, we were tested. I can't explain how—but I was told I have the gift. I've been learning how to use it from Mistress Halima. We all have." Danla motioned to the other young women.

"But we're at war!" Rilam said. "If all of you are healers, where are those who are protecting you?"

"We're quite safe, I assure you," Halima said.

After what Pendr experienced, he could not suppress this doubt. "I mean no disrespect, Mistress Halima, but there are those in the forest who would not hesitate to kill you … or capture you." He didn't want to think what could happen if these women were prisoners. Men did unspeakable things during war.

"That's where the blue *myelur* is of the most use," Halima said. "It is a protecting power—a shield of sorts."

"What can it do?" Eladrel asked. Perhaps he had learned only of the green *myelur*, the power he could use.

Halima squared her shoulders. "At its most basic, it can protect the person who can draw upon it."

"Could it stop arrows from piercing your body?" Rilam asked.

"It can, yes. Though that usually takes practice."

Rilam reached over and smacked Pendr on the arm. "I knew it! Ayab told me what you did, and how he saw the arrows bounce off you. You can use the blue *myelur!*"

Chapter 21

The arrowhead in Wyjec's hand, the one which had recently been in his side, was barbed. It was no wonder he could not pull it out—it was designed to prevent such an action. *Once it is in, it is meant to stay in.* That thought was not unlike what else he had been contemplating. He still controlled the large wolf which lay at his feet, but only by exerting his will. In time, Wyjec would need to sleep, or even use the red *myelur* on something else. If he released his hold on the wolf, it would certainly attack him.

If only there was a way to get the wolf to remain loyal without my direct influence. But how to get the amber glow to stick to the wolf's heart? It was something Wyjec had puzzled over while the sun climbed into the sky.

Taking a moment to think of something else, Wyjec fingered the hole in the side of his leather tunic where the arrow had entered. It wasn't a large rip, but one none-the-less. It would need sewing, but he lacked needle and thread.

Sewing! It was a skill the masters had taught the chardi, mainly in order to fix their own clothes. It was a way of binding two fabrics together. Perhaps there was a way to do that with the heart of the wolf and the amber glow.

Staring at the wolf, Wyjec probed deeper, trying to isolate the aura which indicated intention. It was there, surrounding the beating heart of the beast, right where he placed it. Wyjec had never before truly examined the amber glow closely. In doing so, he noticed something remarkable. The red *myelur*, the power he perceived as flowing through living beings, consisted of tiny threads, like the yellow thread he had noticed before, only the red was much more abundant. The amber glow, then, was a fabric of sorts, made up from yellow and red threads woven together.

It made an odd sort of sense to Wyjec. The red threads were willpower—life flowing, like blood, constantly moving in an attempt to keep the being alive. The yellow, as Wyjec had discovered, was something similar, a life force, the essence of what separates the living from the dead. When combined, willpower and life force, it created action or at least intended action.

But why would the amber glow around the heart create loyalty? Maybe loyalty was the wrong word. Perhaps self-preservation was more appropriate. *Yes. That's it.* Captain Avadi was not loyal, not truly—instead, he was looking out for his own well-being.

If the wolf at his feet only focused on preserving its life, why had it not run away? For that matter, why had Avadi also not fled? There was a missing piece; something Wyjec did not understand. At least not yet. *Understanding how something fully works and using it are two different things.* Wyjec could not explain why water fell from the sky in the form of rain, though he did know uses for the water. The same concept applied.

Looking once again at the amber glow around the wolf's heart, Wyjec probed with his mind until he found the edge of the fabric. *There!* The fringes of the glow were not smooth—tendrils of the red and yellow *myelur* snaked out, almost fluttering after a fashion. Again, exerting his will, Wyjec seized these tendrils and began to tie them to the red *myelur* which flowed around the wolf's heart. The task took effort, and Wyjec double checked all the tendrils were secured before he dared to try the next phase of his plan.

Though the yellow *myelur* from the now dead wolf had helped Wyjec's energy, he was still drained from losing blood, as well as drawing on so much of the blue *myelur* to protect him in the tower before he had been shoved off. *But I have to try.*

Wyjec took a deep breath and then pulled the blue *myelur* around him, protecting him from head to toe. The effort nearly made him lose his grip on controlling the wolf. That was the end goal, but not until Wyjec felt ready.

Several heartbeats later, Wyjec knew he had to try now before he lost consciousness. Staring directly into the wolf's golden eyes, Wyjec released his hold on the amber glow.

The wolf twitched, then twitched again. It jumped to its feet. For a moment, Wyjec thought the beast would attack him, or bolt. Instead, the wolf did something he did not expect. The wolf walked next to Wyjec, turned around and laid next to him, though it still did not touch him.

Fascinated, Wyjec watched the wolf, making sure he was not exerting any part of the red *myelur* on the animal. *It worked!*

Whether it was the comfort of understanding what he had done, or his body had given all it could at the time, Wyjec fell into a deep sleep.

Chapter 22

Me? Able to use the blue myelur? Pendr thought it was possible, though he did not want to believe it to be true.

Danla stared at Pendr, her blue eyes wide. "Is it true, Pendr?"

Oddly, Mistress Halima did not appear surprised. He noticed the older woman watching him carefully when he responded.

"I can't say if it's true or not," Pender said. "As I said in my account of what happened, I ran back into the open field to rescue Rilam. Ayab claims, or claimed I guess…" A moment of grief pierced him. Logically, he knew Ayab was dead, along with the others: Lunz, Tikan, Wescro, as well as soldiers he had met recently. Emotionally, the realization of their loss came in spurts, and when it hit, it took a moment for Pendr to compose himself.

"It's fine, Pendr," Halima said. "Take your time."

From his peripheral vision, he could see Rilam's head turned away from the group, with his hand wiping away tears. *I'm not the only one who feels their loss.*

After taking a few deep breaths, Pendr continued, "Ayab claimed to have seen arrows hit me and then bounce away. I didn't feel them, nor did they leave a mark."

"And did you feel anything before and after?" Halima asked.

Pendr considered the question before answering. *What happens to me if I'm found to possess this power?* Though it had only been less than a season, he missed the days of working side-by-side with his father at the forge. A blacksmith. That is what Pendr was meant to be. Not a soldier, and certainly not someone who can wield the blue *myelur.*

Still, if Danla could accept her ability …

"Before heading out to the field to get Rilam, I felt a cool sensation in my mind," Pendr said. "I'm not sure how else to describe it. It was refreshing, yet tiring at the same moment. Strange, odd, but not unpleasant."

Halima nodded. "And after you returned with the other young man?"

"I was tired, yet in a different way than caused by running. The weariness was … deeper. I suppose that is as good of a word as any. However, what I know of the *myelur*, which is precious little, is that it is passed down from parent to child. Neither of my parents could use it, and to my knowledge, the same was true with Danla's parents. I can't believe my parents would lie to me."

"I asked the same question," Danla said.

"Yes, she did," her teacher confirmed. "It's possible for someone to have the gift and not know it. Until a few days ago, neither you nor Danla knew of your abilities. There are accounts of individuals not discovering they could use the *myelur* until much later in life. Often, it is a traumatic event which can trigger it."

"Perhaps what I felt during battle and the arrows missing me are a coincidence," Pendr said. "That is more likely."

"Possibly, but answer me this," Halima said, leaning forward noticeably. "What did you feel when you entered my tent upon first arriving at camp? Be honest."

Pendr thought back to that time. "It was similar to the cool sensation I felt before," Pendr answered. "But I can't say why. I didn't feel the same fear as before. I mean, I didn't feel like I needed protection."

"No, but *I* did," Halima said.

Eladrel spoke up. "From us?" He sounded startled.

The elderly lady's gaze moved from Pendr to Eladrel. "That's correct. The blue *myelur* can do more than protect a single person—though it's at its strongest when focused on the person who can wield it. It can also be used to create wards."

"Wards?" Rilam asked. "I don't know that word."

"It's like a shield, of sorts," Eladrel said.

Halima smiled. "That's correct. These wards vary in strength. Some of the simpler ones can tell the creator of the ward when someone actively uses the *myelur*, any of the types, within a certain area. One similar to that, somewhat harder to cast, can detect if someone who can use the *myelur*, any of the types, passes through it. The last of these passive wards—"

"Passive?" Pendr interrupted this time. Up until this point, he had been following along, but now Halima was using words with which he was not familiar.

"Passive is the opposite of active," Halima said. "Let me give you an example. When cooking a stew, you have to combine all the elements into a pot, create a fire, and then set up the pot so it will heat up the contents. Those are all active actions. However, the stew is still cooking if you let it be. This is what passive means, in a sense. After the wards are set up, they remain in place, doing their jobs, until you intervene."

The explanation helped, though the overall concepts were still foreign. *Maybe this is what she meant when she said the* myelur *was simple, yet complex.* Pendr tried to stay focused on the basics. The process of learning something new was an experience he faced many times when working at the forge. Pendr's father, Osbrik, drove home the truth of learning the fundamentals before moving on to the complex. Each of the basic metalworking skills built on each other, and when used together effectively, amazing items could be created.

"That explanation helps," Pendr said. "Thank you. As you have said, there are these … wards … which can be set up to alert the wielder of the *myelur* being used or even if a person has the ability. Correct?"

"That's right," Halima said. "Those of my order have been experimenting with imbuing this power, at least to some degree, to objects—like the one Danla wore when she went to find you. Three other initiates were given similar pendants, yet Danla was the first to return. She was able to sense you, and find you."

"That's a pretty big coincidence that it was Danla, someone from our hometown, had found us, isn't it?" Rilam said.

Halima's eyebrows raised. "Is it? Or is it possible that because of your common background and association that the pendant pointed her in your direction—especially since Pendr can wield the blue *myelur*? There are elements we do not know about yet with the imbuing power. I am anxious to tell my order what we have discovered."

"But being warned about danger isn't the same as protection," Rilam said.

If Halima was becoming frustrated with Rilam's brusque questions, she did not let it show. "There is one other passive form of the blue *myelur*—the most challenging to learn, and also the most powerful. It can sense if a person, or animal for that matter, intends harm—whether they can wield the *myelur* or not. It prevents the malevolent being from even passing through the ward."

"And that is the type of ward you placed around your tent?" Eladrel asked.

Once again, Halima appeared pleased when one of the young men pieced together what she was trying to teach with the realities of what they were experiencing.

Pendr snapped his fingers. "And that's why you don't have soldiers here in the camp. You, Mistress Halima, are protecting them."

"Correct, once again."

"But … aren't you tasked with teaching these young women to be healers?" Eladrel asked. "Does that mean you can wield the blue and the green *myelur*?"

The excitement in Danla's voice was unmistakable when she said, "Oh, it's more than that. Though she cannot wield it, Mistress Halima knows much about the third aspect: the red *myelur*!"

Pendr stared into the fire pit as he thought. The green *myelur* had healing powers—something which Eladrel, the soldier from Brentwood, could use. The blue aspect of the *myelur* could create protective wards, as well as a shielding to those people. *No. Not* those *people. I'm one of them.*

But what of the red? What could it do? Despite being taught as a youth that the *myelur* was something of which not to speak, Pendr found a certain anxiousness at wanting to learn more. If Mistress Halima knew of all three, as Danla had stated, then the elderly woman would be the one to ask.

"Is that true, Mistress?" Eladrel asked. "Do you know of all three?"

"After a fashion," she said. "Using the *myelur* is not an all or nothing talent, no more than if a person can lift *a* rock from the ground, they can lift rocks of *any* size. My gift is strongest with the blue, though I've worked hard to increase my skill with the green. I know of the red but cannot wield it myself. What I can explain—"

Mistress Halima didn't finish her sentence. Her head jerked quickly toward the east. "They're coming," she said, just above a whisper.

Chapter 23

The sound of tearing flesh woke Wyjec. In those moments of first regaining consciousness, he feared the flesh might be his own. *Maybe my hold on the wolf failed.* There was no pain, though the blue *myelur* still covered him which would prevent any feeling. *But how could the wolf get to my flesh if I'm protected?* A cry of agony assaulted his ears—a sound which did not come from Wyjec's throat.

After snapping his eyes open, Wyjec tried to understand what he saw. The noon-day sun shone down on a man, dressed in leather armor who lay on his back among the trees. The wolf, the one Wyjec had tied the amber glow around its heart, had its jaws clamped around the soldier's left leg.

Instead of the soldier's armor displaying a crescent moon, as Wyjec expected, green with silver trim distinguished the protective clothing. It was the same type of uniform worn by the enemy soldier who had come to the gates of Iredell.

The enemy had found Wyjec in the trees—at least *one* of his enemies.

"Kill it!" the soldier cried out.

It was then Wyjec spotted the other man—also dressed in well-worn leather armor. He held a long sword in one hand, and a shield decorated with the symbol of a leaf-adorned tree in the other. A quick inspection of the other man's red *myelur* and amber glow surprised Wyjec. The soldier's intention was neither on the wolf nor his wounded companion—it was directed away, to the north. *He's afraid. He wants to flee.* A small nudge from Wyjec's mind triggered the man to act on that intention.

"Osolde! Wait!" The wounded man called but to no avail.

Wyjec was tempted to let the wolf kill the man, but he thought back to when the Masters died. The mistake Wyjec made then was not to have witnesses to spread the word of his power. Yes, the other soldier, Osolde apparently his name, saw the wolf attack, but he did not know it was Wyjec who controlled the wolf.

By this time, the wolf had nearly removed the man's leg below the knee. He would not survive much longer unless Wyjec intervened. Careful as not to undo the weave on the amber glow around the wolf's heart, he nudged the focus away from the man. It worked as the wolf stopped his attack. It backed off, blood dripping from its jowls.

Wyjec knew soldier would die if he kept losing blood. Thinking over his abilities with the blue, red, and yellow *myelur*, he had no idea how he could use them to help. A more conventional solution was needed.

The soldier's sword and shield lay on the ground, out of reach, dropped when the wolf attacked. Part of the wounded man's uniform was a sturdy, leather belt. Wyjec stood, and watched his foe carefully. The man did not move. Wyjec could see he was still breathing, though his eyes were closed. *Perhaps he passed out from the loss of blood.*

Kneeling next to the man, Wyjec could see a solid metal buckle which fastened the belt. It was fairly simple to remove the belt, and then wrap it around the mangled leg. Cinching the belt as tightly as he could, Wyjec stopped the life-giving fluid from seeping from the wound. Cutting off the circulation would cost the man his leg, but it would save his life.

What to do with him now? Wyjec felt refreshed from his brief nap. Perhaps he could wrap the amber glow around the heart of the man who lay before him like he had the wolf. Searching the soldier's red *myelur*, he looked for the accompanying amber glow. It centralized on the injured leg. Wyjec began to pull on the representation of intent, but it would not move. He pushed harder with his mind, feeling his heart beat faster, and still the amber glow remained located around the wound. Drawing in even more of the red *myelur*, Wyjec began to feel dizzy, as if he might faint. *Too much! Too much!*

Unsure how he knew, Wyjec understood he was using too much of the red *myelur*, and it was going to kill him. He shunted the power, limiting it to a simple dribble, and his heart began to slow. He did not like that he was limited in what he could draw from the *myelur*, or that the amber glow from the man's leg would not move.

Deciding to take another approach, Wyjec elected to see instead if the amber glow reacted the same way as in the wolf when it came to tying it to a certain location. Shifting his focus on the essence of the amber glow, Wyjec was immediately taken back.

Whereas the glow in the wolf consisted of distinct strands which Wyjec could manipulate and tie together, the man's aura was significantly more complex. There were individual strands, yes, but instead of them numbered in the dozens, the threads were in the thousands, if not more. And there was something else. The strands which created the amber glow in the man vibrated almost to the point of being violent. *There is no way I could tie these together.*

Considering the issue further, it correlated with what he had learned previously. From Wyjec's experience, animals were much easier to control than humans. This realization strengthened the perception of why Avadi betrayed Wyjec. Men's will was too strong to control absolutely. But wolves, they were different.

That meant men were dangerous. While the man before him was not a threat, it would not remain that way. The other soldier who had fled could return with more men, and Wyjec and one wolf would not be enough. He considered dragging the man with him to make sure he knew it was Wyjec who had beaten him. *But where?* Wyjec had no place to go.

The forest thickened toward the west, away from Iredell. The soldiers who had come upon Wyjec and the wolf came from the north. Iredell was to the south and east. *West it is.* He would leave the injured man behind. The soldier had seen how the wolf had defended Wyjec. That would have to be enough for now.

Wyjec stood, and took several steps to the west. The wolf followed without any prompting through the red *myelur*.

It was an unexpected, yet welcomed action. There was still much Wyjec needed to learn about what the wolf would and would not do.

For much of the afternoon, Wyjec and the wolf traveled deeper into the western wood. Food and drink, as well as shelter, were issues that needed addressing soon. Yet, for the moment, Wyjec began to feel a sense of liberation.

That emotion did not last long. A low whining, not human, came from up ahead and a little to the right. Following came a similar sound, this one from behind and to the left. Growls from each direction joined the chorus.

Wyjec stopped and sought to locate traces of the red *myelur*. His heart began pounding harder in his chest, not only from pulling on the red *myelur*, but also when he realized there were six different creatures which surrounded him and his wolf.

All of the whines changed to hostile growls, and a powerfully built red wolf came out from behind a tree. More wolves followed, surrounding them.

Worst of all was when Wyjec's wolf joined the other wolves by growling aggressively.

Chapter 24

Straightening her back, Halima took on an air of authority. In a stronger tone, she commanded, "Yarma, Shrevna: put out the fire. Nya, get everyone to my tent. Now!"

"Who? Who is coming?" Rilam asked, a quiver in his voice.

"Who do you think, Rilam?" Danla said. "Be quiet and do as you're told!"

Pendr stood and turned toward the east. He could sense nothing different in the woods, neither could he hear anything. The women of the camp followed their leader's instructions without question.

The two young women, Yarma and Shrevna by name, wasted no time in dousing the campfire. Appearing older than the other women, Nya directed the rest of the group toward the tent. Including Pendr and his companions, he counted a total of sixteen people who would need to go into the shelter. It did not look large enough to fit everyone.

Rilam jumped up right away and sprinted to the tent, passing several of the females along the way. Eladrel, showing more restraint, hung back with Pendr.

"I'd feel better if we had weapons," Eladrel said.

The empty sheath still hanging from his hip made Pendr realize he felt the same way. "I agree," Pendr said. Once captured, their weapons had been taken from them. In fleeing with Danla, retrieving their short swords was not practical or, most likely, even possible. Pendr had not learned much when it came to swordplay, but holding steel in his hand did offer a sense of comfort, even if it was somewhat of an illusion.

In short order, everyone aside from Eladrel, Pendr, Nya, and Mistress Halima were inside the tent. As Pendr predicted, it would be a tight fit.

He could see the thick woolen fabric stretch in places.

"Get in, young men," Halima said.

Pendr hesitated. He knew his height and muscular frame would take up more area than a normal sized person. "I'm not sure we'll all fit."

"Not all of us will need to," Halima said. Switching her focus to the other woman still standing outside, she said, "Nya, go. May the Light guide you."

Nya nodded, her blonde curls bouncing a little with the motion. She turned and began sprinting to the north through the trees.

"Now, get in," Halima said with such force that Pendr found he could not resist the direction to enter the shelter.

While those in the tent were already packed in tightly, they somehow found room to allow Pendr, Eladrel, and Halima to enter and close the flaps of the tent.

"Where is Nya going?" Eladrel asked. "Should one of us go with her?"

"You would do more harm than good," Halima said. "She is well rested. You two are not. You may be feeling energized now, but that will not last. Fear can give the delusion of power, though it is fleeting. Now please, remain quiet. I need to focus."

Sweat began to bead on Pendr's forehead. The heat generated inside the tent affected him right away. Working in the forge and standing all day on his feet was not an uncommon occurrence. However, as the moments drew out, he felt a desire to sit—though that would not be possible. Halima made a strong point about Pendr and Eladrel, as well as Rilam for that matter, not resting much the previous night. *Danla must be exhausted as well.* She had traveled with them all night, and Light only knew how long before that.

The snapping of twigs and hushed voices came from outside the tent. Pendr noticed those in the cloth structure tense up—everyone aside from Halima. Her eyes were closed, and serenity masked her face.

"In there!" Pendr heard a deep voice say.

"Obviously," another voice answered, this one with a bit of a lisp.

Feet shuffling sounded around the tent, as well as swords drawn from scabbards.

"Come out from there," the lispy voice demanded.

No one inside the tent moved.

"We see you," the man said. "Don't make this bloodier than it needs to be. Come out now, and only a few of you will die."

It was as if everyone in the tent was holding their collective breaths. Pendr thought ahead. They were safe, at least according to Mistress Halima. He wanted to believe her, but logically the tent's fabric would do little to prevent the enemy's long spears or swords from piercing those inside with him.

Even if Halima could protect them, for how long? They could not last forever inside the tent. The enemy only needed to wait them out. *But Halima knows that. She must have sent Nya to get help.*

"Looks like they need motivation," the deep voice said, after a time.

"Yeah. It does. Wanse, use your spear to show them we are serious."

"No!" Rilam called out. Pendr saw his townmate was up flush against one of the tent's walls—a position he earned from racing inside the tent first. *He's vulnerable, at least he thinks so.*

"Quiet!" Danla hissed.

"Easy for you!" Rilam said. "You're sheltered in the middle!"

"Come out of there!" Lispy shouted. "Last warning!"

Rilam pushed and twisted until he was away from the edge of the tent. But he did not stop there. Catching everyone inside the shelter by surprise, he pushed onward, toward the tent flaps and then out into the morning light.

"I surrender!" Rilam called, raising his hands above his head and dropping to his knees.

"Get back in here!" Danla called.

It was too late.

Though Pendr could not spot the enemy soldier through the gap in the tent flaps, he did see when a spear was thrust forward and into the left side of Rilam's neck.

Chapter 25

Wolves surrounded Wyjec and continued to growl threateningly. Several of them crept forward, teeth bared, closing the distance.

The wolf at Wyjec's side, the one over whom he thought he had control, was also growling. It was a minor relief, of sorts, when Wyjec realized that his wolf was growling not at Wyjec himself, but rather at the other six wolves.

Using the blue *myelur* as a protective shield to encase his body, Wyjec then located the amber glow of the largest of the wolves—the one directly ahead of him. The wolf's focus was on Wyjec's throat. Thinking back to the soldier who he caused to flee earlier, Wyjec decided to see if he could get the wolf to flee in a similar way. Pushing with the aid of the red *myelur*, the wolf's intention was shoved forcefully in the opposite direction. Without hesitation, it fled, crashing through the underbrush as it ran away.

The remaining wolves' growls lessened some with the action. Picking the next larger wolf, this one with a patch of fur missing from his left rear leg, Wyjec shoved again with the red *myelur* which had the same effect as with the previous wolf. *How long will the wolves flee?*

Four wolves remained, each smaller in stature and build than the wolf at Wyjec's side. Without prompting, Wyjec's wolf leaped at the closest of the remaining wolves. One of the smaller red-furred beasts appeared genuinely surprised when attacked. It was not surprised for long as Wyjec's wolf ripped out the smaller creature's throat.

Before the other three wolves could counter attack, they all dipped their collective heads to the ground and began to whimper.

It was the same position the first wolf struck after Wyjec had subdued it. *But the wolves aren't cowering before me.* They were showing respect to the wolf. *It* had dominated them.

No, not it. *The wolf is a male.* Wyjec knew this earlier, of course. It was not hard to tell by looking at the wolf's features. But, for whatever the cause, it was not until this moment that Wyjec considered the beast more than an *it*.

What had changed? Something significant. It seemed that just as men rose in standing with a showing of power, so had the wolf. The lesson here, Wyjec realized, was not dissimilar to the day he first used the blue *myelur*. Death was the key. He who controls who lives and dies has power.

A rustling of trampled foliage brought Wyjec from his thoughts. In between the gaps of the trees and bushes, a wolf, the largest of the original pack, was returning. As before, Wyjec could see through the red *myelur* that the wolf fixated on his neck, meaning the wolf intended to attack.

Before it could get to the small clearing where Wyjec stood, his wolf, as well as the three remaining living animals which had backed down, all reacted as one. They gathered together in front of Wyjec and began to growl. Hair bristled, and bodies tensed as they took a defensive position.

The returning wolf, seeing the other wolves' stances, came to a skidding stop. Its ears stood straight up in the air, and it bared its teeth. It made a sound, a combination of whines and growls. To Wyjec's ear, it was a mixture of confusion and outrage. Wyjec's wolf, the first one he had controlled, responded with a mixture of similar vocal utterances. He, too, stood up straight and tall, with his tail pointed skyward.

Talking? Are they somehow communicating with each other? At first, the idea was absurd. However, there was no denying that something was happening between the two wolves. How deep of a meaning, Wyjec could only guess.

For a moment, the growling/whining continued, with the younger wolves chipping in now and again in support of their new master.

Wyjec could see the amber glow of the returning wolf was no longer on his throat; instead, it was doing something fascinating. Through the red *myelur*, Wyjec watched the red wolf's amber glow flit back and forth between its heart and the neck of Wyjec's wolf. *It's deciding whether or not to fight for dominance.*

A sharp bark from Wyjec's black wolf settled the debate. The red wolf tucked his tail and flattened its ears. It also lowered its head and gave a similar whimper as the other three wolves had done. Moving slowly, the large red fell in beside the other three red wolves. It kept its eyes to the ground and pawed gently at the forest floor.

Wyjec was impressed by the black wolf, and at the same time, a bit envious. *But why should I be?* It was from sheer willpower that his wolf dominated the red wolf which had returned. In a sense, that is what Wyjec had done, though he used the red *myelur*. The show of power here with the wolves was more primal in nature—though just as effective.

Still, Wyjec did not want the other wolves dedicated to his pet. No, the beasts needed to understand who truly ruled. He decided he would weave the amber glow around each of the wolves' hearts, just as he did to the black.

Whether from the vigor created by the recent attacks or from Wyjec's recent nap, he still felt energized. Food, water, and shelter could wait. For now, the wolves would become his. Remaining standing, Wyjec focused all his attention on the largest red's heart. As before, he began to tie the strands of the amber glow, making sure each was secure before moving on.

To Wyjec's surprise, he found himself stumbling forward a couple of steps. Splitting his attention away from the red wolf for a moment, Wyjec understood what happened.

The other wolf had returned.

While Wyjec focused on the work of securing the amber glow, he had been hit from behind. The blue *myelur* protected him from any harm, though the force was strong enough to move him physically—not unlike when Avadi's men had thrown him from the tower wall.

Before Wyjec could react, the rest of the wolves attacked.

Fur and blood flying, along with jaws snapping open and shut, and the howls of pain from the wolf which attacked impacted Wyjec's senses.

Almost as quickly as it started, the battle concluded. The wolf which had done the most damage, as evidenced from the gore on his teeth and claws, was the black wolf. Standing proudly, the wolf's eyes met Wyjec's stare: an unspoken message sent. *The wolf will defend me, even to the point of endangering himself or his pack.*

The wolf displayed something Wyjec had not seen before. Pure devotion, and not only from fear. An idea struck Wyjec. *If this wolf would show such honor and respect, then certainly the other ones will as well once I weave the amber glow around their hearts.* It would take time, but it would be worth the effort.

This wolf, the first one, needed a distinction. *I shall name him.* Wyjec considered what name would be right for the wolf. And then, it came to him. The perfect name.

I will call him Alpha.

Chapter 26

A cry of surprise mixed with anguish came from one of the women inside the tent upon seeing Rilam impaled in the neck. Pendr had witnessed the youth from his hometown murdered, and based on the woman's reaction, he was not alone.

"Close the tent flaps," a female voice said firmly. Pendr was not sure who said it, but he obeyed without questioning.

Mistress Halima continued to remain quiet, eyes closed. *She remains focused on keeping the enemy out.*

"We can help Rilam," Eladrel said. "*I* can heal him."

"Not if you're dead," Pendr said. "I didn't see how many of them were out there, but we can't win."

"I need to do *something* to help," Eladrel said. His eyes displayed an almost pleading nature.

"That's because you are a healer, or will be," one of the women said. Pendr recognized her as Yarma, one of those tasked with dousing the fire before they came to the tent. She was smaller in stature than most of the others, though the way she held her shoulders squarely made her seem taller. Her hair was also cut shorter than the rest of the women, not even touching her shoulders. "It's in your nature to—"

"You see!" the man with the lisp shouted outside of the tent. "You see what you made us do? The longer you wait, the more of you will die. Come out now!"

Yarma shook her head fiercely, whereas Eladrel fidgeted, glancing back and forth between the occupants of the tent and the flaps which led outside.

"We're not waiting! Wanse, do it now," Lispy said.

Movement toward the southeast corner of the tent caused everyone, aside from Mistress Halima, who remained in a trance-like state, to face that direction. Pendr heard the shuffling of feet, something he took as one of the men outside as lunging forward. The next sound he expected was the ripping of fabric, followed by a scream of pain. What happened instead was unlike anything he had experienced before.

An angelic resonance rang through the air. Not only did Pendr hear it, a section of his mind, where he had felt the cool trickle before, *felt* it.

"What the …?" the deep voice said outside the tent. Pendr guessed it belonged to Wanse.

Another ring of the sweet sound emanated, followed by another, then another.

"This makes no sense!" Wanse yelled.

"What?" Lispy said.

"It's shielded somehow." The surprise in Wanse's voice was unmistakable. "Gravatt, try it yourself."

Gravatt must be the name of the man with the lisp. Pendr noticed that Halima had neither moved nor changed expression. When more blows were deflected, accompanied with the awe-inspiring sound which followed, Pendr thought he saw the older woman twitch, just perceptibly.

"You're right. It *is* shielded," Gravatt said. "Get Somner up here."

The command was echoed by a male voice, some distance from the tent. Gravatt swore, then said, "You may feel safe in there, but you aren't the only one who can wield the *myelur*. Somner, get the shielding down!"

The women in the shelter tensed up noticeably. Pendr searched out Danla among the others and spotted her looking in his direction. *She's afraid. They weren't expecting this.*

"He's … he's fighting me," Halima said. Her breathing started to become labored.

Pendr looked around the room, trying to spot anything he could use as a weapon. All he could see were the bodies packed inside the tent. Thinking back, he did not remember seeing any weaponry when he had first visited Halima.

"Can she hold it?" Eladrel asked.

"She's trying," Yarma answered.

"Are any of you able to help?" Eladrel asked.

Each of the women shook their heads. "We're training as healers," Yarma said. "None of us have the gift of the blue *myelur*."

"How long can you keep the shield up?" Eladrel directed this question directly to Halima.

She kept her eyes closed, though her eyebrows knitted in deeper concentration. "He is attacking ... random spots ... trying to create a small opening. It ... it is getting harder to mend the spots he has weakened. It won't be ... much longer."

Her words struck something inside Pendr. In recent days, he had seen too many people die—people he should be protecting. He had escaped each time, and still, he had been hunted. *They won't stop. They intend to kill us. We did nothing to them. I will not let this happen!*

With that singular thought, one of unwavering determination, Pendr felt a cool sensation wash over him, just as when he had run back to the battlefield to rescue Rilam. At the same time, he felt his inner energy begin to wane. *I must act now!*

Pendr pushed open the tent flap and stepped out into the light. On the ground, only a few steps away lay Rilam's corpse. The soil around his head was stained deep red. Three men stood around the tent. Two wore solid leather armor; crescent moons emblazoned on their chests. Both held spears in one hand and swords in the other. The other man wore a blue robe, shimmering in the daylight.

"There's one!" the man directly in front of Pendr said, his voice slurring on the "s" sound.

That's Gravatt. He's the one giving the orders. Pendr would put a stop to that.

A victorious grin spread over Gravatt's face. "Aren't you a big one? And not even armed. You must be one of those who we captured before. I can't wait—"

Pendr refused to let him finish. He charged Gravatt, lowering a shoulder. Startled, the leader of the enemy group was still able to bring his spear up in time. Instead of the sharpened point skewering Pendr through his chest, the weapon struck solidly and skidded off to one side.

Though Pendr felt no pain from the blow, he had felt a slight pressure at the point of impact. Confusion filled Gravatt's eyes and then understanding as Pendr barreled into him. The force of Pendr hitting the man was enough for him to fall to the ground, and in the process, it caused him to drop his sword and spear.

Kneeling quickly, Pendr grabbed the spear while Gravatt remained dazed. Pendr had sensed movement behind him before he heard it. *Wanse is coming.*

Spinning while still on his knees, Pendr tucked the spear under his right armpit and faced his oncoming foe. Wanse's spear struck Pendr first, but as before, it deflected off to the side. The man's momentum, however, kept him moving forward and directly into Pendr's spear. A grunt of surprise was the only sound Wanse made when the spear pierced him just below the ribcage and exited out his back. He tipped to one side, breaking the shaft of the spear in the process.

Gravatt was getting to his feet, clutching his sword in his right hand. Without considering a plan, Pendr *acted*. Still close to the ground, he pulled the sword from Wanse's grip as the newly dead man fell. Remaining low, Pendr swung his newly acquired weapon in an arc. Gravatt was still in the process of standing when Pendr's sword connected with his shin. So powerful was Pendr's strike that Gravatt's leg separated into two parts, his booted foot twisting at an odd angle now that it was no longer holding up Gravatt's weight.

Again, Pendr sensed movement just out of his field of view. Turning his head, he saw the man in the robe, Somner, running for the trees. It would not be possible for Pendr to catch him in time. *If he gets away, we remain at risk. He can bring down Halima's ward around the tent.* There was nothing Pendr could do. Throwing his sword would only mean losing a valuable weapon, and chances were slim he would do any real harm to Somner.

Frustration boiled inside Pendr, and with it, a knot of energy formed.

It continued to build inside his chest, and unsure how or even why he would do such an action, Pendr stretched forward a hand toward the fleeing enemy. He released the energy knot. Pendr's physical eyes saw no evidence of the knot leaving his body through his hand, but he sensed it fly across the distance between him and Somner.

The man in the shimmering robe flung forward as if hit by a powerful wind, only much stronger. The force slammed him against a tree, and from the angle of his neck when he came to rest on the ground, was dead.

"You … you," Gravatt said. He was on the ground, clutching his severed leg.

Pendr spun and faced his enemy. "I, what?" Pendr asked.

"It's not possible for you to—"

Aware there were more dangers in the forest, Pendr silenced the injured man by bringing his sword down, removing Gravatt's head from his body.

Chapter 27

It took the better part of the afternoon for Wyjec to weave the amber glow around the hearts of the remaining four wolves. Wyjec had moved the pack deeper into the western wood, away from the corpses of the two wolves killed during the encounter. During the process of tying the loose strands of the glow, he found it interesting how each of the beasts was unique, even though the three smaller red wolves were similar in appearance.

The smallest of the group, which would normally be considered the runt of the pack, had a heart slightly larger than the other wolves of the same size. Wyjec decided to name him Pluck. The other two of the smaller red wolves were nearly opposite when contrasting them. One kept flitting about as if he had bundled up energy which made it unable for him to remain still. This one would go by the name of Jittery whereas his companion was almost serene in nature. *Tranquil—that is what he will be called.*

The largest red wolf, the former leader of the red pack who had since relinquished authority to Alpha, was powerfully built. His heart was the strongest, by a good margin, than the rest of the red wolves.

He was older than even Alpha, Wyjec understood somehow, though he was not sure how he knew. *He's strong, yes, but he's also wise enough to realize that Alpha is more dominate.* Acumen—*yes that word fits well as a name for the large red.*

By the time Wyjec finished securing the amber glow around the wolves' hearts, he could no longer ignore hunger and thirst. Water was easy. The bubbling and gurgling of a nearby brook acted as a beacon, of sorts. Wyjec readily answered the call, and soon he and the wolves were drinking their fill.

The water flowed west to east, and as Wyjec studied the terrain, he understood why. In general, the further west they traveled, the higher in elevation they climbed. The Masters had spoken little of the land around the palace, but from what Wyjec could remember there was a vast land of water, an ocean it was called, to the east. The west contained mountains, whatever they were. These mountains were land formations—that much Wyjec could guess—but what kind? *Are these mountains something I should fear?* Perhaps they could offer shelter.

With a belly full of water, Wyjec felt strong enough to continue deeper into the western wood. He and the wolves stayed close to the brook. The running water appeared to be a popular spot as Wyjec noticed small trails running nearby.

Not far into the trip, Acumen stopped and sniffed at some animal tracks left in the soft earth. They were smaller than what wolves made, by at least half. From what Wyjec could tell, Acumen was not alarmed by the tracks—though he did act in an enthusiastic manner. The large red wolf whined/growled at Alpha as if asking a question. Alpha, in response, looked up at Wyjec, his eyes conveying—what? Permission? *But to do what?*

Using the red *myelur* to examine each of the wolves, Wyjec sensed no intention of aggressiveness toward him. Focusing his attention back on Alpha, Wyjec nodded his head, as well as trying to send a sense of authorization through the red *myelur.* Whether it was the head nod or the transmitted approval, Alpha reacted.

The leader of the pack whined/growled to the other wolves, and two heartbeats later, they all ran off in different directions. *What is this? What have I let them do?*

Wyjec searched out with his senses, trying to find any of the wolves, but they had disappeared into the thick forest foliage. The sun now angled in from the west. It was not Wyjec's imagination that with each passing moment the light dimmed. Instinctively, Wyjec called on the blue *myelur,* covering his body in a protective coat. Without the wolves by his side, he was subject to attack.

Hunger once again began to gnaw at him. There were plants around, and some roots which Wyjec could dig up, though he had no idea which would help and which would harm. Small fish flitted in the stream time and again, but they were too quick for Wyjec to snag either with his hands or the red *myelur*.

Insects and other creeping things were found under rocks and by tree roots, but Wyjec found he could not bring himself to put them in his mouth. He was hungry, yes, but not so much as to stoop to eating bugs.

Thoughts of the meals prepared for him by the chardi, and those later served by the captains, taunted him. When Wyjec was a chardi, the Masters withheld water and food, and once he was free from their control, he vowed never to take water or food for granted. *How quickly I fall into compliance.*

A sense of self-pity, as well as frustration, joined hunger as Wyjec's dominant sensations. Time passed, the day turned into twilight, and with each heartbeat, his resolve not to eat bugs wavered. *I need food—at least some form of nutrition—or I will not be able to retain the shield from the blue* myelur.

Wyjec sat next to the brook, cross-legged, and reached for a moss covered rock. Upon lifting it, he saw various types of squirming creatures. It was dark enough now that Wyjec could not make out many details of the bugs. *It's probably for the best.*

Before he could pick the least disgusting of the bugs, leaves crunching and small branches snapping to Wyjec's left caught his attention. He dropped the rock and stood, double checking his shielding was intact.

Alpha emerged from the woods, holding something in his mouth. It took a moment for Wyjec to realize it was a rabbit, fairly plump, and quite dead. Alpha lay the hare at Wyjec's feet. Where Alpha had bitten into the rabbit, its fur was torn, revealing the red meat beneath.

I have no way to start a fire, but ... does it matter? Unsure why, the thought of eating raw rabbit was infinitely less repulsive than eating bugs. Hunger overrode any other sense of concern as Wyjec fell to his knees and tore into the rabbit.

While he feasted, Wyjec became aware that each of the other wolves returned. Recently dried blood on their jowls indicated they, too, had found an answer to their hunger. Upon eating his fill, Wyjec offered the rest of the rabbit back to Alpha. The wolf's golden eyes once again transmitted a message: approval.

Chapter 28

Pendr ached—a bone-deep type of weariness that even the longest days of working at the blacksmith shop could not create. Halima said that would happen because Pendr used a large amount of the blue *myelur* when defeating Gravatt, Wanse and Somner. After the initial battle, the rest of the men led by Gravatt, who had been standing a good distance away, fled into the woods. Halima sensed no danger, so for the moment, they were supposedly safe.

Danla had relit the fire, and then Halima instructed her, Pendr, and Eladrel to rest beside the flames. The sun was close to setting, and the campfire offered more light than any other source. Eladrel's shoulders stooped, and his head hung low.

"I could have saved Rilam," Eladrel said. "I wanted to. Wait, it's more than that. It was as if I *needed* to. It was hard standing back and doing nothing."

"No one is blaming you," Danla assured. She had been assigned to stay with Pendr and Eladrel while the other young women worked on different tasks—including burying the dead. Pendr felt it was wrong, for whatever reason, for women to do such hard labor. Yet, the more he learned about Halima and her group, the more his biases changed. *They are strong. Stronger in more ways than I could have imagined.*

Eladrel, indeed, had tried to revive Rilam, though Halima told him it would be of no use. His insistence to at least make an attempt impressed Pendr, and from what he could tell, Halima as well. The effort nearly caused Eladrel to pass out, which is when Halima stepped in.

"Remember the words of my teacher," Danla said. "Using the green *myelur* draws from your strength and health to heal others. You've not been taught how to build up a reserve, so trying to heal too much too soon can kill you."

Eladrel looked up at Danla. "A reserve? I don't understand. Is this what Mistress Halima has been teaching you?"

"Yes, as well as other things which *you* will need to learn."

The young man's reply was not to respond at all, at least not verbally. His eyebrows knitted, and a troubled look indicated to Pendr that Eladrel considered where his future might take him.

If Danla had the notion that Eladrel would receive training, what did that mean for Pendr? Twice now he had used the blue *myelur* to save others. If he learned to hone the skill, he could become a formidable warrior. *But that's not me. I'm a blacksmith, not a killer.* However, he had killed people. Reflecting back on the attack, Pendr realized that when in the heart of a battle, he did not hesitate to do what he previously thought was unthinkable. *I killed three men today.*

"What of Pendr?" Eladrel said, bringing Pendr out of his thoughts. "Will Halima teach him as well?"

A voice from the darkness spoke before Danla could. "I will train neither of you." It was Halima.

She stepped closer to the fire, the red and orange flames illuminating her face. Her hands were clasped in front of her. Though she wore the same serene expression as normal, Pendr could see the weariness in her face and shoulders. She slouched, barely perceptively, and her eyes pinched in the corners.

"But Danla said that—" Eladrel began.

"Danla said you needed to be trained. And of that, she was correct." Halima sat next to Danla and touched her lightly on the knee. "Danla has displayed great potential in the use of the green *myelur*. Thank the Light we found her. She will play an important part in the battles ahead. As I suspect, will both of you."

The thought of more battles made Pendr feel even wearier—something he did not think possible. Once the remaining enemy soldiers had run away, and Halima assured everyone they were safe for now, she also claimed help would arrive shortly. How she knew, exactly, was something Pendr still struggled to comprehend.

Halima leaned a bit closer to the fire. "I won't train you because I am unable to do so. Men and women are different, especially when it comes to using the *myelur*—any form of it. Only those of the same sex can truly provide the correct training."

"I don't understand," Eladrel said.

Danla spoke. "May I explain, Mistress?"

Halima nodded.

"A woman cannot create a child without a man. Neither can a man create a child on his own," Danla said. "While men and women are similar in many ways, there are inherent differences. The way the *myelur* flows through a woman is just different enough that a man cannot fully comprehend it. The same is true for women understanding a man's use of the *myelur*. Yes, the end results of the power can be the same, or very closely the same, but the methods are different."

"Different, how, exactly?" Eladrel asked. "I still don't understand."

Danla's lips curved upwards. "That's a question, as I understand it from my lessons with Mistress Halima, which has been debated and studied for generations."

"In simple terms," Halima said, "it's not unlike trying to get someone who primarily uses their right hand to do the same activities with their left. They are both hands, yet different."

Pendr imagined doing some of the work at the smithy using his left hand. He could try, though he did not have the same control or strength. This did not help him begin to understand the complexities of the *myelur*, but he could accept that there were differences.

"You mentioned upcoming battles," Pendr said. "I'm afraid I know little of what has happened since we were first attacked."

The edges of Halima's eyes tightened a bit more. "I know we're still at war," she said. "The forces from Sothcar have taken Iredell and continue to hold it."

"That much we knew," Eladrel said. "It's why we were conscripted."

"Aye," Halima said. "But what wasn't known until recently is that the leaders of Sothcar have created bands of fighters—ranging from a few men to dozens—to infiltrate our kingdom. There are an unknown number of these bands roaming the land, creating havoc wherever they can. Sometimes the enemy group bands together for larger attacks—like those who attacked your camp."

"To what end?" Pendr asked.

Halima's tone contained an underlining bitterness. "Power. War and conflict are about power. Those who want it, and those who have it. But it is an unquenchable thirst. Those driven to gain more power can never get enough. Under King Viskum's rule, the Light has shone upon us. He's a man who understands the corruption of power. His goal has always been to protect his people—not gain more lands."

"But, who determines which people belong to which kingdom?" Pendr asked. "As I understand it, the town of Iredell has been part of several kingdoms over the generations."

"Ah, let me guess," Halima said. "You must have grouped with someone from Umstead."

Eladrel tossed a twig into the fire. "Rheq—the little guy. He was from Umstead."

"Aye, we did have a young man from that area with us for a time," Pendr said. "He disappeared right before we were captured."

"I see," Halima said. "I wish I could say that everyone could agree on which lands belonged to which kingdoms. Alas, borders do shift over time. Even your village of Logs Pond has belonged to other realms. What King Viskum achieved was fair borders with the other leaders of the region. Those to the north and west have honored these agreements. Sothcar, however, has been different."

Pendr knew little of other kingdoms. Aside from Sothcar, he knew the land north was called Virqyna. Most of his life, his world had consisted of Logs Pond, which had been fine with him. Halima had not mentioned the east. Pendr vocalized the question.

"The east?" Halima sounded surprised. "Nothcar is bordered by the land of waters. Ships from other parts of the world trade along the coast, but there have never been any invasions by way of the sea."

"But previous attacks have come from Sothcar," Eladrel said. "Correct?"

Halima nodded. "Those in Umstead are under constant harassment. When the borders were being drawn, Umstead was originally supposed to be in Sothcar. But the town leaders petitioned to be part of King Viskum's rule, and their efforts were rewarded. Many from Sothcar are still resentful."

"Then why did those from Sothcar capture Iredell instead of Umstead?" Eladrel asked.

Halima unclenched her hands and turned her palms upwards. "I can't say for sure. From what I understand, Iredell is a walled city. Umstead is much like Logs Pond: not much more than a village. Iredell is a more strategic target. From there—"

The leader of the campsite stopped talking abruptly and turned her head sharply. Pendr could see her tense, but almost as quickly, she relaxed. "Ah, good. They're almost here."

"Who?" Pendr asked. "Who is coming?"

"Nya. The one I sent when we were under attack," Halima said. "She's brought soldiers from a nearby campsite to help. They will be quite delighted to find you two young men here."

Pendr felt the back of his neck tense up. More than anything, he wanted to sleep. After that? A strong urge to return home coursed through him, though he knew that would not be possible—not after what he had seen and learned.

"Why will they be happy to see us?" Eladrel asked.

Halima smiled, one which touched her eyes. "Because they are those who will be teaching you how to use your skills with the *myelur*."

Chapter 29

At first, Wyjec was not sure he could live off raw rabbit. It was not the taste, nor the texture which created the issue. Hunger had a way of eliminating those factors. Instead, it was the pains emanating from his stomach—often causing him to taste his food a second time as it made a return trip up his throat.

Of all the wolves, this seemed to concern Alpha the most. The black wolf brought squirrels, and even a fat trout once, though the results were the same. After one particularly rough evening when Wyjec heaved more than he slept, Alpha did something unexpected: he delivered a rabbit which was still alive.

The hare's back legs bent at strange angles, broken, but its heart was still beating fiercely. Through the red *myelur*, Wyjec could see the rabbit's life force flow through its small frame. When Wyjec reached out and touched the rabbit, he spotted it—the yellow threads he had seen before. It was like the red *myelur*, but different. Instead of remaining inside the animal, as did the red, the yellow strings ran between Wyjec and the rabbit once he touched it.

Instinctively, Wyjec pulled on the yellow threads. Two things happened at once. The pain and aches vanished from his system, while at the same time, the rabbit's heart came to an abrupt stop.

I've taken its life to heal myself. That is the power of the yellow myelur. A brief sensation of grief attempted to sink into Wyjec, but he quickly dismissed it. There was no point grieving over food, especially when it can heal as well as nourish.

For the next several days, Wyjec and the wolves continued deeper into the western woods, spending as much time climbing as walking.

The younger wolves took turns scouting ahead for potential dangers, as well as paths they could take.

Wyjec sensed no doubts from the wolves. He checked them each night to make sure the amber glow remained around each of their hearts. Not once did he have to retie any ends which may have frayed. Their dedication was unquestionable. *More than I can say about men.*

While the wolves may not question why they headed west, or what would happen next, Wyjec could not say the same for himself. *What do I want?* He did not think of it as running away, though he had no other explanation of what drove him west. He found comfort in the company of wolves. More than that, he began to feel safe, though not completely so.

What will *make me feel safe?* The four wolves could protect him from one or two foes, perhaps more. But there were *armies* of men—men who could not be trusted, men who needed to pay for betraying him.

Plans and schemes came to mind of how Wyjec could take his wolves and infiltrate Iredell, though each was dismissed as being too risky or foolhardy. Wyjec trusted these wolves, and he was not willing to sacrifice them for his quest for vengeance. What he needed was his own army.

That singular notion remained with Wyjec for the next three days. At night, he would curl up between Alpha and Acumen. Their fur and body heat kept him warm. Oddly, when he touched the wolves, the threads of the yellow *myelur* did not appear—even when he was feeling ill from eating raw meat. *Perhaps it's because they are linked to me through the power I possess.* Regardless of why, he was glad the yellow threads did not form when coming into physical contact with his wolves. It could be too large of a temptation to drain one of them if he felt sick or was injured.

The wolves continued to find food easily enough—brought to him still alive so he could drain them using the yellow *myelur* to keep the ill effects of eating raw meat at bay. Wyjec even became better at spotting and recognizing rabbit tracks.

Early one afternoon, nearly a quarter moon after Wyjec had fled from

Iredell, his pack came upon a different type of tracks—wolf tracks.

His wolves moved more cautiously, and neither Tranquil nor Jittery scouted ahead. Alpha and Acumen whined/growled to each other in subdued tones as if planning a strategy. Pluck, the smallest of the wolves, remained by Wyjec's side watching the rest of the pack's actions.

The sun was beginning to set when Alpha came to a stop. His ears pricked up, and his body tensed. Squinting through the foliage, Wyjec spotted glimmers of the red *myelur* ahead. Alpha began to growl, and Acumen, Tranquil, Pluck, and Jittery soon followed. Immediately, Wyjec coated himself in the blue *myelur*.

Alpha whined/growled toward the creatures just out of sight, becoming louder and more aggressive with each passing heartbeat.

Then, from behind a tree, stepped a brown wolf. There was something different about this one. Once it came fully into view, Wyjec inspected the wolf through the red *myelur*. He then understood what made this one different. This wolf was female.

She approached slowly, head kept low with her tail tucked behind her legs. Wyjec had come to learn such a stance meant submission, yet the amber glow from the female wolf flitted back and forth between her heart, and those behind her.

Wyjec reached through the red *myelur* to secure the female's glow around her heart, thereby securing her dedication. The response was something he did not expect. Manipulating the red *myelur* was different. The sensation was like touching silk compared to the coarseness of the male's glows. It made it more of a challenge, but after a few attempts, Wyjec succeeded. *Why should she be different?* He thought back to the other women who he manipulated and then realized while he had noticed the red *myelur* and amber glow in women before, this was the first time he had tried to insert his will on a female. *Interesting.*

The female wolf joined the pack. She would need a name. *Silk works as well as any other for her.* Alpha whined/growled a few times to Silk. In response, four more wolves came into sight—each of them female.

Wyjec set about making each of these other wolves dedicated to him.

Before beginning, an answer to a problem he had been contemplating came to him. The men in Iredell, those who had tried to kill him, had an army to protect them. Now, with a pack of wolves consisting of both males and females to do his bidding, Wyjec knew what he would do. *I will create an army of my own.*

Chapter 30

The soldiers of Sothcar moved around camp unaware someone watched them. It was a smaller band, only five men. Their camp formation appeared as if the soldiers took little care in setting it up—two small canvas tents, side-by-side, faced the fire pit. Provisions leaned against trees and tents, and the men relieved themselves wherever was convenient at the time.

Rheq wondered, not for the first time, how soldiers like these could have been successful in their attacks. *They lack focus. Something I can exploit.*

Several days had passed since Rheq escaped capture. He knew that staying with Pendr's group would be dangerous. Aside from Pendr, and perhaps Eladrel, the others in the party also lacked focus. Rheq felt it would only be a matter of time before another ambush—and that prediction came true.

Once Pendr's group entered the copse, Rheq, who had been leading the way, spotted the enemy soldiers lying in wait. At that moment, he had two options: warn the others and risk being killed or captured, or run. He chose the latter. *That doesn't make me a coward. It makes me a survivor.*

Rheq had always had the knack of spotting prey or enemies when hunting. He tried to explain once to his older brother, Groq, that he saw a glimmer of red shining in others. Groq openly mocked him for believing such things and claimed it was pure luck that Rheq was a better hunter. Rheq knew differently.

Even now, as he watched the men from the south laugh and drink around the campfire, he could see the red glimmer flowing through them. It lacked brightness, yet its presence was consistent enough to help Rheq stay attentive.

The packs strewn around camp contained food, as well as other supplies Rheq needed. Though he held on to the short sword assigned to him from the quartermaster, he was far more comfortable with a bow and arrow. Fortunately, a bow and quiver of arrows were some of the items leaning against a tent. All he had to do now was wait for dark.

Growing up in Umstead, Rheq had learned how to move silently through the forest. Not only was this skill used to hunt food, but also for pure survival. Attacks and raids on the areas around Umstead were common and had been since the town's leaders had petitioned for inclusion in King Viskum's land.

When the knights came to Umstead to conscript young men for the army, the town's reaction was mixed. Some were glad that the king was finally going to put a stop to the attacks, while others were bitter that it took the fall of Iredell to prompt the action. Rheq and his family fell into the latter category. *Where were the king and his men when we were being attacked over the many seasons?*

Now, it seemed, the fighting had escalated. Bands of southern fighters in their blue uniforms with crescent moon emblems swarmed over this part of the land. It was an invasion, though less direct than previously experienced. *I'll wager the king never expected this.*

The singular thought which drove Rheq was to return to Umstead. It was not desertion, at least that is what he kept telling himself. The rest of his original squad died in the initial attack. It was dumb luck that Rheq ended up with Pendr and the others who had survived. He doubted any of them were still alive after the ambush, but that was not Rheq's fault. With them captured, Rheq was a soldier without a squad or leader. It only made sense for him to return home to protect his people.

Somehow, those thoughts were not as reassuring as Rheq wanted. Did he feel guilty for surviving while the other conscripts died? *No, it's not my fault they died.* Like a mantra, Rheq kept telling himself that as he waited for night to arrive.

Just as Rheq predicted, the enemy soldiers were unorganized in their sleeping plans. They argued which of them would have first watch.

The smallest of the group got the assignment, mainly because he was in no position to enforce his will otherwise.

Watching the larger men bully the smaller soldier struck home. Rheq was small, even compared to those in Umstead. It was hard not to be intimidated by someone like Pendr who towered over him, as well as had a large, muscular build. However, Rheq refused to be bullied, and he found extra contempt for the particular enemy who allowed such behavior. *He'll be the first to die.*

The back of Rheq's legs began to ache as the moon climbed slowly, yet steadily, toward the middle of the sky. He knew he would have to move soon, but it would be foolish to attack too early. Finally, convinced the four larger men were asleep, and the guard was sufficiently bored, Rheq made his move.

Using the techniques learned as a young child and perfected over his life, Rheq slipped silently between trees, shifting the weight of his feet from the ball of his foot to his toes as he moved. The small soldier was unaware when Rheq stepped up directly behind him. In one fluid motion, Rheq used his left hand to cover his enemy's mouth, while with his right he used the short sword's sharp blade across his throat.

Only the smallest of groans escaped from the dying man, not nearly loud enough to wake the others. Convinced the sentry no longer posed a threat, Rheq moved toward the campfire.

Two of the soldiers slept under the stars, while the other two had commandeered the tents. Using the same technique as before, covering their mouths as he slit their throats, Rheq killed the two men by the dying fire. Neither were able to make enough of a stir to warn the others.

The two men in the tents would pose more of a problem. Heavy canvas door flaps could make enough noise to alert the occupants. *Perhaps I'll leave them here so they can discover their dead companions.* The idea intrigued Rheq, but leaving them alive meant two more enemy soldiers would be a threat. Scanning over the campsite, Rheq got an idea.

First, he gathered the bow and quiver of arrows, along with a pack full of provisions, and placed them near a tree away from the campsite.

Next, as quietly as he could, Rheq stacked the firewood the men had previously gathered in front of each of the tent's door flaps.

The fire which had been started earlier in the evening was nearly out now, though it had enough embers to light a torch Rheq found among the soldier's possessions. Once the torch roared to life, Rheq quickly lit the stacks of firewood which now blocked the tents' respective exits.

Racing, not worrying if he made noise or not, Rheq went to the tree where he had placed the bow and arrows, as well as the stolen provisions. From this vantage point, he was far enough into the wood where he could not be spotted, yet he could still see the camp.

The man in the left tent awoke first, as indicated by his shouting and flailing against the tent—a tent which had caught fire. The one thing the soldiers had done well was bury the tent spikes deep enough that it was near to impossible to pull them out from inside the tent.

The shouts of surprise turned to shrieks of pain as the tents became fully ablaze, burning the men inside. Rheq watched long enough to ensure that neither man would survive. It happened faster than he imagined.

Secure in the knowledge that this threat was eliminated, Rheq gathered his new weapon and provisions and headed south—toward Umstead.

Chapter 31

"I guess this is goodbye, again," the large man in front of Danla said. *He looks like he'll never see me again.* Though she did not want to admit it, Danla conceded that it was more likely than not. The camp where they had stayed was nearly broken down and ready to move. Soldiers had come for Pendr and Eladrel. The leaders only gave them a moment to say their farewells.

Danla squared her shoulders, forcing herself to look brave. "Now, you listen here, Pendr," she said. "You gave me that same look when we were first separated once we left Logs Pond. And we found each other again, right?" Only a fortnight had passed since that day, yet to Danla it felt much longer. Whereas Pendr and the rest of the boys from Logs Pond were sent off to become soldiers, Danla's path had been much different. *I had no idea how much I was missing from living in that small town.*

"Yes, you're right," Pendr said softly. "Just promise me you'll stay safe, will you?"

For her entire life, she had known Pendr. Not until she was away from him did she realize two things. First, Pendr was not only tall and strong compared to those in Logs Pond, but also compared to all the others she had met since. His size made him an intimidating figure, which completely countered who he was as a person. She liked that he was gentle-hearted—and that led to the second thing she realized from their separation: she missed him when they were apart, more than she thought possible. *Should I tell him? Or will that only make his leaving harder?*

Deciding not to make things more complicated, Danla redirected the conversation. "Mistress Halima will protect me. You've seen what she can do."

"Yes, but had we not been here when—" Pendr began to say.

"But you were," Danla said. "And from what I heard, we will be moving our camp next to a group of soldiers. We will be there for mutual protection."

Pendr frowned. "Why were you so far away before? It seems like an unnecessary risk."

"I asked the same question, back before I knew what Mistress Halima could do," Danla said. "She said the answer for keeping the men and women separate while training was quite simple. Can you guess it?"

She watched as Pendr tried to puzzle it out. After a moment, she understood he probably would not come to the answer on his own. *It's not who he is.* "I'll tell you," she said finally.

"Thank you. Aside from what Halima said about women not being able to train men, and the other way around, I can't think of a good reason," Pendr said.

"Young men do stupid things around young women to try to impress them," Danla said. "More than once has a soldier in training been hurt from trying to do more than he was prepared to do from showing off."

The answer failed to satisfy Pendr, based on his continued confused expression. Eventually, he shrugged, accepting it. *Maybe it's because his best friend has always been a girl.* That is when Danla recognized that explained much about Pendr, as well as her feelings toward him. They were as brother and sister, yet different. They had always been close, yet that changed somewhat once they grew older. They did not grow apart once their bodies began to mature, though he began to treat her with more respect.

"I guess you'll be able to practice your healing skills more if the soldiers get hurt while trying to impress you," Pendr said. His lips displayed a smile, though it did not touch his eyes.

Danla poked him in the chest. "If there are young women where you will be training, don't be one of those doing stupid things."

"Of course not," Pendr said. He looked genuinely surprised she would even suggest a thing. "And to be honest, I'm not even sure what kind of training I'll be doing."

He made a good point. Danla's training consisted of breathing and concentration exercises, but that was to help her develop her skills with the green *myelur*. She knew little of the blue version of the power, aside from what Mistress Halima had demonstrated recently.

"Whatever it may be," she said, "I know you'll do well. You've always succeeded when you put your mind to something."

Pendr's gaze moved to the earthen floor beneath them. "That may be true for things I've wanted to do …"

"Does this newly discovered talent scare you, Pendr?" Danla doubted she would have been bold enough to ask anyone else the same question. Still, she knew him well enough to know he would not take offense.

For several heartbeats, Pendr said nothing. His brow furrowed a little, and he continued not to meet her eyes. "It does, yes. I didn't ask for this, nor did I want it."

"Is it because you see it as a weapon? A way to hurt people?" Danla suggested.

"I guess that's a big part of it, yes." At this moment, he lifted his head enough to look at her. "I've seen things, Danla. Terrible things. Light help me, *I've* done some of these very things."

She reached out and placed her right hand on his muscular arm. "You did what you must to defend yourself as well as others. You didn't seek to hurt people. You saved all of us here in the camp. How is that a bad thing?"

Pendr did not have a response for that. If anything, it made him even more pensive. Once again, he averted his eyes.

"Pendr, look at me," Danla said.

Reluctantly, he did so.

"Think of our families back in Logs Pond," she said. "If we don't stop the enemy here, they will be at risk. They are depending on us."

"And when the war is over?" he asked. "We will return, yes?"

For the first moment since they began talking, she saw something appear which had been missing in his eyes before: hope. After learning more about the larger world around her, Danla was quite certain she had no desire to return to the small village of her birth. But to tell him now would not be wise. He *needed* hope.

"Yes, Pendr," she said. "Once the war is over, we can return."

He smiled at that, a smile which Danla found to lift her spirits.

"Pendr! Time to go!" a voice called from the far side of the camp. It was Eladrel, standing next to a handful of men wearing the king's colors.

"I'll be right there!" Pendr answered, waving to the men. Facing Danla once again, he said, "I'm going to miss you, Danla."

Her response surprised even her. Stepping closer, she wrapped her arms around him, at least as far as they could reach, and hugged him tightly. With her head resting on his chest, she said, "I'll miss you as well. Now, go. Learn all you can about your gift. Become strong. We'll need your talent to end this war as quickly as possible. Will you do that, Pendr? Will you honestly do your best, even though it might fight against your natural tendencies?"

He hugged her back, gently, as if he was afraid he might break her. "I will, Danla. I will."

Chapter 32

Nestov watched the sunlight flow through the clear crystal—a gemstone cut with sharp angles to produce a specific effect. Though the sunshine shone through a window in the abbey, the particular beam which fascinated Nestov had been redirected by a curved mirror, narrowing the beam.

"What do you see, Nestov?" Friar Janus asked. His gray, bushy eyebrows raised toward the heavens. His dark robes were a contrast to his nearly alabaster skin.

The white light entered the crystal on one side, yet something different appeared from the other side, as displayed on a blank sheet of parchment affixed to a wooden box at the end of the table. "Red, green, and blue," Nestov answered. "The crystal has changed the sunlight into other colors."

"But how can that be?" Janus asked as he walked closer to where Nestov sat on a stone bench, facing the crystal placed upon a limestone table. Small, metallic prongs, formed to make a sturdy base, held the crystal in place. "The light from the sun is white. The crystal is clear. Then, pray tell, from where does the red, green, and blue light come?"

Three winters previous, Nestov had come to the capital city of Virqyna to become an initiate for the church—as was the custom for the third boy in each family. The first lesson he learned was a simple mantra: "Nothing comes from nothing." Truth be told, it was the only thing taught for his first moon cycle. Each day he would arrive for training, alone, and each day Friar Janus would say the same thing, "Nothing comes from nothing. Meditate on that principle."

Naturally, the first lesson Nestov gleaned was that *something* must come from *something*, yet the more he reflected on the mantra, the more he considered the nuances. A child comes from two parents, something from something. Simple in concept, but not complete. The same parents could create more than one child, and not every child was the same. The different traits—from eye and hair color, height and thickness, and even sex—each of these had to come from somewhere.

Using that as a guide, Nestov considered the light. "It takes both the sunlight and the crystal to create the separate colors," Nestov said.

"Oh?" The friar did not elaborate.

"Yes. Remove either one of the elements—the light or the crystal—and the effect disappears." Nestov placed his hand between the sunbeam and the crystal, and indeed, the parchment went blank.

The friar's expression remained impassive. "But which of the elements contains all three colors?"

Nestov looked again more closely at the three distinct hues on the parchment. Each color was separate, yes, but where they converged, he could see evidence of even more shades. Still, that did not help him pick one element over the other.

This was a test; Nestov knew as much. If he were to move to the next level of his training, he would have to pass. Based on what he saw, he simply could not say which, if either, of the elements was more dominant. He considered the second mantra, one only learned once he passed the first test: "Compare the unknown to the known."

When faced with new things in the world around him, Nestov learned to relate them to things with which he was familiar. Creating a basic foundation of understanding allowed him to seek into deeper unknowns.

But what can I use to compare? The room was warm, and Nestov and the friar had been at this for some time. While he considered the friar's question, he recognized his body began to thirst. At each meal, novices were given a glass of juice created from the vineyards located on the abbey's grounds. It was one of Nestov's favorite moments of the day. *The juice.*

134

The drink served with their humble meals was created using grapes, but not before the seeds and pulp were filtered out. Thick cloth allowed the juice to pass during the creation process, while at the same time retaining the other elements. *It's the grapes from which the juice comes, not the cloth.*

"The light, Friar," Nestov said. "The light contains blue, red, and green. The crystal acts as a filter." He tried to sound as confident as possible in his answer, though even he heard a hint of uncertainty in his voice.

"Of this, you are certain?" Janus asked.

Instantly, the third mantra sprang to Nestov's mind. "A hesitant answer is always wrong." Of the first three mantras, this one gave Nestov the most trouble. Certainly, a correct answer to a question was always correct, even when given hesitantly—or so he thought. In moments of crisis, he learned, inaction could create more problems than a wrong answer. If asked a question when immediate action was needed, like on a battlefield, a hesitant answer could produce doubt in the mind of those needed to act. Therefore, even a correct answer could not have the needed result if given too late.

More than that, often there was more than one correct answer, and the only way for it to be successful was for people to believe in it. Or so that is how Nestov understood the third mantra.

Nestov was approaching his eighteenth winter which made him one of the youngest novices to face this particular test. He wanted to be successful, as well as make the friar proud. There was only one way to do that.

"It is a certainty," Nestov said, this time, stronger than before. "The light *is* the source. The crystal is the filter."

In response, Janus said nothing. Instead, he reached inside the box to which the parchment was attached. He removed another crystal, different in shape and shorter than the one which already sat on the table.

Carefully, the friar placed the second crystal a specific distance from the first. The light from the sunbeam now went through the first crystal, and then partially through the second crystal. The blue light still appeared on the white parchment, but instead of green and red below it, the light was a vibrant yellow.

"And what make you of this?" the friar asked.

Nestov ran through the first three mantras once again in his head in an attempt to understand what his eyes saw. *The yellow has to come from somewhere, but what of the red and green? Where did they go?*

In the moon cycle previous, Nestov had been given a similar test with colors, using paint instead of light. In that lesson, however, he learned that any color could be created by combining red, blue, and yellow—not green. When adding enough of each color, the result was black. *There has to be a reason the friar is showing me this. What lesson does he want me to learn?*

Why would the friar use two different methods to teach the same lesson? It was not something Nestov had experienced from his teacher previously. Something was different. But what? *Perhaps that is the point of this test.* At that moment, an idea popped into his mind—a possible solution. Recalling the third mantra, he reached out and picked up the second crystal.

Janus made no attempt to stop him as Nestov lifted the second crystal a bit higher, and closer to the first. The result, as clearly displayed on the parchment, was white light.

Speaking with as much fervor as possible, Nestov proclaimed, "Like paint, different colors of light can be combined to create new colors. Unlike paint, it is red, *green*, and blue—and the result is white, not black."

For the first time since he had known Friar Janus, Nestov saw an expression on the elderly man's face yet to be displayed. The old man smiled.

Chapter 33

For three days Rheq made his way south. The land rolled with hills and forest, making traveling slow. Still, it offered ample cover to protect him from being spotted. By fortune or chance, Rheq had yet to come across another band of enemies.

Yesterday, not long after his mid-day meal, Rheq found the Timber River. Before being conscripted into King Viskum's service, this waterway had been as far north as he had traveled. It was not hard to understand from whence the river earned its name. Red maples, harvested upstream, were placed in the river to be transported to the south and the east, where such wood was scarce. Even now, during war, Rheq could see men on flat boats using long poles to guide the timber downriver.

Rheq had to wait until nightfall to cross one of the high, stone bridges which spanned the Timber. Once again, he made it undetected, again by either fortune or chance. *Or perhaps neither. I am a skilled hunter, after all.*

Unsure of who claimed ownership of the bridge, seeing that war reigned upon the land, Rheq thought it best not to approach any of the men in the meager dwellings which were common on either side of such a man-made crossing.

From there, the land became more familiar, and Rheq's confidence grew that he would make it back to Umstead safely. By his best guess, he would arrive by the morning of the following day if he were to remain undetected.

The provisions he had poached from the enemies' camp ended up being exactly what he needed. A mixture of salted pork, hard cheese, and rock-like biscuits allowed him to keep his strength. The streams found everywhere in this part of the land made water a non-issue.

Pushing hard, Rheq made it to Fairmont, a hill of decent size, and one often used as a landmark for travelers. Southwest of the hill contained a small village, not much more than a trading post, though it did have an inn.

Rheq was tempted to find room indoors. Sleeping in the wild, especially with the thunderstorms which occurred almost nightly, drained him. For the most part, he knew where to find dry shelter among the trees and hills, but few things were as relaxing as sitting in front of a blazing fire found in a common area of an inn while rain pounded the roof. *I'm too close to home. I can't risk it.*

Up until the sun fully set behind the tree line in the west, Rheq debated about the inn. His survival instincts won, though he questioned the victory more than once when rains came that night—falling harder than any day previous.

At first light, Rheq set off again. He ate as he walked, and considered what he would do when he first returned to Umstead. The answer came readily enough: he would make sure the enemy did not occupy the town. If soldiers from Sothcar patrolled the streets, he would have to slip in undetected. *I know my hometown far better than any enemy.* Getting in would not be a problem. What to do after that? He would leave that to his father. His older brother, Groq, had experienced enough winters to avoid being conscripted. Both his father and brother should be in town, and both of them would know which course of action to take.

With Fairmont a good distance behind him now, Rheq felt a sense of excitement that he was nearly home. *But I must remain vigilant. No use getting caught this close to my destination.*

Instead of traveling by the main road which led to the heart of town, Rheq skirted to the north and picked up on a hunting trail he and his brother would frequent. It was isolated enough that Rheq felt he could approach undetected.

More familiar landmarks appeared as he continued to travel. A mossy stone, shaped roughly like a pear, was one of the first. A thick tree root which spanned the trail, worn down in places from being stepped upon over the seasons, meant he was nearly home. And that was when Rheq smelled it.

Ash.

The scent was not unfamiliar, especially from all the campfires which Rheq had sat around during his lifetime. But this was different—and stronger. Never before had such a smell been present at this part of the trail, even when all the hearths were ablaze in town during the colder times of the seasons. *Something's not right.*

Rheq pulled the bow from over his shoulder, removed a feathered arrow from the quiver, and nocked it. Crouching, Rheq moved ahead more carefully, looking for signs of others in the forest around him. He saw none.

Each step closer to town increased the smell of ash, and with it, a knot in Rheq's stomach grew. At last, he came to the final knoll before town. Once he ascended it, he would be able to assess what caused the unwelcomed odor.

Carefully, Rheq climbed the small hill, still keeping his bow and arrow at the ready. When he finally reached the summit, it became clear why he smelled ash.

Umstead was a smoking ruin.

Only stone chimneys stood taller than a man's height. Everything else—the bakery, smithy, tanner, homes, all of it—were piles of charred wood.

Rheq's mind shouted for him to be cautious, though the message did not make it to his legs. He ran to where his home had stood, dropping his weapon on the way. *They couldn't have been here when it happened. They couldn't!*

The fire even destroyed the rough wooden fence erected at the front of their property. Rheq jumped over the remains of the barrier easily enough. His mother's garden was gone, uprooted, leaving an empty hole which had teamed with vegetation for as long as Rheq could recall.

He wanted to cry out, to call for his family. This time, his mind was able to override his natural reaction. The destruction of his town was no accident. This damage had been systematic, and enemies could still be within listening distance.

The charred wood was not hot to the touch, so Rheq did not worry about being burned as he moved fallen beams and parts of the roof aside. He found no evidence of his family among the collapsed house. *They may have fled. They may yet still live.*

Convinced he had searched thoroughly enough among his family's property, Rheq moved on to the neighbor's home. He did not spend nearly as much time in this search, but enough to be convinced no one had died in the fire there either.

More cautiously now, Rheq moved among the other burnt buildings. His house sat on the northern side of town, closer to the tree line of the wilds. The only movement Rheq detected was ash floating to and fro from the slight western breeze. After passing through the town center, where the fountain now ran dry, Rheq's nostrils detected a new smell. It was familiar, but not quite. *It smells like cooked rabbit, only ... not.* Perhaps the ash and smoke in the air tainted the smell. If someone was preparing a meal close-by, they could know what happened here. *Or perhaps I could punish them if they are the ones to blame.*

Before investigating the source of the new smell, Rheq returned to where he had dropped his bow. Armed, once again, he made his way back to the town square. The breeze had picked up a little, and with it, he could sense the smell came from the direction of old man Carq's farm. It was by the largest open field in the area, which would make it a perfect place to set up a camp.

A small copse had been left untouched between the town and Carq's farm. Rheq had heard the old farmer call it his natural fence. It also gave Rheq a place to approach the farm without being in the open.

Perhaps he would find another group of five or so soldiers as he had before. *But it would take a lot more than that to do what was done here.* Rheq stopped, and listened for voices, yet heard none.

The smell of cooking meat was stronger here, and it began to make Rheq's stomach churn, though he did not know why.

Finally, he made his way closer to the open field to get a view. When he did, Rheq understood. No enemy camp was in the field. No one was cooking rabbit. Point of fact, no one was doing anything at all. They *could* not. From what Rheq could see, every townsperson's body had been burned to death and left to rot in a giant heap.

Chapter 34

Danla woke to someone shouting. Prying her eyes open, darkness still prevailed. How long she had slept, she could only guess. The ache in her body told her it was only for a short period.

"To arms!" a male voice shouted. "To arms!"

Is it a test? Only two days had passed since Mistress Halima moved their camp next to where male soldiers were training. Surely those who had witnessed the attack before, in which Pendr fought them off, would not be back so soon. *Maybe that's wishful thinking.*

Yarma and Nya shared the tent with Danla. Her eyes adjusted to what light was available to see both of them sitting upright.

"You heard him," Yarma said. "Best get up, quickly!"

Neither Nya nor Danla questioned her. Yarma's experience surpassed the other two women, hence, the reason she was assigned to watch over them.

Wearing only a night dress, the same cut and style as the other initiates, Danla stood and followed Yarma out of the tent. A slight chill in the air cut through the cotton clothing, causing Danla to shiver. What she saw next caused her to shiver even more.

Twenty or so men, most wielding long spears in one hand, and swords in the other raced from the trees. A few of the men dressed in robes held nothing in their hands. *Those have to be men who can use the* myelur.

"To me! Now!" called Halima.

Danla recognized her voice right away. The elderly leader of her group stood by the fire pit, arms stretched outward with her palms open. Behind her were the rest of Danla's fellow initiates.

Grabbing the folds in her dress near her thighs, and lifting the cloth a little so she would not trip as she ran, Danla followed Yarma and Nya. On the way, she noticed two fighters from the other friendly camp, wearing full chain mail, and armed with long swords and shields standing in front of Halima. *Where are the rest?*

Confidence reflected in the enemies' faces. Two men, armed though they were, and a group of women were not match for their forces. Danla could see the crescent moon symbols on their armor now, the silver thread gleaming in the moonlight.

In a matter of heartbeats, the battle would be engaged. Then, the two allied fighters did something unthinkable: they turned and ran behind Halima. Laughter at such cowardice gurgled from the onrushing soldiers—and then came to an abrupt end.

The first of the charging soldiers came to a sudden stop as if they had run headfirst into a wall. Which, in a sense, they had. Though Danla could not see it with her physical eyes, she knew there was a barrier, one created by Halima using the blue *myelur*, between them and their foes.

The rest of the men slowed and eventually stopped before hitting the magical barrier. One of the men who had fallen let loose a string of curses, followed by yelling, "Mages! Bring this barrier down. Now!"

Three robed men stepped forward. Each stretched forth their arms and opened their palms, mirroring Halima's stance.

Based on Danla's previous experience, she knew Halima would not be able to hold the barrier for long—especially not against three men who could attack the invisible defenses. *I'm not trained for combat! I'm a healer!* A quick glance at the other initiates indicated that they, too, felt the same. The only two people behind Halima who did not look afraid were the soldiers. *Is it because they are armed?* Cries of surprise from the enemy made her realize it was something else.

The three mages, as the enemy soldier had called them, fell to the ground. Multiple arrows protruded from their bodies—arrows which came from the southern side of the forest. More arrows flew, most hitting the enemy in vulnerable spots.

In the open, the enemy had no place to take cover. Without awaiting orders, several of the men went to race for the northern tree line to seek cover. That was, until, a dozen men, dressed in the king's colors charged from their hiding place. The two fighters behind Halima sprinted forward.

The battle was joined.

"Remain behind me!" Halima shouted to the initiates.

Some of the young women looked away as limbs were chopped off, swords found passages through armor, and the work of death commenced before them. Danla remembered hearing once that time slowed down while in battle, but for her, it did not. Perhaps it was because she was only an observer and not an active participant.

Sooner than she thought possible, the battle ended. Shouts of "No quarter!" sprang from the lips of the winning soldiers. *Her* soldiers. Their forces had won, but not without cost. Several of her allies lay wounded— some crying out in pain, others moaning deeply.

"Now, initiates, now!" Halima ordered. "Use what you've been taught. Heal the injured."

Yarma was the first to rush out to where men had fallen. Danla followed closely behind. She jumped over a fallen enemy to reach a man who held a hand to his stomach, trying to stop the oozing blood.

Kneeling, Danla reached to the man and placed her hands over the wound. She tried to shut out everything else around her, as had been taught. There, from the center of her being, she found the green *myelur*. She coaxed it forward, through her hands and into the man's wounds. Soon, she could feel the gash in his middle closing, and with it, her energy began to wane. The soldier would be as new in a moment as long as she could remain focused.

A sharp pain in her left shin interrupted the process. *Something hit me.* The green *myelur* slipped from her grasp. She turned her head to see a dagger embedded in her leg, just below her knee. The enemy soldier which she had jumped over was propped up on one arm, grinning victoriously. His grin did not last long.

One of Danla's allies reacted to the attack, shooting an arrow into the back of the man's neck. Her rescuer rushed to her, and looking her in the eyes said, "I need to remove this blade. It may be poisoned."

Without waiting for confirmation, he grasped the handle and yanked the dagger free from her leg. Spots danced in front of Danla's eyes. The pain was unlike anything she had felt before.

"I need a healer!" the soldier cried. "Here! Now!"

I still have a task at hand. She tried to shunt the pain and refocus on the man she had been healing before. *Someone can heal me after I've healed him.* The idea offered her enough comfort that she directed her full attention on her patient. When she did, something unexpected happened.

In addition to the green *myelur* flowing from her inner self, she noticed something else. Yellow threads stretched between her and the wounded man. They glowed in a similar fashion to the green *myelur*, yet differently. Whereas the green acted more like a balm, the yellow threads vibrated with a sense of urgency.

What is this? What does this mean? Then, from the recesses of her mind, she remembered what Halima had said. The *myelur* consisted of red, green, and blue. But that was not all. Yellow also existed, though it was dangerous and should be avoided, no matter the situation. Halima had never explained why.

Danla again fixated on the yellow threads. They did not appear to be dangerous. If anything, they seemed to call out to her—begging her to let them help. The urge to pluck one of the threads grew stronger, and with each heartbeat, Danla's resolve weakened. *How can something so beautiful be dangerous?*

Mentally, she reached out toward one of the threads, not quite touching it. Then, she felt a hand clasp her leg, where the knife had pierced her. Immediately the pain lessened, and with it, the yellow threads began to fade. When the pain in her leg was gone, the threads vanished completely.

Danla turned her head, enough to see it was Mistress Halima who had healed her.

"Go ahead, Danla," Halima said. "Finish healing your patient. And from there, we'll heal the rest."

"Yes, Mistress Halima," Danla said.

A hard look appeared in her teacher's eyes. "After this is over, you and I need to talk."

Chapter 35

"You are now ready to learn the fourth mantra," Friar Janus told Nestov. "As with the others, you are required not to share it with anyone. Of this, will you accept?"

"I accept, Friar Janus."

Once again, the friar smiled. It was odd to see again an expression which until two days ago Nestov had never seen from the older man. Muted light came in from the windows set high into the limestone walls. Clouds crept in during the evening and seemed content to remain over the abbey. Normally, Nestov found the hard, stone bench in the training room to be uncomfortable. This morning, he hardly noticed it at all.

Two days previous, Nestov had passed the test of light. The other thirty initiates of his age reacted in differing manners. A few were openly happy for him, while most made no acknowledgment of his achievement. Only a couple were outwardly hostile, though not in front of any of the church leaders.

As a reward for his efforts, Nestov was given two days of freedom to spend as he wished inside the abbey. Naturally, he chose to visit the library. He read books on the history of Virqyna, as well as the battles fought with Nothcar and Murlund. These were texts expected of him to read, though, on the second evening, Nestov indulged in burying himself in the pages of *The Tales of Grorage the Brave*.

Many a night as a youngster, before the land of dreams took him, Nestov would fantasize he was Grorage, off on a noble quest of no small importance. As a third boy born to his parents, it was not a life he could lead. No, he was committed to the church upon his birth.

To be fully honest with himself, heroes in the stories did not have his skinny frame and shorter stature.

In a way, Nestov found himself on an adventure of a different kind—one of knowledge. Unlike fighting with swords, or mastering horseback riding, this was something in which he excelled. And now, he was about to learn even more: the fourth mantra.

"In your last test," Friar Janus began, "you learned of light. You divined that light can be separated into three basic elements: red, green, and blue. You also discovered how by combining all these elements any color could be created."

"Yes, Friar."

"Is that all there is to be learned from light?"

Nestov considered the question. Answering only in the affirmative would bring nothing new to the discussion. *What else do I know of light?* There were many points, and he filtered through is possible answers. He selected two. Remembering the third mantra, he stated them confidently.

"Two more key elements are to be considered when learning about light," Nestov said, his voice strong. "First, there is a connection between the three colors of light and the *myelur.*"

Surprise flitted across Janus's face. "Oh? And of what do you know about the *myelur?*"

"I have heard stories, as most children have, I'm sure," Nestov said. "Though it is from the texts in the library where I have learned the most. Scattered throughout the holy works are references to the power to do good. They are given different names, some in the ancient tongue, yet in each case, the words can be translated or referenced to one of three colors: red, green, and blue."

Janus clasped his hands behind his back. "And what makes you think this is related to light?

"Light we praise," Nestov recited. "Light brings life. Light brings hope. Light helps us see the things otherwise hidden."

"You are only repeating what each first level initiate knows." The scowl which Nestov knew well had replaced the friar's smile.

Lifting his hands in a gesture to pacify his teacher, Nestov said, "If light is good, and the three elements of the *myelur* are good, the connection cannot be a coincidence."

The older man still scowled, though not as deeply. "What is your other main point?"

"As I stated, light helps us see the things otherwise hidden. What, then, causes something to be hidden? Shadows—created when light is obstructed."

"Meaning?" The friar's voice did not have the same critical tone as before.

Nestov took that to mean he was on the right path and sat up a bit straighter. "There is a connection between light and shadow. Shadows cannot exist without light."

For twenty or so heartbeats, Janus said nothing. He simply stared at Nestov, his expression giving away nothing. Then, he asked, "If, as you said, light is good, does that mean shadow is evil?"

The point made sense, after a fashion, though something in the way the friar phrased it seemed … *off.* Unlike the previous three mantras, what his teacher said now did not possess the same resonance of truth.

"No. The shadow in and of itself is not evil. To state as much indicates that good creates evil. It does not." Nestov said. Friar Janus's lips twitched as if he were about to speak, but Nestov continued. "I will concede evil survives better in shadow than light. Therefore, it is light we seek. But where there is light, there will be shadows."

Janus rubbed his hand over his mouth before speaking again. When he did, his words were soft, thoughtful. "You say light and shadow are connected, yes? And you state shadows are created when light is obstructed, correct?"

"Yes, Friar Janus."

"What, then, obstructs the light?"

It was yet another question which Nestov could take literally, or metaphorically. None of the others with which he trained were purposely trying to limit their learning, but literal interpretations were what most of his fellow students could not see beyond, and hence impeded their progress at the abbey. *Obstacles can be passive in nature.* That triggered the next thought: *Sometimes the barriers are intentional.*

"Obstructions, or barriers, can be benign in nature—such as ignorance," Nestov said. "Obstructions can also be created or positioned to block the light deliberately. An example would be withholding the truth to those in need of it."

Janus took three steps to his left, then faced Nestov once again. "Barriers are different, you say?"

"Yes, Friar," Nestov said. He began to feel an excitement build within his chest. *I'm on the verge of learning something important here. I can feel it!* "Using the second mantra of comparing the unknown to the known, consider a leaf. It can block out some, or all, of the light, depending on its character. Or look out the window today. The sun is in the sky, yet the clouds prevent all of the light from passing through. Thicker storms, violent storms, can make even mid-day appear as night."

Janus took three steps back to his right, which seemed odd to Nestov. *Why move to one side, just to return?* Then again, he had never known his teacher to do anything without a reason. "So, it is the nature of the barrier which determines the characteristics of the shadow?"

The first response to come to Nestov's mind was to answer in the affirmative. But then he paused. Once again, an element of truth was missing. Yes, some obstacles allowed a portion of light through, while others prevented any. However, if the shadow and light were directly connected, then it was more than the barrier which determined the shadow. It was then Nestov understood.

"No, Friar Janus. The nature of the shadow depends not only on the barrier, but also the amount or brightness of the light."

Janus took two small steps, placing him in the middle of where he had walked before. Unblinking, he said, "The fourth mantra is thus: Brighter the light, stronger the barrier, darker the shadow."

Chapter 36

Pendr stood in the back row of the formation, shoulder to shoulder with men who he did not know, but swore to protect—even if that meant dying for them. *No, not for* them. *For the people I know and love.* He could see clearly over the first two rows as the shorter men stood in front. Glancing quickly to his left and right, he noticed he stood taller than any of the rest of the trainees. There was one man who was almost of a height with him, but his skinny frame made him look like a child in an adult's body.

"This is not the war we thought it would be," the man standing before them said. His stature was average, perhaps even on the smaller side. However, his hard facial features and steely gaze made for a commanding presence. "My name is Captain Mux, and I am tasked with making you into the weapons we need to win."

A few of the trainees stood a bit more proudly at the declaration, though Pendr was not among them. It took four days of traveling from sunrise to sunset for Pendr to arrive at the training camp—a camp close enough to the king's castle that they could see the top of the tower spires above the trees. Pendr had never been to the capital of Nothcar, and seeing even a bit of the castle was awe inspiring. *I had no idea men could build something so tall.*

The trip to the wooded campsite was not entirely unpleasant, at first. Eladrel was in the same caravan, though he left with those who could wield the green *myelur* on the second day. None of them were told where they would be going, to avoid leaking information upon capture, Pendr supposed.

For the rest of the trip, Pendr had kept to himself. Others were making friends and getting to know each other, though he had no desire to do so. *Perhaps it is because those I've known, or who I get to know, have ended up either dead or separated from me.*

More than once his thoughts dwelled on Danla. But each time, he remembered his promise. He would not do anything stupid in an attempt to impress anyone—including her. If he was to protect her, as well as his family in Logs Pond, he needed to learn what Captain Mux would teach him. He may not like the role he was in—he missed the satisfaction which came from bending and shaping metal—but he could not return to that life knowing the risks that could come to his village.

"Each of you has demonstrated the ability to access the blue *myelur*," Mux said, snapping Pendr out of his wondering thoughts. "Though some of you have displayed a stronger aptitude than others. I need a volunteer to tell of an experience they have had."

A man in the front row raised his hand. "I would be honored."

"Step forward, and tell us your name and from whence you come," Mux said.

The trainee did as commanded, turning to face the rest of the men. His dark hair was cropped short, so much so that it looked like a skullcap. "I am Dosfogal, of Seven Lakes. It happened while training with my squad after my conscription. We were practicing swordplay. Though we used wooden swords, they could leave quite a mark. On the first day, as the battle commenced, I could feel a cool sensation in the center of my head. It was unlike anything I'd felt before. After each day, I was physically exhausted, though I slept well each night. By the end of the third day, I was the only one in my squad not marked with bruises or minor cuts."

Pendr noticed a number of the trainees nodding their heads as if indicating they had similar experiences.

"I knew I had taken several hard blows," Dosfogal continued, "and had no reason why they didn't show. The next day, I was summoned to my captain's tent. After describing my experience, he ordered me here."

Mux's expression did not change when he said, "That will be all. Return to formation."

As Dosfogal did so, Mux asked, "Who will be next?"

This time, a man from the third row pushed his way forward. Though he was a handspan shorter than Pendr, his physique was similar. Pendr thought perhaps he had also been a blacksmith once.

"I'm Sadem, from High Falls. I was shield bearer for Sir Noffton." He paused for a moment as if waiting for that statement to mean something. When no one reacted, Sadem frowned, then said, "We were headed toward Iredell when the ambush came. Twenty-five of the king's men died that day, including Sir Noffton. When we were first attacked, the cowards peppered us with arrows. My liege had no warning before his horse was struck twice—once in the leg, the other in the neck. The horse collapsed, throwing Sir Noffton onto a solid boulder. I rushed to his aid, and in so doing, felt the same cool sensation as Dosfo— Dosfog— whatever his name was, described. I, too, felt drained, until I realized that the arrows bounced off me, not even leaving a mark."

Sadem smirked. "This was *real* combat, not slapping each other with wooden swords. While I felt powerful, I knew my duty. Sadly, the fall had broken Sir Noffton's neck. He was dead before I could even get to him."

The young man from High Falls stood taller. "While those around me fell, I continued to ward off the arrows. I took up Sir Noffton's sword and went to attack those shooting at us from the wood. When they saw I could not be harmed, they ran off. Yes, I was a bit tired after that, but based on the stories I'd heard growing up, I *knew* I had the warrior's power. It was only logical I would be sent here to help all of you."

Though Sadem looked nothing like Lunz, the mayor's son who had died during the ambush on Pendr's small group, his pride certainly matched. It was not confidence which Sadem displayed; it was arrogance. Pendr pondered a moment on the difference, thinking that confidence was displayed when a person knew something about themselves to be a strength, whereas arrogance was not knowledge as much as a belief.

Sadem thought highly of himself, and being able to use the blue *myelur* could only make it worse. *I won't let that happen to me.*

A few other men came forward after Sadem, recounting stories of a similar nature. In each case, there was some peril involved. None of them described the experience of feeling the blue *myelur* build up inside of them, and then release it as Pendr had done. Neither did any of the others describe the ability to create wards, both of warning and protection, like those made by Mistress Halima.

"Is that all?" Mux said after the sixth man told his story. "Did none of you experience anything different?"

Pendr hesitated, waiting to see if anyone else would speak up. No one did. Finally, he raised his hand, only high enough to catch the captain's attention.

"You, the tall one," Mux said, pointing. "Come forth."

"Pardon me," Pendr said. He waited for the men in front of him to move out of the way. With a pathway clear, he stood next to his new captain.

"Explain," was all Mux said.

Pendr looked at the soldiers before him. Most of them were a bit older, and none looked younger. *Perhaps the power doesn't come to us until a certain age.* A few of the group waited anxiously, while Sadem continued to smirk.

"I have had similar experiences," Pendr said. "The blue *myelur* protected me in battle. Yet, there was something else."

He looked at the ground, not wanting to see their reactions, yet unsure why. "In one battle, instead of feeling the *myelur* in my mind, I felt it here." He tapped his breastbone. "An enemy was escaping, and I couldn't reach him before he would disappear into the trees. The energy built up inside me, and then ... " *They won't believe me. They will think I'm making this up to impress them.*

"Then, what?" A voice called out. Pendr recognized it as Sadem.

Pendr lifted his head. Raising his arm, palm forward, he said, "I instinctively made this motion. Somehow, I released the power inside my chest. I could not see it, though I saw the result. The enemy was flung against a tree. It was powerful enough to kill him."

"Not possible," Sadem said. "Did anyone else experience this?"

None of the men responded.

I was right. I should have kept quiet.

"Telling falsehoods is not the mark of a knight," Sadem said. "You should—"

"Sadem, come forward," Mux said, cutting off whatever the soldier was going to propose.

Once again, Sadem shoved his way through the crowd. "The blue *myelur* protects. It is not a weapon," he said once he stood in front of Pendr and Captain Mux. "That is the light's truth."

"That is the light's truth," a few of the other men echoed.

Mux, still as stoic as from the moment Pendr had met the man, answered, "You are correct, Sadem."

The statement hit Pendr as hard as any blow from a sword. *Even the captain doesn't believe me.*

"Sadem," Mux said. "Stand there. Three paces to my side."

Smugness masked Sadem's face as he followed the instructions. Once in place, Mux raised his arm, mimicking Pendr's earlier stance. The hair on the back of Pendr's neck began to bristle, only slightly, and then something remarkable happened. Sadem flew backward, landing hard on his hindquarters.

Surprise replaced Sadem's haughty expression. He went to speak, but Mux spoke first.

"You are right in that the blue *myelur* by itself protects. That is when it is used in a passive manner. However, when combined with the red *myelur*, something new is created. It is an active power, sometimes known as the purple *myelur*." Motioning to Pendr, Mux said, "Rare are those who can wield the blue *myelur*, yet rarer still is one who can do as Pendr described."

The men all turned to Pendr, most with awe showing in their eyes, though several held fear.

Chapter 37

Wyjec sat upon a throne of stone. Here, among the high trees of the mountains, was his kingdom.

When the Masters had referred to the mountains, Wyjec did not understand. Now he did. These were giants among the hills and plains— a perfect location both in isolation and symbolism for Wyjec to establish his dominance.

After the female wolf, Silk he had named her, joined his pack, along with her female companions, Wyjec thought about how he would force the wolves to create more of their kind. His intervention turned out to be unnecessary. The wolves acted on instinct, and shortly, Wyjec could tell by using the red *myelur* that each of the female wolves was carrying young inside them.

What Wyjec found fascinating is that each of the females would produce more than one pup at a time. Silk, the biggest and strongest female, had seven distinct heartbeats growing inside of her, whereas the others had in the range of four to six.

Admittedly, Wyjec knew little about how the process worked in humans, though he had deduced that most children were born one at a time. Because the wolves could create more per pregnancy, it would not take as long for him to build up is army—an army he would use to take revenge on those who had betrayed him.

In the mountains, the wolves found caves in which they made homes, including a large one for Wyjec. The air higher up in the mountains was colder, and heavy rains were not uncommon. The caves provided enough shelter to keep them dry, and Wyjec still relied on sleeping next to the wolves for warmth. But it was not enough.

The cold and damp air made Wyjec weak. During the days, he would shiver and was miserable in the process. Using the yellow *myelur* to drain the life from the still-alive food the wolves brought him helped, yet the power inside the rabbits and squirrels was small—usually enough to fight off the sickness from eating raw meat with a little to spare.

Now, in between rainstorms, Wyjec sat on a rock smoothed over the seasons by falling rain and gusting winds. Enough moss grew upon it to make it comfortable. From here, he could see the small gorge where they had settled. When not scouting or hunting, the wolves often ran free in an open meadow nestled within the gorge.

The land formation was an oddity, to find an open expanse among the rocks and trees seemed out of place. *It's just like me. I'm unique among other men.* Moreover, it felt like home. It needed a proper name, Wyjec decided, though he could not pick one which truly represented it. *It will come to me in time.*

Thunder boomed in the distance, heralding another storm. The wolves stopped their activity in the meadow. Even from Wyjec's vantage place, he could hear Alpha whine/growl to the others. Immediately, the wolves headed toward their caves.

For the most part, the wolves had paired off. It did not surprise that Alpha and Silk became a pair. Wyjec shared their cave, where they kept him warm during the coldest of times. The impending rainstorm meant yet another long afternoon in the cave. Wyjec had little to do, now, with the wolves providing him food, the mountain springs offering clear water, and the cave giving shelter. For the first time since his exodus from Iredell, Wyjec realized something—he was bored.

It was an odd sensation. *I could have never imagined this feeling.* As a chardi serving the Masters, Wyjec usually worked from the time he woke until after the sun dipped passed the horizon. While he did have small breaks now and again, the times when he would eavesdrop on the Masters, they were never long enough for him to experience what he felt now—not having anything to do.

He sighed, and stood. Down a path, he had created an area where he discarded the bones and fur from the rabbits the wolves provided. It was far enough away from the caves, and his rock, for the smell of decomposing to stay away.

Today, as he headed to the cave, he paused while passing the area. He had eaten that morning, as well as later the day previous. Through repetition, Wyjec had become good at using sharp stones to separate the rabbit's fur from its body. It made eating them much easier. The two pelts of the most recently consumed rabbits lay side by side. Strangely enough, the pelts of the animals he had drained using the yellow *myelur* did not decay like the bones and sinews of the corpses—the fur remained intact. *Perhaps the* myelur *has something to do with that.* A moment of inspiration hit.

The wolves and rabbits had fur to keep them warm. Wyjec's clothes, those he had worn when at Iredell, were shredded and threadbare—they did little more than cover him. The rabbit skins by themselves were too small to cover his body unless he combined them somehow.

His clothes, tattered as they were, still stayed together because of thick stitching. Wyjec reached down and picked up one of the rabbit's hides. Upon inspection, Wyjec imagined he could use one of the sharp rocks to punch small holes in the fur. Using the same technique as employed on his current garments, he could tie the hides together to make something larger. *But what to use for thread?*

Then, another answer came to him. His clothes consisted of cloth and thread. He could use that for starters, and perhaps, over time, he could figure out a way to make thread from rabbit fur.

The idea excited him, though he was unsure why at first. Soon, he understood. *Because it will give me something to do, as well as solve one of my problems.* He picked through the pile of discarded bodies and gathered the rest of the pelts. Remarkably, each of the hides showed no signs of decay. *This shouldn't be.* Then again, there were many aspects of the *myelur* Wyjec did not fully understand. A spring returned to his step, one he did not realize he had lost, as he carried the pelts back to the cave.

Fat raindrops, falling heavily, began hesitantly at first, but by the time Wyjec made it to the cave, it was as if his shelter existed behind a waterfall. Fortunately, the floor of the cave's mouth sloped toward the meadow, and a giant rock outcropping jutted over the top. This prevented the rain from gathering in Wyjec's shelter.

Alpha and Silk were already in the cave, snuggled up next to each other. They gave him curious looks as he sat in the faded light and squinted at the collected pelts. Neither of the wolves moved nor made sounds aside from their breathing while Wyjec sorted through his assortment of sharp rocks.

One rock, which was stark in its blackness, had a fairly fine point as well as a wide base. It took Wyjec a few attempts, but eventually he created a small hole in a hide. He smiled triumphantly at the wolves, neither of which seemed to comprehend the significance of the accomplishment. *No matter. It's not for them to understand.*

The work was slow and hard, but his time as a chardi prepared him for such tasks. Soon, Wyjec found a rhythm in his work, and then did something he had not done since … since … it had been so long he could not remember the last time he did it. He began to whistle a merry tune.

At that, the wolves *did* react. Alpha perked up his ears and lifted his head. His golden eyes stared at Wyjec with complete attention. *That's odd. Why would Alpha react that way?*

Wyjec shrugged and went back to his work. He whistled three more notes and was interrupted when Alpha leaped to his feet. Instinctively, Wyjec called upon the blue *myelur* to protect himself. Alpha did not attack. Instead, he did something which chilled Wyjec more than the coldest night.

Alpha, whining, recreated the same three notes at Wyjec.

Chapter 38

Revenge, vengeance, justice. Each of these words tumbled through Rheq's mind as he walked. Instead of moving stealthily, as he had done when returning home to Umstead, he simply placed one foot in front of the other. A particular destination did not drive Rheq's movements. What motivated him was the need to get away from *there.*

The bodies of the dead, arranged like a giant haystack, had been charred—some beyond recognition. It was those Rheq *could* identify which haunted him: people he had known, people with whom he had grown up, faces twisted in agony from being burned alive. None of these villagers deserved such a horrific death. But those who did this to them? Yes, they were the ones who needed to suffer as they made others suffer. *Revenge, vengeance, justice.*

What was stranger still was that the crows had not been feasting on the dead. Rheq had seen them, circling overhead, but they had kept their distance. Of that, Rheq had no answer. Neither did he understand why there was no enemy present. Using the tracking skills learned as a youth and honed through his life, he could tell that a great number of men had walked through the field and then had headed south.

Initially, Rheq thought to follow them, to make them pay for what they had done. *But if a whole village full of people could not stop them, what chance do I have?* Burying the dead had felt like the proper thing to do. Logic overruled sentiment. The body count was much too high, and taking the time needed would have made Rheq vulnerable. He would have to honor the dead a different way. *Revenge, vengeance, justice.*

Numbly, Rheq headed north. The primary motivator was to get away from the horrors which had been his home. Rheq considered his next course of action. He needed to find help. Recruiting assistance would not be easy. *But I don't need to recruit soldiers; they have already conscripted* me. He realized now that his goal was to return to King Viskum's army—there he could tell the leaders what he saw. Certainly, they would help him do what he could not achieve on his own: *Revenge, vengeance, justice.*

Even after the sun dipped below the horizon, Rheq continued onward. He hardly noticed the forest around him. Though he tried to put the images of his ruined hometown out of his mind, they kept returning. Finally, even using the light from the moon and stars, Rheq could not see the ground in front of him. Twisting an ankle now, or possibly some other careless injury, would prevent him from reaching friendly soldiers.

He snapped out of his reverie enough to look for a place to rest for the evening. The rumbling of another approaching thunderstorm helped expedite his decision. A large oak, wide enough to cover him from the western winds and rains would suffice.

Rheq began to search for dry leaves or other soft material to cushion his bed for the night when he heard something aside from thunder—music. A jaunty tune, one played at festivals or celebrations, sifted through the trees. Its location was northwest and close enough that Rheq figured it was worth a look, if for no other reason than to see if it posed a threat.

For the first time since leaving Umstead, Rheq used the techniques of walking silently through the forest. Light soon accompanied the music, as well as a distinct sound of singing. *I recognize that song.* Rheq felt his shoulders relax—he had not realized how tense they had become. If the source of the music came from whence he thought, his luck may have turned once again for the better.

The singing and playing of musical instruments—lutes, tambourines, recorders—were loud enough now to where Rheq no longer had to worry about moving quietly. Stepping around a thicket of briars, he got his first good look at them: Gymads.

From Rheq's previous experience, he knew Gymads were a group of people who roamed from town to town, earning their living from trading goods as well as news. They were also entertainers who were more than happy to accept payment for those who wanted to hear their music. For Rheq, the most important thing about the Gymads was that their home consisted of wherever their travels took them at the time; they were not subjects of any particular king or ruler. It meant he could find shelter with them for the night.

Rheq counted fourteen wagons, a good omen, circled around a blazing fire. Children, dressed in bright colors, ran around the fire, while the adults—dressed in a similar fashion—played instruments, sang, or simply chatted with each other. Horses, along with a few goats, were penned up nearby.

Raising his empty hands, as was customary when entering a Gymad camp, Rheq stepped out from the shadow of the forest. Not only did it show the Gymads he wanted permission to come into their encampment, but it also showed that he meant them no harm.

A tall, thin man leaned against one of the wagons. He appeared disinterested, though Rheq new better. While the Gymads were peaceful by nature, they were also renowned for their fierceness in defending themselves. Throwing daggers, some coated with different types of poisons, were their weapons of choice. Rheq spotted several more men around the campsite, each watching without appearing to be on guard duty.

The closest man casually dropped one of his hands to his side as Rheq approached. No doubt he had daggers hidden out of sight.

"I ask for permission to enter," Rheq spoke loudly enough for the thin man to hear.

Without looking at him directly, the man asked, "What is it you seek?"

"Shelter."

"No more than that?"

Even during a simple exchange as this, Rheq noticed that bargaining was part of the process. "Perhaps to swap news as well as supplies."

"And what news do you have which would interest us?"

"Why build a wagon when you can ride on one for free?" Rheq answered. He would show this man that he, too, could bargain.

At this, the man looked up. He studied Rheq for a moment, keeping his hand to his side. "You're a soldier. We want no part of your war."

Rheq realized he still wore the uniform provided him by the king's army. He began to chastise himself for making such an error, then realized he had no other clothes to wear. The chance to rest with the Gymads was slipping out of his hands.

"I have not sought out war. *It* sought out me," Rheq said. "I honor your desire for peace. I wish for the same. Please, I ask of you, allow me to enter. I will share what I can in exchange for a place to rest for the evening."

Thunder boomed, and the night lit up with arcing flashes of light. Rain began to fall now, a few drops at first, yet enough for the Gymads to stop playing their instruments. Adults ordered the young ones to their wagons. Still, the thin man did not move.

"A storm is coming, yes. An angry one by the smell in the air," he said.

Rain began to fall harder. Rheq continued to stand in place, hands held high.

The thin man sighed, and then said, "Come then, in with you. But first, give me your weapons."

With little choice, Rheq removed the bow and quiver of arrows slung from his shoulder. "Thank you," Rheq said. He quickly moved toward the camp. Upon reaching the man, he handed the bow and quiver, as well as his short sword, to the Gymad then asked, "Where may I rest?"

Shrugging, the man motioned to the wagons. "Pick one."

"But, won't the owner of the wagons mind that I will be sharing their home?"

With that, the thin man barked out a laugh. "Oh, you misunderstand. You may sleep *under* one of the wagons."

Chapter 39

Danla sat cross-legged in front of Mistress Halima, who sat in a similar fashion. Only the two of them were in her leader's tent, a point on which Halima insisted.

The pain from the stab wound in Danla's leg was gone. Once Halima had finished healing her, no trace of the wound remained. That was not to say all was well with her. After she had completed using the green *myelur* to heal the wounded soldier, her whole body felt drained of energy—which of course is exactly what happened.

"How do you feel?" Halima asked.

"Tired," Danla said. "I've never treated such a severe wound before. I didn't realize how taxing it would be."

"It's quite a change from the scrapes and bruises you've been practicing with, isn't it?" Halima said. Despite having healed Danla's stab wound, she looked as refreshed as ever. "Now you can see why it is important that you learn to build up a reserve of energy."

Danla had been told this before, but in light of her recent experience, it truly meant more to her now. "Yes, Mistress Halima. I am inspired to work harder."

Her leader said nothing for a moment. The expression on her face was serene, with a hint of expectancy. Danla recognized the countenance as Halima's way of trying to get her initiates to think for themselves on the next course of action. Other initiates had healed soldiers, yet after the battle, Danla was the sole person asked to meet with Halima. *Why me? Did I do something wrong?* The only thing different was of all the healers, only Danla received an injury.

"Mistress, was I too hasty to go to the soldier's aid? Should I have been more cautious around the enemy?" she asked her mentor.

"Others did as you," Halima said. "In battle, not all is as it first appears. There are risks, yes. What would have happened had you waited to make sure there were no threats?"

"The soldier I healed had been bleeding profusely," Danla said, picturing the events in her mind. "When I reached him, time was already short. And honestly, I thought the enemy who stabbed me was dead. How can I be sure that no threats remain?"

"You can't," Halima said. "At least not without the aid of the red *myelur*—a power you do not possess."

"I don't understand."

"One ability of the red *myelur* is to be able to discern the state of living creatures," Halima said. "Had you that skill, you would have been able to tell if the man who stabbed you was still alive."

Danla had no experience with the red *myelur*, so she had a difficult time trying to imagine how it would do as Halima said. *Then again, until I used the green* myelur, *I didn't understand that either.* "Then I was wrong to act so quickly?"

"Were you? As you said, the man you healed was fading swiftly. Would he be alive had you waited?"

"No. I don't believe so."

Halima reached forward and placed her hand on Danla's knee. "There are risks in being a healer. Many times, healings need to be performed while the battle is still engaged. Often healing the injured while the fighting continues around you can make the difference between winning or losing."

"Can I develop the skill of using the red *myelur*?" Danla asked. "That way I could sense danger before it arrives."

Halima leaned away from Danla, a glint of sadness in her eyes. "Alas, that is not possible."

"Why not? After all, you can wield more than one aspect of the *myelur*," Danla said.

Her leader reacted in a way which Danla found odd—she reached up and ran her fingers through her hair. "What color is this?"

"Gray," Danla said.

Halima sighed. "'Twas not always so. When I was younger, I had hair as golden as the morning rays. Time has changed that. Now, what color are my eyes?"

"Light blue, nearly gray."

"And my skin?"

"White."

"Quite right," Halima said. "Now think of initiate Nya. How would you describe her?"

Danla imagined the other woman in her mind. "She is dark of hair, nearly black. Her eyes and skin are brown."

"Meaning?"

She wants me to figure this out. It's one of her ways of teaching. Danla decided to speak her thoughts out loud. "Each of us is different, yet the same. Some of us are born with certain traits—that makes us who we are." She made the connection. "You are saying the aspects of the *myelur* is something we are born with?"

"Yes. And it is more common than most people realize. From what I have learned, one aspect of the *myelur* resides in everyone, though the vast majority of the time it is so small that they will live their whole lives without realizing it. Being born with the ability to access and cultivate the *myelur*, as you can with the green, is quite rare."

"And accessing more than one aspect is rarer still, correct?"

"That's right," Halima said. "I can access the blue and the green, though I am stronger in the blue. The red, however, is beyond me. I can't will myself to use it any more than I can will myself to have brown eyes instead of light blue."

All of this still did not explain why Danla was the only initiate called to Halima's tent. She knew her leader well enough that there was another reason behind their meeting. She thought back to the battle. Halima had healed more than Danla, so that was not it. *What makes me different?* And then she remembered. *The yellow threads.*

"And what of the yellow *myelur*?" Danla asked, just above a whisper.

"What of it?" If Halima was bothered by the question, she did not let it show.

"How rare is it, that is to say, how uncommon is it to have access to both the yellow and green?"

Halima leaned in closer. She narrowed her eyes and said, "Yellow is the most uncommon of the *myelurs*. Extremely rare, as a point of fact. But for those who have the ability, it is tremendously powerful. While I can't use it, I am trained well enough to recognize when it is present—like a cloud passing in front of the sun."

"You sensed I could use it after I was stabbed," Danla surmised.

Her teacher's face marked a seriousness Danla had seen on few occasions. "Yes, I sensed it."

"You said it was dangerous, though you haven't ever explained why," Danla said. "Why wait until now?"

Halima inhaled deeply, held the breath, and then let it out slowly. "As I said, the yellow is very uncommon. But let me first explain the nature of the yellow. Whereas the green *myelur* uses energy from your body to heal others, the yellow acts in an opposite way, of sorts." She paused to let Danla absorb that bit of information.

"Meaning … if I were to use the yellow *myelur*, it would take someone else's energy, and in turn, I would be healed?" Danla said.

"Exactly."

Danla considered this for a moment. *How is that a bad thing?* If someone else had energy to spare and was willing, and she was wounded, certainly it could be useful. Also, when Danla saw the yellow threads, she sensed nothing malicious. Moreover, the yellow threads appeared inviting. "Mistress, forgive me, but I can't see what makes the yellow *myelur* dangerous, as you have said."

"And that is why you and I are speaking," Halima said. "You were not ready to be taught, yet the battle escalated the timetable. Of all the initiates who healed men after the battle, several were injured in minor ways, but only you were able to see the yellow *myelur*. The dagger was indeed poisoned—I could tell as I healed you. You would have been dead in a few more heartbeats. That is why the yellow *myelur* called to you so powerfully. It felt good, didn't it?"

"I won't lie," Danla said. "It was beautiful."

"Often the vilest things in the world are wrapped in pretty packages."

"But had you not been there, it could have saved me," Danla said.

Halima's tone took on a harder edge. "Do not be fooled. *Never* use the yellow *myelur*."

"I'm sorry. I still do not understand why."

Her mentor took her hand again, and this time squeezed it hard. "From what I have read and have been taught, once a person sets the yellow *myelur* in motion, it will not stop until the other person's energy is completely depleted. It kills them. There is something worse still."

How could anything be worse than being unable to stop yourself from killing someone? "Tell me, please," Danla pleaded.

"It is said that using the yellow *myelur* is highly addictive," Halima said. "It can become bad enough that users will intentionally hurt themselves and find others to drain just to feel the power."

"Could you sense the yellow *myelur* when you healed me?"

"Not as much as I could sense the signs, again, based on what I have been taught," her teacher said. "Even injured, your connection to the wounded soldier through the green *myelur* would have been strong. When I healed you, there was a connection, but not one I could see. That led me to fear that you were about to go down a path from which you could not return."

The statement hit Danla hard. "What is done with those who can wield the yellow *myelur*?"

"If they do not wield it, then nothing," Halima said. "That would be like putting someone in a dungeon because they *might* kill someone someday, though they had done nothing wrong to that point."

"And if they do use it?"

Halima looked directly into Danla's eyes. "They would be killed. As I said, the yellow *myelur* causes a person to seek it out. They would not be able to help themselves."

All of this was hard for Danla to consider, yet she could not deny seeing the yellow threads when the soldier had stabbed her in the leg. "How often are people put to death because of this?"

"That's the most interesting part of all of this," the mistress said. "You are the first person to be able to use it that any of our order has come across in several generations."

Chapter 40

The abbey's bells rang out, loudly and deep, as they did each morning, yet instead of stopping after the customary three peels, they continued to sound.

Nestov sat up from his cot and rubbed his eyes. The morning's first light shining through the room's frosted glass windows were strong enough to illuminate the initiates' sleeping quarters. Thirty other young men were also waking, each with expressions of confusion.

"What's this about?" Cron asked. His cot was across from Nestov. "Why are the bells still ringing?"

"Something's wrong," Nestov said as he swung his legs off the cot and placed his bare feet on the cold, stone floor.

Cron remained in a sitting position, keeping his legs covered. "Why do you think—"

The door to the sleeping quarters slammed open. Friar Janus stood in the frame, his form silhouetted against the morning light shining behind him. Shadows hid the leader of the Abbey's face, preventing Nestov from judging the friar's mood.

"Initiates," Friar Janus said. "Get dressed, quickly. Come to the eating hall as soon as you can." He left before anyone could question him.

Nestov leaned to the end of his cot where a small, wooden crate stored his cloth robe and leather sandals. He put on his footwear first, appreciating the warmth, however small, they provided. As he continued to dress, he could see Cron in his peripheral vision. The other initiate, one who had been particularly critical of Nestov's quick advancement in his training, moved slowly.

Normally Nestov would take care in making his cot, but this morning he simply pulled the woolen blanket flat. Not waiting for the rest of the initiates, he took quick strides to the open door.

The eating hall, the largest room in the abbey, was located down a long passage. Like the rest of the abbey, the walls and floor were made from limestone, something which Nestov found comforting compared to the wooden frame of his childhood home. Today, as the bells continued to ring, Nestov found the walls pressing in on him. Entering the open space of the eating hall helped dispel the feeling until he saw Friar Janus standing upon a dais at the end of the room. His arms were folded, and a deep grimace, deeper than normal, dug into his face.

A few other initiates, those younger than Nestov, were already there. All of them remained standing. Nestov walked up to the area right in front of the dais. Within a few moments, the hall filled up with the rest of the young men—nearly one hundred in all.

"Darkness is coming," Janus intoned as an introduction. "We no longer have the luxury of waiting until you are all fully trained. Word arrived late in the evening that the Light we provide is needed now."

Nestov felt an uneasiness wash over the hall. All of them knew that one day they would leave the abbey, but if they were like him, they still felt like they had many seasons before that day came. During his time, he had seen the older initiates get their assignments. Those who did well were sent off to prestigious destinations. Personally, Nestov hoped to be sent to one of the coastal regions because many of Grorage the Brave's adventures took place near the land of waters.

"Those of you in your primary seasons of training, go to the kitchens. Your first task will be to ready supplies for everyone's travels," Janus said. "Secondary initiates, you will report to the quartermaster. There, you will prepare the packs each of you will carry."

The friar peered over the group, with his eyes finally resting on Nestov. "Now go, your assignments will be given to you once preparations are completed."

Nestov turned to follow the other secondary initiates when he heard

Friar Janus say, "Nestov, not you."

Some of the other boys gave Nestov weary glances as they left him standing alone in the hall.

"Follow me," was all Janus said as an explanation.

Of all the initiates currently in the abbey, Nestov knew he had advanced the furthest in his training. It was the only reason he could guess for being singled out. Though the urge to ask questions spurred inside him, he thought it best not to speak until the friar presented more information.

With Nestov walking several steps behind the friar as a show of respect, he followed his teacher out of the hall and down a passage normally off-limits to initiates. It did not look different from any of the passages Nestov had seen before which made him curious what made this one different.

The passage made a sharp right, and when Nestov turned the corner, he understood. A staircase, made of stone like everything else in the Abbey, led up to the second floor—a place no initiate had been, at least to Nestov's knowledge, which was the cause of much speculation.

"As with other things you've been taught," Janus said, "you are not to speak of what you see or hear to anyone unless given permission."

"Of course, Friar."

Curiosity overrode anxiousness. *What does the friar mean when he said darkness was coming? And, what, possibly, can I do about it?* The steps led to a large wooden door covered in symbols carved into the surface. Nestov recognized a few of the images—he had seen them in several of the books he had read—though their meanings were unclear.

"Say nothing unless you are asked a question," the friar said. "Understand?"

Nestov nodded, choosing that moment to remain mute.

Using only his right hand, Janus pushed against the edge of the door. It opened smoothly and silently, something Nestov would not have guessed possible based on its size.

The room beyond lacked windows, at least none Nestov could see.

Tapers, most wide with long wicks, provided the only light.

A feathered bed, made from a stone base and covered in thick quilts, sat in the middle of the room. Propped against the headboard was the oldest man Nestov had ever seen. Despite his age, he had a full head of hair which continued down the side of his face and merged into a long, neatly combed beard.

"This is the one?" the bed-ridden man asked. His voice was strong, conflicting with his physical stature.

"Yes, Your Holiness," Friar Janus answered.

Your Holiness? I'm meeting with Abbot Aydomus? Of course, Nestov had heard of the leader of the church, yet no one—at least to his knowledge—had seen the abbot for longer than Nestov had been alive.

"Come closer, young one," the abbot said.

Nestov did as instructed. Anxiety switched positions with curiosity, as indicated by the shaking in his legs, as he approached.

"You are Nestov, correct?"

"Yes, Your Holiness."

The abbot smiled, showing off straight, white teeth. "Friar Janus speaks highly of you. I pray his faith is not misplaced. We will need your strength."

My strength? Nestov was small compared to others of an age with him, sometimes being mistaken for an initiate in his primary seasons by those who visited the abbey.

"I can see you have questions," the abbot said, leaning forward. "As well you should. I want you to understand something important before I explain what will be required of you. You, Nestov, are a blessing during such times as we now face. You see, you are the first initiate in three generations to progress enough to learn the fourth mantra."

Chapter 41

The view from the tower made Pendr's stomach flutter, a feeling he normally associated with fear. Never before had he seen such a view. *I wonder, is this what a hawk sees when searching for food?* Pendr had counted one hundred and fourteen stairs when he climbed to the top of this, one of the towers next to the castle entrance. From here, he could see the greenery of trees stretch outward toward the horizon, to an edge which seemed to curve a bit at its most extreme. Patches of blue, which later he realized were lakes and ponds, interrupted the sea of green. Granted, there was a town of no small size surrounding the castle, but beyond that, nature ruled.

If the other soldiers training with him knew that being this high off the ground affected him so, perhaps they would not be so leery around him. Three days and nights had come and gone since Captain Mux demonstrated the power of the purple *myelur*, a force Pendr had used in his last battle. Though Pendr had yet to recreate the experience, Mux never wavered in his belief that Pendr spoke truly.

"Sometimes, it takes extreme emotions to trigger the *myelur* at first," his captain had explained. "But as with any skill, the more it is practiced, the better you will become."

The concept made sense. It was not that many winters ago when Pendr began working with his father by the forge. On that day, Pendr watched his father heat, bend, and hammer metal into something new. When his father gave Pendr a chance to try, the task seemed nearly impossible. *Not unlike how I feel with trying to learn to use the* myelur.

Metal boots clanging against the stone stairs indicated that his time alone in the tower was ending. The room where Pendr stood was round. Four expansive openings faced in each direction.

On the far side of the room, twenty paces from where he stood, the floor opened to the curved staircase—a twisted flight of steps which hugged the wall of the tower.

A conical metal helmet was the first thing to arise from the opening of the floor, followed by the rest of Captain Mux. The older man did not breathe heavily after the ascension, a testament to his strong health.

"Now that you've had time," Mux said as a greeting, "what are your thoughts?"

Pendr had no quick answer to the question, and his leader said nothing else while he removed his helm. When Mux had told him to climb to the top of the tower and wait, he had not said why. Perhaps it was to allow Pendr to think without the distractions the training camp provided. *Should I tell him I feel fear?* After a moment of selecting the right words, Pendr answered, "From up here, I see more than I thought possible. It's frustrating."

"Frustrating, you say?" His captain strode toward him and stood next to one of the open windows. Gesturing to the view, he said, "What is frustrating about seeing so many trees?"

The question was not asked mockingly; it begged clarification.

"There is so much land out there," Pendr answered immediately. "The town around the castle is large, yes. Certainly larger than my home of Logs Pond. When compared to the land around us, it seems ridiculous for men to fight over something when there is plenty enough for all."

The edges around Mux's eyes tightened. "You think we are at war over trees?"

"Not trees, specifically. The land on which the trees grow. After all, kingdoms are divided up by imaginary lines. When someone wants more, as with the attack on Iredell, men die. It's pointless."

"Tell that to the people of Iredell," Mux said.

"I'm sorry, Captain," Pendr said. "I meant no disrespect."

Mux shifted his shoulders and faced south. "Of that I'm certain. It's not in your nature to be disrespectful, which means teaching you to use your power will be more difficult."

"I— I— don't understand."

Pointing to his chest, Mux said, "The ability to combine the red and blue *myelur* comes from here: your heart, the source of your emotions. Those quick to anger or to react without thinking are those who can learn to grasp the *myelur* quicker."

"Then, are you saying your efforts are better spent helping someone else?" Though Pendr did not want to admit it, the idea of avoiding the *myelur* appealed to him. *It's a power I didn't ask for, nor want.*

"Pendr, I'm not saying that at all," Mux said, his voice softened. "There's a reason there are so few who can wield the purple *myelur*. It's powerful, so much so that it can be destructive to the user."

"You mean to the target of the user, correct?"

Mux shook his head. "I meant what I said. When a person draws upon both the blue and the red, it builds up, as you described. At what point did you release it?"

It took a moment for Pendr to think back on the incident. "I released it, not fully knowing what I was doing, right before the enemy was about to find shelter in the trees."

"And what would have happened if you were in an open field without a place for him to hide?"

The question was odd, and not something Pendr had pondered. "I honestly do not know."

Mux tapped Pendr's chest. "What could have happened is that you would have let it continue to build inside you until your heart burst."

"Wh— what?"

"Those who are not trained do not know the strength of the power and its limits. Most of them die the first time they try to use it."

"I've never heard of such a thing," Pendr said.

"That's because most healers do not know what to look for after it has happened. They wield the green *myelur*, which while related, is as different as a leaf is to water or fire. The point is this: you have a special talent, one which can help prevent the killing of more people. By the Light, we found you before the worst happened."

Pendr found the statement to be odd in context. He had been forced into an army, left his home, seen friends he had known his entire life die before him, Danla, a girl for whom he cared more than he thought, was in danger, and now he discovered a power which could potentially kill him. Or, worse yet, he could be turned into a weapon. *In many ways, the worst has already happened to me.*

"Tell me, Pendr, what is it you want?" Mux asked after a long pause.

"To be with my family and the ones I care about. To not see more senseless deaths. To live a happy life, doing what I love."

"Unless you help us," Mux said, "that can never be."

"I don't see what I can do which can make a difference. From what I've heard in camp, the siege on Iredell worked."

"I've heard the same, and that's because it's true."

"Then why—"

Mux interrupted. "What I share with you now is to be kept between us, understand?"

"Of course, Captain."

"We have reclaimed Iredell. The enemy soldiers left the town at night and rushed one of our encampments. Many died on both sides, but reports say that their leader and a handful of his men made it back to Sothcar. But this war was never about Iredell."

"That's not what we were told when we were conscripted," Pendr pointed out.

"Because at the time, that was an honest belief. We don't know everything, but from what we have been able to gather, the Masters who ruled Sothcar are dead, including one who was at Iredell. A new leader has taken over, Avadi is his name, and with him, the rules have changed."

Pendr felt himself frown and then tried to force his face back to a more neutral expression. "I'm sorry, Captain. I'll admit I know little of the rules of war."

"Let me clarify," Mux said. "In the past, large armies gathered and fought each other over the right to rule parts of the land. Not this time. The soldiers from Sothcar are attacking at random—sometimes with small forces, sometimes with several dozen soldiers. The result has been the same. The lands where people are killed are not occupied by the enemy. They just move on and kill more."

"Why would they do that?"

"That, Pendr, is a good question. Unfortunately, the answer is simply this: we don't know."

Chapter 42

The wolves communicated to each other using a combination of whines and growls—that much Wyjec had observed, though he could divine no meaning. That began to change.

Over the last several days, Wyjec had methodically sewn together the rabbit pelts to create a cloak of sorts. He habitually whistled when he worked, and much to his surprise, Alpha had begun to imitate the notes perfectly. Granted, there was not a meaning associated with the sounds at first. Soon, he began to recognize that the wolves would make certain sounds when they were about to go hunting—specifically when Alpha instructed the other wolves to do so.

It took some practice, but Wyjec was able to approximate the whine/growl combination when *he* wanted the wolves to hunt. It was not much, but it worked.

Today, while Wyjec sat on the stone he had dubbed a throne, he watched the wolves run around the open field, as well as through the forest of the gorge which they had settled in the mountains. The sun had been up long enough that Alpha should have brought Wyjec a rabbit or squirrel, yet there was no sign of the large wolf. Wyjec had told Alpha to go hunting before the sun came up. It was unlike the wolf to take so long.

Trying to ignore the hunger pains, Wyjec considered his next move towards revenge. He did not know how long before the females would give birth, let alone how long it would take the wolves to mature enough to be able to fight. *It could be many seasons.* The concept was frustrating, yet Wyjec had no idea how to accelerate the process. Would Captain Avadi still be alive when Wyjec was finally ready? The last time Wyjec had seen his betrayer was in Iredell—a town surrounded by the enemy.

If he lives, I'll find him. Then, he will know the price for treachery.

Wyjec stood, deciding that getting at least a drink of water would help chase away his hunger. A stream flowed not far from his throne. The water was cool and refreshing, and Wyjec took his time to savor as the liquid washed down his throat. Dipping his cupped hands for another drink, he heard movement behind him. Unlike the times when wolves approached him, this was different. Whatever was moving did so quickly.

Gathering the blue *myelur* as protection, Wyjec then stood to face what approached. When the animal came into sight, Wyjec took a step back, nearly falling into the stream. It was Alpha, bloodied with three deep grooves cut into his fur. *He's been hurt!*

Wyjec rushed to Alpha's side. The wolf whined/growled urgently. Whatever the wolf was trying to communicate, Wyjec could not understand. Alpha stepped backward, continuing his urgent attempt to communicate. Wyjec took a step towards the wolf, only for Alpha to back away even further. The animal was not acting afraid, but rather in a way that he wanted something. *He wants me to follow him.* With a flick of his hand, Wyjec indicated for Alpha to go. Seemingly satisfied that his master would follow, Alpha turned and headed down the path.

Instead of going toward the cave where they had made their home, Alpha led Wyjec further north along the mountain side. Traveling was more difficult here, with no real path to follow. The blue *myelur* still surrounded Wyjec, a wise precaution he thought because of the recent attack on Alpha. The unfortunate side effect was that the protection was weakening his already low energy.

While they traveled, Wyjec scanned for any living thing from which he could draw strength. Insects flitted by, their red *myelur* twinkling like stars in a night sky. *It wouldn't be enough.* Abruptly, Alpha came to a stop. His hair bristled, and his whole body taut. Ahead was the mouth of a cave—larger than any they had found thus far.

Alpha growled menacingly toward the gaping maw on the side of the mountain. *Whatever hurt him must be in there.* For a moment, anxiety skimmed over Wyjec, but he dismissed it. *I'm protected with the blue* myelur.

Nothing can hurt me. Those thoughts fled, however, when a giant, black bear charged from the cave.

Stunned by the sight, Wyjec stood transfixed as the beast barreled into him. Although the *myelur* protected him from feeling pain, it did not stop him from being knocked over and against a rock outcropping.

The bear roared, flashing his teeth. A huge paw raised and with claws extended, the bear swiped at Wyjec. The result should have been Wyjec's disembowelment. Instead, the claws raked across his middle without leaving a mark—at least on Wyjec. The action of the bear hitting an impenetrable force caused two of the bear's claws to bend backward at an unnatural angle.

If it was possible for a bear to show surprise on its face, that is what Wyjec perceived. More than that, he searched out for the bear's red *myelur* to control it. It was easy enough to spot, though another idea came to him: the yellow *myelur*. He reached out a hand, touched the bear, and the yellow threads appeared. He pulled on the threads vehemently.

Right away, Wyjec felt better. His strength began to return. Harder and faster, he continued to drain the energy from the huge beast. The use of the yellow *myelur* seemed to paralyze the bear. Shortly, Wyjec felt as alive as he could remember—and still, there was more he could draw from the dying bear who had collapsed at his feet, twitching.

Alpha chose that moment to join in by jumping on the back of the bear and sinking his teeth into the larger animal's neck. Though the yellow *myelur* refilled Wyjec's energy, the scent of blood and raw meat appealed to Wyjec's base need to eat. Alpha clawed away at the bear's hide, revealing red meat beneath.

Instinctively, Wyjec climbed next to Alpha. Together, they feasted on the bear, its heart still beating. Wyjec continued to draw upon the yellow *myelur* to offset the effects of eating raw meat. He realized he could end the bear's life quickly enough now, but decided against it. *Let the bear understand what happens to those who hurt my family.*

Chapter 43

Sleeping under a wagon would be a welcome change to huddling against a tree during normal circumstances. It was not the rain which fell during the night which made Rheq curse his luck, but rather that the wagon he picked was slightly downhill from the pen containing the horses and goats. The storm was strong enough that water flowed from high ground to low, and it brought with it whatever was in its path—including animal dung.

At first, Rheq thought those who had slept in the wagon above him had emptied their chamber pots, thereby creating the foul odor which surrounded him. That would have been a harsh jest from the Gymads, and based on what he knew about them, something within their character.

Instead, when his hosts discovered him sleeping in filth, they found the situation even more amusing. Rheq had emerged from under the wagon in time to almost be run over by the tall, thin man who he had met last night. Once those around the area were done laughing at Rheq's soiled clothing, the man who allowed him to stay asked, "Why pick that wagon?"

"It was the largest," Rheq answered. "I thought it would offer more protection from the storm."

The man laughed again and turned to walk away.

The sun was high enough from the horizon to offer light to the Gymad's camp, though low enough that any direct rays were blocked by the tall maples which surrounded them. Already, the camp was a buzz of activity. Their horses were hitched to wagons which meant that they would soon be on the move.

"Wait!" Rheq called out. "Why are you leaving?"

The man stopped, turned, and responded, "Why would we stay?"

Rheq considered the question. There was nothing here but an opening large enough for the fourteen wagons to create a camp. Rheq was not aware of any villages nearby, though he had to admit his exact location was unknown.

"What about a morning meal?" Rheq asked hopefully.

A puzzled expression covered the man's face. "We don't eat until we can see the sun. It's bad fortune to do otherwise. How can you not know this?"

"My people do not … follow such customs," Rheq said carefully. Though he knew something of the Gymads, it was clear there was much yet to learn.

"And your people are from where, exactly?" the man asked.

Rheq noticed a few of the other men in the camp slow down or stop to hear the answer. Outwardly lying about his home, could make things worse. After all, from what Rheq recalled, his village had always been on friendly terms with the Gymads. Thinking over the events of the previous night, Rheq realized he had not introduced himself, and neither did he know the man's name.

"My name is Rheq. I'm from Umstead, though I was recently conscripted into King Viskum's army. And what shall I call you?"

Each of those watching him reacted in different ways, though a common trait was one of which Rheq would describe as pity.

"My name is Brishen. When was the last time you were there?" he asked. His tone was softer than before.

"A few days," Rheq said. "I—" Grief hit him hard at that moment. He had been so focused on getting revenge that he had buried the realization of what had truly happened to those he loved. "I— that is, they—"

The tall man approached Rheq. Despite the state of Rheq's attire and the smell that accompanied it, Brishen embraced him. "We saw what happened. Most of us only heard it. The screams, the pleading for mercy—all of it. Our scouts warned us to stay clear. We did, and fortune smiled on us as those who killed your family and friends did not know we were close. If nothing else, the experience strengthened our resolve not to become part of this or any other war."

Rheq pushed himself away. "How can you not respond? You said you heard them! No one there earned that type of death. It was beyond reason!"

"Is any war within reason?"

In response, Rheq turned to walk away, but Brishen reached out and grabbed him by the shoulder. "Where will you go, eh? What will you do now?"

Rheq tried to shove off the man's grip, but it held him too tightly. "I will see my people are avenged. I will find those willing to help me."

"We will help you."

Slowly, Rheq faced Brishen. "You? But you said you don't—"

"Do not misunderstand," the Gymad said. "We will not attack those who killed the villagers."

"Then what kind of help can you be?"

Unblinking, Brishen looked directly into Rheq's eyes. "We can help you become a better you. Join us. There is much you can learn."

The idea seemed ridiculous upon first consideration, but then it occurred to Rheq that Gymads were known for their defensive combat skills, as well as their knowledge of poisons. These were skills Rheq could use. More than that, he realized that he honestly had no idea where to go aside from heading north. Chances were he would run into enemy soldiers before finding those loyal to King Viskum. Yet, the Gymads never did anything without them gaining something in return.

"What is it you want from me in exchange for your help?" Rheq asked.

Brishen smiled. "Good. You see that everything comes with a price. My price is simple. You have a skill which we lack. Teach us what you know, and we will teach you what we know."

What I know? What could I possibly know that they don't? Rheq sensed no deception from the man, but he was a Gymad—traders known for their skills in bargaining. "And what is it you think I know?"

"You can move silently. I have men watching the camp to prevent exactly what you did last night—you approached us without prior warning."

"*Your* men?" Rheq clarified.

"Yes, my men," Brishen said. "Who else would be the leader?"

For that, Rheq had no answer. He doubted Brishen was elected. It did not seem a manner in which the Gymads would select a leader. *Maybe he was born to it, or maybe he fought his way to dominance.* Regardless, Rheq changed his focus to the other question: why the leader of this group thought that Rheq could move silently. *That's because I can. I'm a hunter and a tracker.*

"To be clear," Rheq said, "If I teach you how I can move silently, you will teach me what you know?"

"It will be more than that," Brishen said. "You will be required to do those things necessary to maintain camp."

"But I will have food to eat and a place to sleep?"

This was the bargaining stage, something which Rheq knew he was overmatched. Still, he had to try.

"Food, shelter, and teaching in exchange for your promise to work and show us how to move silently," Brishen said.

Rheq did not consider long before answering, "Deal."

Chapter 44

"Chaos is a powerful weapon," Mistress Halima said to the initiates sitting on the ground before her. "It is one which the enemy employs. That is why we are losing this war."

It was her final statement which caused the greatest reaction among the women who sat by Danla. She, herself, felt shocked at the revelation.

After the morning meal, instead of working on training exercises to help the initiates further their skills with the green *myelur*, the diminutive leader told her fourteen trainees to follow her to an open field, just north of the main campsite. Once there, she had instructed them all to sit. It was then that she told them of their situation.

"We're *losing*?" Initiate Nya asked. She tugged at the fringes of her long, brown hair. "How is that possible? To my knowledge, our soldiers haven't lost any battles. Did we not reclaim Iredell?"

Halima folded her hands over her lap. Her response was not to speak at all—a sign Danla had learned to mean the leader wanted the initiates to consider the situation and come up with possible conclusions.

"To understand why we're losing," Yarma, another of the young women in training. said, "we have to know what we're fighting for."

Nya folded her arms across her chest. "Isn't that obvious? We're fighting to keep our land safe."

No, that's not it. Danla realized there was something fundamentally wrong with the statement—though she could not decipher what was off. Iredell was safe, yes, after its recapture. The cost, as she understood it, to retake the city was not without the loss of life. That is when she made the connection.

"But we're not fighting to keep the land safe," Danla said. "We're fighting to keep the *people* from harm."

"It's the same thing," Nya countered.

"No, it isn't," Danla said. "The land was here long before we were. Who knows, it may be here long after we're gone. But the enemy isn't attacking the trees or dirt—they are attacking the people."

"To what end?" Yarma interjected. "Why spend the resources to arm, feed, and support an army just to kill people. Isn't the point of war to take something that someone else has?"

Danla considered the statement. Why would the enemy continue to attack villages and homesteads, and then abandon them before reinforcements could arrive? If what Yarma said was true, what would the enemy gain? Often the reports stated nothing was taken from the places attacked. *At least nothing physical.*

"Mistress Halima," Danla said. "You stated the enemy is using chaos. Perhaps what they want right now is not land nor possessions. They want to take away something more precious: our freedom."

The corner of her leader's mouth twitched. "Why would they want to do that?"

"I can't speak for everyone else," Danla said, "but I haven't felt safe since I heard we were at war. I'm constantly anxious, and I almost expect to be attacked at any moment. It makes me realize how much I took for granted when I was growing up."

"I feel the same," Yarma said. Most of the other initiates nodded or vocalized their agreement.

Danla continued, "Perhaps the enemy wants us to feel this way—that we aren't safe, and there isn't anything we can do about it."

"But we *are* doing something about it," Nya said. "We chase them off with greater numbers after each attack."

"The damage is already done by then," Danla said. "People have already died. Word spreads. Fear grows."

Nya tugged harder at her hair. "That doesn't explain why they are doing it. What do they have to gain by creating fear?"

Then, at that moment, Danla understood. "I know." *But how to vocalize it?* "Mistress Halima, may I try to explain?"

"Please do." The leader motioned for Danla to stand next to her.

Unfolding her legs from beneath her, Danla stood and then weaved her way to the front of the clearing. Though she was one of the youngest of the women in training, she was not intimidated by standing before them.

"In the village where I grew up, Logs Pond it was called, we rarely had anyone new move to that part of the kingdom. Late one spring, oh, four winters ago or so, several families petitioned to build houses on the edge of town. It caused quite a stir. The idea of having new people live close by was exciting—at least it was to me."

"I don't see how this connects," Yarma said.

Danla did not take offense to the statement. Yarma was as level-headed as any in the group. "It will make sense soon," Danla said, "I needed to set up the situation.

"It took me several moon cycles of asking and listening carefully, but I finally found out what had happened. Those who moved to our village were part of a small homestead to the west, towards the mountains. It had been an especially wet winter, and with the spring thaw came severe flooding. It wiped out most of their farms."

"That happened once to my family," a young woman named Clo said. "We didn't move. That was our home. We just rebuilt."

"Aye," Danla said. "That was my reaction as well—at least initially. I learned that this was not the first time it had happened recently. Point of fact, the land where their farms had been settled were in constant danger of flooding. It became too much, so they left to find a safer place to live."

"I still don't understand," Yarma said. "Are you saying that the enemy wants us to abandon our homes because we don't feel safe?"

"No, not our homes," Danla said. "Think about it. Who is supposed to keep us safe?"

"King Viskum," Nya said. "He directs our soldiers."

"Exactly!" Danla said. "And if people don't believe he can keep them safe?"

Nya stopped tugging at her hair. Her expression displayed the grim reality of what Danla had realized. "Then they will follow someone else."

Chapter 45

The carriage bounced and jostled Nestov, though he hardly noticed. The ride had been smoother at times than others. Friar Janus warned Nestov of the uneven road, but the information helped little to make the ride more comfortable.

"The road from here to the castle in Nothcar was once maintained and well paved with stones," Friar Janus had told Nestov before he left. "But after the war between our lands, travel and trade reduced significantly."

Of all the things Friar Janus had told him before he left, the condition of the roads was the least of Nestov's worries. *I'm not ready for this.*

"Are you going to keep your breakfast from returning whence it came?" asked the only other person in the carriage.

Brother Mey was dressed in a simple brown robe, cinched at the waist. It was almost an exact copy of what Nestov wore, though the other man riding with him was much larger. While the robe covered the man's physique, Nestov knew that Brother Mey was strong and quick enough to act as his protector.

"I'm fine, Brother Mey," Nestov answered. "Thank you for asking."

The monk laughed. "You certainly don't look fine. Your face is as white as the purest cloud."

Both Friar Janus and Abbot Aydomus said that Brother Mey could be trusted, though there were certain things which Nestov should keep to himself—specifically the four mantras he had learned while at the abbey. *There are things I can talk to him about. It could help.*

"I'll admit that I'm ... anxious," Nestov said. "Aren't you?"

"What's there to be anxious about?" Brother Mey said. "Is it that we are heading to a land which is at war—not with us, thank the Light—but with Sothcar? Or perhaps it is because you are the first emissary from Virqyna since our war ended with them. Could it be that you are being tasked with not only gaining an audience with King Viskum, but also you need to persuade him of the threat which we all face? Which is it?"

"All of them, I suppose," Nestov said. *And one you did not mention.*

When Abbot Aydomus told Nestov his task, he considered the old man to be joking, or mad—or both. *I am far too young to be an emissary. Did they send me because I was expendable?* Nestov had read enough history to know that misdirection and ulterior motives were commonplace in politics. Was the goal to have him be captured, or killed, to give a reason for Virqyna to attack a land already at war, and therefore vulnerable?

"Hear me, Nestov," Brother Mey said, snapping Nestov out of his ponderings. "My job is to keep you safe. I made a vow to get you to the castle alive, and that I will do. Though I don't know exactly what caused Abbot Aydomus to act now, it has to be serious."

"What have they told you?" Nestov asked. He did not want to reveal anything he should not, but if the monk already knew, then it would not be breaking his vow of secrecy.

Brother Mey parted the thick cloth which covered one of the carriage's windows. In doing so, beams of white light entered in. "They told me precious little, at least in the way of details. Abbot Aydomus said something terrible had happened. A darkness is approaching— something of which we have not seen in many generations. The church knew this could happen one day, which is why you, and those like you, have been trained."

"But I'm not much more than a boy. What can I do?" Nestov asked, realizing after he said it how weak it made him look.

The monk turned his attention back to Nestov. "I know even less about your training," he said. "Mine has been focused on combat and defense. If I were meant to know, then I would have been told. What I *do* know is that when the darkness came before, it reshaped the land.

Whole populations were wiped out. Humanity's achievements were destroyed—erased as if they had never been. Nature reclaimed the land. Only in the past several generations have we begun to rebuild."

Nestov had read of all of this during his studies, though most of the accounts were based on speculation and tales passed down from parents to children. To hear the monk speak with such solemnity of the events— some of which many people believed to be metaphors or parables instead of actual occurrences—made Nestov even more on edge.

"Know this, Nestov," Brother Mey said. "You were selected for a reason. The abbot is old and powerful. He knows of things we can only guess. You should trust in him."

"In him I trust," Nestov said.

"But you aren't sure you trust yourself?"

Nestov realized that was the heart of his concerns. Lowering his head, he responded, "Yes, I have my doubts."

"That's a contradiction, then, don't you see?" Mey said. "If you trust the abbot, and he says you are the one who can do this, then you *can* do it. To believe you cannot means you truly do not trust the abbot. Which is it you believe?"

The question brought to Nestov's mind the last time he saw Abbot Aydomus. He could picture the old man propped up in his bed. With a seemingly large amount of effort, the abbot had lifted a hand and pointed at Nestov. In doing so, he had said, "Darkness is created by many barriers—some stronger than others. The Light in the world is beginning to grow once again. There are those who are growing stronger with its power. But something has happened, a dramatic shift in the *myelur*. A barrier is forming, and with it, a deep darkness. You must find this barrier and eliminate it before what grows in the shadows can once again lead us to destruction."

"But Abbot Aydomus," Nestov had said, "I have not been taught how to do what you ask. I have no idea how to recognize this barrier of which you speak, let alone how to rid it from the world. These are not skills I have learned in my lessons."

It was then that Friar Janus had spoken. The friar had said, "Nestov, the lessons you have learned are more valuable than you understand at the moment. It is true that I have not taught you the specifics of that which our abbot speaks. Instead, I have taught you something more."

"I don't understand," Nestov had answered.

"Not yet," Friar Janus said. "But you will." It was then his teacher said something which resonated with Nestov to this day. "You will understand in time because I have taught you *how* to learn."

Chapter 46

Pendr's heart was close to exploding. Though he knew if he waited a moment longer, his actions would be more effective, he also understood dying would be the least impactful action of all.

With the palm of his right hand facing the enemy soldiers charging him and his men, Pendr released the knot of purple *myelur* building inside his chest. The invisible force flowed down his arm and out through his hand. Instead of it connecting solidly with the man Pendr had targeted, the power pushed three enemy soldiers backward and into the men behind them. The blow had been strong enough that one of the men pushed backward was impaled on a spear by the soldier behind him.

"Keep charging!" their leader screamed.

A quick count told Pendr that the enemy forces were a few more than the fourteen men in his squad. This was the third time Pendr's squad had been attacked in as many days, something which he found to be more than a coincidence.

Sunshine shone brightly in the clear sky behind the enemy. It was a smart tactic, Pendr realized, as it gave them a clear view of Pendr and his men, while somewhat blinding their foes.

"Archers!" Pendr commanded.

The four men he had placed on the flanks of the squad fired into the heart of the incoming enemy. Three more fell—the arrow from the fourth archer went high and wide. While the archers reached for more arrows to fire again, Pendr rushed forward, pulling his sword from the scabbard slung on his back. In his left hand was a stout, metal shield—one he had forged himself during the previous moon cycle in-between training sessions.

Nine sword-brandishing soldiers with Pendr drew their weapons and followed him into battle. Each of them had trained with Pendr during the winter months, and each of them could wield the blue *myelur* to various degrees. From what he could see, the enemy had not brought any ranged fighters, meaning he would not have to worry about bows, slings, or crossbows. That gave him an advantage because he could wait until the last possible moment to embrace the blue *myelur* and the protection it provided.

He had told his men to wait before drawing upon the protective skill, though he was sensitive enough to the power that he could tell that three of them had already begun shielding themselves. *No! It's too early!* None of the rest of them were strong enough to hold onto the blue *myelur* for any significant length of time before it drained them completely of any form of strength.

The enemy kept coming, even though four of them were already wounded or killed. That made the numbers more even, and then odds tipped more to Pendr's favor as his archers mowed down three more just before the melee combat commenced.

Pendr rushed at a man to his left, leaving his right flank exposed. At that moment, he drew upon the blue *myelur* and encased his body in a protective shell. The feint worked as two soldiers turned to attack what they perceived as Pendr's opened side. Both of the men to his right thrust their spears into him. Instead of piercing through his polished breastplate, they both connected with the blue *myelur* shield and the points of their weapons skidded off to the side.

Pendr expected such a result and used it to complete his initial attack. He shifted his target from the man to his left, and instead went to a knee while swinging his sword in a backward arc to his right. The thick iron broadsword found little resistance as it cut through both sets of legs of those who had tried to spear him.

Their screams distracted Pendr's original target enough that when Pendr completed the spin and continued the deadly sweep with a slight upward motion, the man was stunned into inaction as the sword cut into his side and stopped when it hit his spine.

Standing, Pendr pulled the sword out of the dead man and looked for the next threat. Most of the enemy was already dispatched, with the rest of them falling to either arrows or the weapons of Pendr's men who used the blue *myelur* as protection.

This doesn't make sense. The previous two attacks ended in similar results. Certainly, word would have gotten back to the enemy that attacking Pendr's squad was futile. Granted, after each battle his men would be drained to the point of exhaustion, but they had had time to recover.

The soldiers who Pendr had amputated were still screeching in pain. The wounded would bleed out soon enough, but their cries of pain touched part of Pendr he could not shield. He convinced himself it was mercy as he lopped off their heads.

After the battle had ended, quick inspection lifted Pendr's spirits as once again none of his men sported any wounds. One of his soldiers, Dosfogal, came to his side.

"Three days in a row," he said. "You think they would learn."

"Aye," Pendr said. "Are you hurt?"

"No, Sir Pendr," the blond man said. "Though I'm spent. We need to find a place to hole up for a few days."

It was still odd for Pendr to hear the title before his name. Captain Mux had made him a knight before assigning him his squad. Pendr was not sure he was ready for such responsibility, yet his leader felt differently. During the winter season, Pendr trained with the squad. Early on, it became clear that the squad looked to Pendr as their de facto leader. Captain Mux noticed and made it official with the promotion.

As for their current situation, Dosfogal making the suggestion to rest was noteworthy. Of all of Pendr's men, he complained the least.

"Agreed," Pendr said. "I need to send word to Captain Mux to get further instructions. We'll double back to—"

Battle cries cut off his response. From over a hill to the east charged twenty or so armored men riding on equally armored horses. In a moment of clarity, Pendr understood the enemy's plan. The previous attacks were designed to weaken them—and it worked. Even at full strength, Pendr's squad was no match for a cavalry in an open field.

The nearest trees were too far away for a retreat. They would be cut down by the horse-backed soldiers before they could get there.

Pendr considered his options, which were few. Right or wrong, he had to decide to do something—*now*—or they would all die.

"Form up behind me! Drop your blue *myelur*. Reserve your strength!" Pendr called out. He raced to a spot in the open field which placed the recently slain soldiers between the charging enemy and his men. The cavalry would have to skirt around the dead bodies or ride over them. Either way, it would buy Pendr some time.

Rapidly, his men formed up behind him, the archers instinctively nocking arrows, but waiting for instructions. Arrows would do little to stop the men and beasts covered nearly head-to-toe in plate mail. There was only one obvious weakness Pendr could exploit.

"Aim for the horses' legs!" he called out.

The archers reacted immediately. Once again, three of the four archers found success, with the fourth arrow deflecting harmlessly off a horse's armor. The injured animals tumbled, spilling their riders to the ground. The trailing cavalry did not have time to react before they crashed into their fallen comrades—at least the ones who had chosen the direct route toward Pendr and his men.

Five of the riders had skirted around to Pendr's left. It delayed them, but they also avoided the fate of those now trying to pick themselves up from the tangle of men and beasts.

Along with his men, Pendr had stopped using any form of the *myelur* while they waited for the onslaught. He could not wait any longer.

Pendr dropped his sword and shield to the ground. That action had no effect on the men who still charged forward, and Pendr knew it would not. Lifting his arms, with his palms forward, Pendr drew upon the blue *myelur*, but not to create a personal barrier. Creating a protective ward, as Mistress Halima had done around the tent when he first met her, was something that took a lot of concentration and was not something which Pendr had done during battle, only in practice. If his men were to survive, he saw this as his only option.

Pulling almost as much of the blue *myelur* as he had available, Pendr projected the ward just a few footsteps from where he and his men had gathered. The archers continued to focus on shooting at the horses' legs but were less successful than before.

"Pendr?" one of his men called out, fear evident in his voice.

"Hold fast!" Dosfogal responded for his leader.

The ward solidified just as the first horse-back fighter encountered it. The result was akin to the man and beast running into a solid stone wall. The cry of pain from the horse mixed with the angelic resonance coming from the blue *myelur* ward.

It was then that Pendr realized he had drawn too much of the power to create the ward. His vision dimmed as he watched the other four charging soldiers crash into the large, protective barrier. Though Pendr fought it, he could not keep his grip on consciousness. His last thought before being embraced by the darkness was how Danla would react when she heard the news of his death.

Chapter 47

Alpha stood next to his first-born son, beaming with pride. At least, that is how Wyjec interpreted it, and why not? Silk was the first of the females to give birth, followed not long after by the other pregnant wolves. Alpha's mate produced seven pups in her litter. The rest of the births were between four and six. Still, within a moon cycle at the beginning of spring, their numbers had grown tremendously.

Today was one of the warmest of the early spring days to date. Wyjec sat on his stone throne, using only one layer of sewn together rabbit pelts as a cloak. His legs and feet were kept warm from the bear skin breeches and moccasins he had made from the black bear which had attacked Alpha several moon cycles ago. The bear's hide had been difficult to sew, but the durability and warmth it delivered proved worth the effort. As with the rabbit pelts, the hide from the bear remained intact over time, a result of Wyjec using the yellow *myelur* on the beast.

The pup next to Alpha captured Wyjec's attention at this moment— in a surprising and delightful way. During the cold winter, Wyjec had contemplated many times how he would proceed with the pups when they were born. He had the loyalty of the older wolves aided by the power of the red *myelur*. Though still unsure why tying together the loose ends of the amber glow around their hearts would make them steadfast in their dedication, he feared that if he did the same to the pups too early in their development, it could hurt them. It turned out to be a non-issue.

The wolves were born with their amber glow, something indicating intention, already surrounding their heart. By using the red *myelur*, Wyjec verified that each of the pups was already bound to him, seemingly through their parents.

There was something more. And that is what Wyjec focused on now. Alpha's first born son had a strong heart—the strongest Wyjec had seen in a wolf, even when factoring his age. He was not sure what to make of that, aside from it giving him hope that the wolf would grow up to be strong enough to attack when the time came.

Another challenge arose from what to name all the pups. For the older wolves, he had picked names based on their characteristics, but the young ones had yet to distinguish themselves, aside from some variations in the color of their fur—a trait which could change over time and therefore would not be reliable.

While still inspecting the pup's heart through the use of the red *myelur*, an idea came to Wyjec. Carefully, he reached through the *myelur* and added a few extra strands of the amber glow which surrounded the wolf's heart into a singular line on the surface. The process caused no pain, at least based on the small wolf's reaction. When Wyjec finished, he examined his work.

The result was akin to a scar where the skin would be slightly different than what surrounded it. Instead of the scar embedded physically, it resided on the surface of the amber glow. Through the red *myelur*, Wyjec could spot it easily. *He's the first of the new generation. I'll call him "One."*

For the rest of the morning, Wyjec created similar marks on each of the new pups. To keep it simple, he assigned them numbers. During the process, he figured out a system he could use. Four lines were distinguishable, but more than that would be a challenge without taking the time to count. Instead, he decided to add a perpendicular line representing the number five. Using this logic, for the fifth pup he first created a circular shaped design, then put a line under it. Adding the two marks together on this one would add up to five. For six, there would be one line running perpendicular to the other.

Upon completing the process, and verifying that he could quickly determine which wolf was which, Wyjec turned to the next task at hand: to find something to kill.

Wyjec whined/growled to Alpha, letting him know the hunt would soon commence. Alpha responded by escorting his pups back to Silk, their mother, and then gathering up the rest of the adult males.

After killing the bear last autumn, Wyjec had feasted not only on the animal's meat but also its yellow *myelur*. The larger beast had an immense amount of the reenergizing power; it was enough to satiate Wyjec for several moon cycles. The yellow *myelur* acted differently than the red. It aided his physical well-being—allowing him to eat raw meat without getting sick. What it had not done, much to Wyjec's disappointment, was to act as a direct energy source for the blue and red *myelur*. It was as if they were barrels full of different types of liquid.

For the last several days, Wyjec realized that the energy used to maintain him physically was waning, as indicated by the nausea which accompanied eating. This meant he needed to find something to drain using the yellow *myelur*.

Alpha led the hunting party directly to the cave where Wyjec had killed the bear. It was empty. Checking the cave was a good idea, one which Wyjec could understand. If it had once housed a bear, it could house another.

The hunting party continued roughly north, skirting along the mountain side. The other wolves found three rabbits, which were brought to Wyjec alive. He drained the smaller animals using the yellow *myelur* quickly, but it was not enough. Once he had absorbed the bear's energy, he craved more than what a rabbit could provide.

For most of the day, they continued northward. Wyjec knew the further he traveled, the longer it would take to get back to the female wolves and the pups. He did not like to leave them alone, but neither could he help them if he was too sick to move.

Finally, just as the sky began to change to an orange hue, Alpha tracked down a bear. It was next to a stream, swiping fish out of the water with a paw. It was not as big as the bear Wyjec had killed before, but it would do.

The wolves moved in, preparing to attack. The bear was far from defenseless, and Wyjec feared one of his family might get hurt.

He paused at that. *These wolves are my family—more so than I've ever had.* He could reach through the red *myelur* and stop the bear's heart, but that would mean the yellow threads would not last long. Also, the wolves needed the practice of attacking something larger than themselves.

Wyjec whistled a tone. The sound instructed the wolves to stop whatever actions in which they were engaged—a command he had discovered recently. *How can I protect them?* He thought of the blue *myelur*, but his attempts to project the shield on anyone but himself had failed. From the distance he was to the bear, only the red *myelur* would have any power.

And then he understood what he could do. Enforcing his will through the red *myelur*, he pushed the bear's amber glow to focus on a boulder next to the stream. The same tactic had worked when he first discovered this ability—back at the Master's palace when a vermin had gnawed on his foot.

The bear gave up on fishing and instead turned toward the large rock. It butted its head against it, causing it to be dazed. After it had done the same action twice, Wyjec whistled for the wolves to attack.

Wyjec raced after the wolves. Once they were upon the bear, and tearing into its flesh, Wyjec could see the yellow *myelur* calling out to him. Exuberantly, he placed a hand on the dying bear and pulled on the yellow threads. The energy which flowed into his body immediately made him feel better, but it was more than that. *It makes me feel powerful.*

Chapter 48

The Gymads had asked Rheq to teach them how to move silently—to sneak through wooded areas without being noticed. He had tried over the last several moon cycles to do just that, yet none of those he taught could duplicate his actions. Yes, several of them improved much, but not to the level with which the Gymads were satisfied.

This morning, a day filled with the promise of spring and warmer weather, Rheq had just awoken. The wagon in which he slept was parked on the outer edge of the camp, next to the forest line. Before he could start his daily routine, Rheq was confronted by the leader of the Gymads as well as the seven men Rheq had been tasked with training.

"You're holding back," Brishen said by way of greeting. "We've done our part. We've fed you, given you shelter, and taught you ways to make different types of poisons. Yet none of our men can do what you can do." The Gymad's leader folded his wiry arms across his chest and glared down at Rheq.

"I'm not holding back," Rheq said. He stared defiantly at Brishen in return. "It's not enough to move without making noise. Your men aren't recognizing when someone, or something, is close by to avoid it. Often, they step right into the line of sight when it is obvious they shouldn't."

Brishen shifted his glare to the seven men who stood beside him. "Is what he says true?"

One of the Gymads, Prakzen by name, answered. "I've tried my best." He motioned to the men around him. "We all have. You selected us because of our agility, as well as our strong eyesight. I can't explain why Rheq can see things which remain hidden from us."

"How do you answer to that?" Brishen directed his question at Rheq.

Letting out an exasperated sigh, Rheq responded, "I don't know! If you were to tell any of your people to avoid stepping in puddles, and they continued to do so, what would you do?"

"That's not a fair example," Prakzen said. "We all know what a puddle looks like and how to spot one. But if it is completely dark, how could we possibly see where the puddles are?"

"But it's not completely dark—ever," Rheq said. "There is always some light which shines through. You need to look for that light."

Prakzen's thick, dark eyebrows lowered as he scowled. "The puddles reflect the light of the sun, moon, and stars—they do not give off light."

"Agreed," Rheq said. "Yet living creatures *do*."

To that, all of the Gymads tensed up, including Brishen. Rheq had lived with these people through the winter and had never seen them react in such a way.

"What did you say?" Brishen asked, his tone guarded.

Rheq instinctively took a step backward. "I said living creatures give off a form of light. Even in the darkest of nights, part of that light always remains visible—though you need to focus to see it." He gestured at the men he had been training. "They aren't focusing enough."

"You never said anything about a light," Prakzen said. "You only said to look closely in the shadows for those in hiding."

The ridiculous statement added to Rheq's frustration. "How would you see them in the shadows if it were not for the light? Why should I need to explain something so basic? What's next? Someone telling you that fire gives off heat?"

"This light," Brishen said. "What does it look like?"

"What does light look like?" Rheq said. "Are you trying to trick me?"

Prakzen took a step forward. "Answer the question."

"Please tell me you have seen fireflies," Rheq said.

The men nodded.

"It's much the same. Except instead of the green shimmer of light, living creatures' light is red."

Brishen's reaction to the clarification startled Rheq—the leader of the Gymads pulled a knife from his belt and pointed it threateningly.

"Why did you not tell us sooner?" Brishen asked.

Each of the other seven men also armed themselves.

Lifting his hands in the air, Rheq slowly backed up. "Tell you what? I hid nothing from you."

"Those who can touch the *myelur*, in any form, are tainted," Brishen said.

The *myelur*? Rheq had heard of people using a strange power in unnatural ways—even though discussing it at any length was considered taboo in Umstead. "But— but— I can't."

"You *can*!" Brishen shouted. "You just admitted it. Only those who can touch the *myelur* are able to see the red glimmers."

That made no sense to Rheq. If it were true, his parents would have told him. *Or would they?* If they had had the same ability, they most likely kept it a secret. Had it been known, they would have been forced to leave Umstead—their home.

"Honestly," Rheq said, "I didn't know that what I could do was tied to the *myelur*. You must believe me."

"No, I don't," Brishen said. "The only question which remains is how quickly you'll be killed."

"Killed? I've done nothing but help you!"

Prakzen took another step forward, lifting his knife a bit higher. "Let me do it, Brishen. I need to be cleansed."

"No! Me!" Another of the men said. "I can't have the taint remain."

The rest of the men spoke up, demanding to be the one. Brishen turned to address them—that was the opening Rheq needed.

Spinning and ducking, Rheq dashed to his right behind the wagon and toward the forest wall. He heard the swishing of the men's knives slicing through the air as he stepped behind a maple. Sprinting, while continuing to zig-zag as to make a harder target, Rheq began to put distance between him and the Gymad camp.

He thought he was clear when he heard another swishing sound—

a noise Rheq knew instinctively as another knife being thrown at him. Bending at the waist, Rheq made an attempt to dodge the incoming projectile. He was almost successful.

A searing pain sliced across his right shoulder. The knife had not hit him squarely enough to become embedded, but rather the glancing blow bit into the flesh. Instead of pausing to investigate how severe the knife wounded him, Rheq picked up the weapon which rested on the forest floor ahead of him and pushed deeper into the forest. He knew he could lose anyone chasing him—but only if he could get enough distance.

Time passed, Rheq was not sure how much, but it was long enough that he could stop running to see if the Gymads still pursued him. Focusing his eyesight, he searched behind to see if he could spot any red glimmers indicating men close by. Part of his mind realized he was using the *myelur*, but it could not be helped. That was an issue for another time.

While red glimmers popped up here and there from the direction he had come, none of them were strong or big enough to belong to a human. It was time to make sure he lost them for good.

Rheq doubled back, jumping on roots and rocks as much as possible to mask his trail. He then climbed a tree—one close enough where he could jump from one thick branch to a tree next to him. He went from tree to tree, convinced they could not find his tracks. His shoulder throbbed, but he ignored it. There would be time to tend to the wound later.

It was mid-day before Rheq felt comfortable enough to stop for longer than just a few heartbeats. Inspecting his shoulder, he saw the knife had cut through his tunic and into his skin. The wound was shallow and had bled little. However, a closer look made Rheq realize that despite losing his attackers, peril remained a real concern. Around the cut was a greenish tint—one which came from a type of poison Gymads used on their blades.

Chapter 49

The alarm sounded during Danla's morning training.

"A squad has been attacked!" one of the scouts shouted. "The wounded are arriving soon!"

This, in and of itself, was not unexpected. Danla learned that to counter the random attacks on Nothcar, dozens of squads—groups of fourteen men—had been sent along the border to find and destroy the enemy. Danla's camp, consisting of healers and support troops, was stationed far enough to the north as to be considered safe, but close enough to lend help as needed.

Men adorned in the king's colors of green and silver rode in a large wagon drawn by two horses. This was a medical cart sent out to bring in the wounded. The vehicle was large enough to transport a full squad, though now it held not nearly that many. Danla did a quick count as the wagon pulled into camp. Only seven of the squad had lived through the battle.

She, along with the other healers in the camp, went to the long, flat tables designed to hold the wounded. One-by-one, soldiers brought each of the men from the cart to where the healers would do their work.

"This one is already dead," Yarma said, her voice cracking.

Danla wanted to comfort her friend but did not have time as a soldier was placed on the table before her to heal. Remembering what Mistress Halima had taught her, she did not look at the man's face. If it was someone she knew, it could distract her enough from reacting as quickly as needed to save him. Over the winter, Danla had sharpened her skills as a healer. She did not flinch at the sight of blood or broken bones anymore—though this wound was unlike any she had seen before.

She focused first on where his armored breastplate had been pierced just below his ribcage. The blow must have been powerful—more than what was possible from a normal man. A quick inspection of the wound gave understanding. The metal tip of a lance was broken off and still lodged in his body. *He has been skewered by a man on horseback.*

Deftly, Danla reached in and pulled out the tip, causing the man to let out a guttural moan of pain. She ignored it, knowing she could not be distracted. Quickly, she pulled on the green *myelur* which resided in her body, letting it flow from her to the injured man.

With the healing process came a sense of the soldier's overall well-being. She felt a sense of familiarity which meant she had met him before. Still, she remained focused on his wound. He was as near to death as any she had healed in the past. The damage was more than just from the hole in his chest. *His whole body is nearly drained of energy!* That was something which only time and rest could replace, yet he would have neither of those if she did not complete her task of fixing the harm done to him.

The time she practiced and trained over the winter came into play. First, she mended the internal organs, restoring them to their natural state. Next, his skin was sealed together. Upon completion, healthy skin and tissue replaced the wound.

Danla's strength waned from the amount of green *myelur* needed to complete the healing. Blood coated her hands. She fought the urge to wipe them clean on her robes. Instead, she drew in a deep breath and for the first time looked at the face of the man she had healed.

It was Pendr.

That explained why he seemed familiar, and why she had been distracted by his moan. She knew him as well as anyone she had ever known.

With this understanding, the barriers she had developed to shield herself from feeling any emotions while healing shattered. "No!" she sobbed. "No! Not him!"

Someone placed a hand on her shoulder. Danla turned to see it was Yarma. "I recognize him. He's the one who saved us when we were first in training, correct?"

Unthinking, Danla reached up with the back of her hand to wipe away the tears—and in doing so, smeared blood on her cheeks. "Yes. His name is Pendr. We grew up together."

Yarma reached down and placed her hand on Pendr's chest. After a moment, she said, "He'll live. You saved him. Why are you upset?"

It was a fair question. Danla had healed numerous people since she had learned to use her gift with the green *myelur*. Never before had she reacted in such a strong manner. Pendr was a soldier, just like the rest of them. *No, he's not. He never wanted this. He has a gentle spirit.*

Trying to save face with Yarma, Danla responded, "You're right. I should be happy he's alive. Are there any others who need to be healed?"

"You are in no position to heal others," Yarma said. "I sensed that when I touched you. Healing him took nearly all your strength."

"But, the other men. Are they—"

"Only three others could be saved," Yarma interrupted. "None of them are coherent enough to tell us what happened. Mistress Halima has sent scouts to the other squads to pull back and protect this camp. We need to rest up, heal, and find out what happened—as well as await further instructions from Captain Mux."

Danla could not find reasons to argue with that course of action. Her initial shock of realizing it was Pendr who she healed began to wear off, and with it, she recognized how drained she truly had become.

"Can you arrange it so that I can rest close to Pendr?" she asked. "I'd like to be there when he awakes. He'll talk to me. I can find out what happened and report it."

"Of course," Yarma said. "I'll find where we can place you. Stay here."

After the other healer had walked away, Danla rested her head on Pendr. She could feel his chest rising and lowering with each deep breath. In studying his face, she found some comfort in its familiarity.

Yet, there was something different about him. Even in a relaxed state as in now, she could see it: a hardness in his jaw and around his eyes.

The horrors of war were changing him. *How could it not?* With that thought, Danla realized that she, too, had changed. Just moments ago, she pulled part of a weapon from Pendr's side. While they lived in Logs Pond, she had never seen such a wound, let alone reacted in such a decisive manner. *I couldn't have done it back then. I would have been too afraid.*

At that moment, Danla understood that there was no returning to her previous life. Neither she nor Pendr could return to live as they had once before—a time of blissful innocence. With that, Danla felt a profound sadness for the loss of who they were and could have been.

Chapter 50

Nestov hoped with each new sunrise that today would be the day. Last night he had once again been told the same news since he had arrived: King Viskum had been too occupied with important matters to receive visitors. At first, Nestov graciously accepted the explanation. However, after being told the same thing each night through the winter moon cycles, Nestov felt as if he had failed his mission.

Friar Janus had tasked him to be the envoy to Nothcar, to inform the king of the impending darkness which would cover the land: news for the king's ears only. No one else in the castle, aside from Nestov's protector, Brother Mey, knew the reason why Virqyna had sent a representative.

With each passing day, Brother Mey grew more frustrated. He considered the lack of a response for so long to be an insult. Nestov pointed out that the king's men knew they were here. After all, they had a room in the castle to stay, were fed three meals a day, and Nestov had limited access to the library where he spent his days studying texts not found in his homeland.

Though Nestov could not explain why, he felt that today was the day he needed to see the king—the news could no longer wait. He expressed his thoughts to Brother Mey as they woke. The monk responded with a dubious expression.

"And what, pray tell, are you going to do today which we have yet to try?" Mey asked.

"I will be persistent to the point where we can't be ignored any longer."

"Oh? And how are you going to do that? Throw a tantrum?"

The comment was ironic because Nestov rarely showed any strong emotions—a trait which seemed to baffle Brother Mey. Many a time his protector noted how a normal person would be upset by any number of situations which they had experienced since the start of their trip, but not Nestov. It was not part of his character.

"No, I won't throw a tantrum," Nestov said. "Even if I did, do you honestly believe that would grant us the audience we've been seeking?"

"Of course not," Mey said. "But I don't know what else you can do."

It was a fair question. Nestov considered standing outside King Viskum's throne room all day until they let him in but doubted that was enough. He had to say something to make an impression. The idea of being so forceful created a tight knot in his stomach. It would be much easier to spend the day in the library…

With that thought, an idea came to Nestov which should work.

"Get dressed," he told Brother Mey. "We're going to see the king first thing this morning."

"You have an idea," Mey deduced.

Nestov reached for his brown robes. "Yes. I have an excellent idea."

The two readied themselves to see the king as quickly as possible—even to the point of scarfing down the morning meal of ham and biscuits left outside their door.

A guard stood outside the room where they slept—as had been the case since their arrival. The guard was there to protect them, or so they were told, though the constant presence of someone at their door made Nestov feel like somewhat of a prisoner.

There were several guards who took turns watching over Nestov and Mey. This morning, the guard was a man named Reginal. He was of a height and build of Brother Mey, but that is where the similarities ended. The guard's skin was dark—the darkest Nestov had ever seen. He wore a neatly trimmed mustache and beard. Though Reginal rarely smiled, on the few instances when Nestov had seen the big guard grin, his white teeth were a stark contrast to his ebony skin.

"Reginal," Nestov said in greeting. "We will be seeing the king today."

The guard appeared to notice the statement was not in the form of a question. "I will place your request in front of the magister," Reginal said, in clearly enunciated words.

"It's not a *request*," Nestov said. "Take us to the magistrate now."

Reginal paused for only a brief moment before nodding. "Follow me."

The room in which Nestov and Mey resided was on the third floor, near the far back corner of the castle. The throne room sat in the center of the castle on the first floor. In the past, Nestov had admired the tapestries which lined the stone walls of the castle. Not today. At this moment, he needed to stay focused.

Their guard led them down two flights of stairs and around to the front of the throne room. The entrance was a large stone archway. Two, stout wooden doors were closed, blocking the view into the room. Nestov had never seen the doors open. That needed to change today.

Sitting at a desk outside the doors was an older man, as indicated by his wrinkled features and silvery hair. He was using a quill dipped in ink to write something in a tome laid before him. Nestov had been introduced to Magistrate Cason when they first arrived, and it was this same man that delivered the news each night that the king was too busy to grant an audience.

"Ah, Envoy Nestov and Brother Mey," Cason said, greeting them in a pleasant voice. "You are up early this morning. I'm afraid that—"

"Does Nothcar need all its resources to fight the war with Sothcar?" Nestov interrupted.

"I— what? Why do you ask such a question?" For the first time since Nestov had known the magistrate, Cason looked confused.

"Nothcar is at war with Sothcar. That is what we have been told is keeping the king so occupied," Nestov said. "Per the treaty with Virqyna, either one of our lands could request aid from the other in time of need."

"Yes, that is in the treaty. But, we've made no request of Virqyna," Cason said. "And yes, we do need all our resources for the war."

"Then unless I am granted an audience with the king right now, I will invoke Virqyna's right of requesting aid from Nothcar to help us in our time of need," Nestov said.

Cason's eyes grew wide. "Your ... *need*? I'm unaware of any such need that you claim. Why have you not said something before now?"

"My orders were to tell the king directly," Nestov said. "With the winter we experienced, such resources would have been hard to move. Now that spring has arrived, it's possible."

"Seeing the king is, well—this is not a good time." Cason's words were not nearly as convincing as they had been in the past.

Nestov took a step closer to the table. "Then I have no choice. I will draw up a list of our needs and present them to you by the end of the day. The violation of ignoring such a request is war. Is Nothcar ready to fight a battle to the north and the south?"

The magistrate stood. "Please, you do not understand."

"It is *you* that fails to understand," Nestov retorted. "I was sent by Friar Janus to see the king on a manner of the utmost importance. We have been more than patient. We simply cannot wait any longer."

Cason said nothing for several heartbeats. Finally, his shoulders slouched noticeably. "You will be given your audience with the king," he said. "However, you will find the experience ... unsettling."

Chapter 51

The protective ward held fast. Most of the enemy cavalry could not stop their horses from charging into what became like a solid wall. Pendr's ability to remain conscious slipped for a moment after he had projected the ward created from the blue *myelur*, but was jarred back to his senses as he collapsed to the ground.

Some of the horseback riders were killed or injured gravely upon impact with the ward, coupled with being trampled by their horses or those who followed them into the unmovable protective shield.

"Stand ready, men!" Dosfogal cried out. As second-in-command, he took charge due to Pendr's inability to do more than struggle not to pass out.

Through the blue *myelur*, Pendr could sense the ward he had created. It surrounded his men, like a dish covering a plate of food. In theory, the ward should hold as long as Pendr remained conscious. He had learned that those more advanced in their skill to make a ward could create it to stay in place for much longer periods of time—even past their death— though Pendr was nowhere near that level.

Then, like a pinprick, Pendr felt a small pressure against the ward to his right. He glanced to the spot and saw nothing out of the ordinary to explain the sensation. Focusing his sight beyond the ward, he understood. The enemy had brought a man—a mage they called it— who could wield the blue *myelur*, and thereby damage the ward.

At first, Pendr tried to fight it, but it was impossible with his current level of energy. He was simply too tired to do more than watch the ward start to collapse.

"It won't hold much longer," Pendr called out. "I— I can't—"

The ward fell, and with it, the remaining enemy soldiers rushed in. Pendr picked up his sword and shield which he had dropped to create the ward. He stood just as a heavily armored man on horseback holding a lance pierced him in his breastplate, just below his ribs. With that, Pendr lost all sense of time—until now.

He sat up quickly, his hand reaching down to where the lance impaled him. His armor was gone, and in its place was a crudely spun cloth tunic. He lifted the shirt and found that there was no sign of the wound.

Comprehension replaced confusion. He was inside a large tent—the kind found in a healers' camp. Ten or so cots lined the walls, each of them filled with either a recovering soldier or a healer resting from what Pendr assumed was the aftermath of their battle.

Directly to his left was Danla. His heart leaped upon seeing her, though she appeared to be asleep. *She's safe. I'm safe. What happened?*

The images of the battle were still fresh in his mind—as if he were just there. Perhaps they were dreams. With a sickening feeling, Pendr understood they were not dreams. *They were memories.*

Pendr sensed movement outside the tent, but none of it seemed frantic as to indicate they were in any immediate danger. Taking his time to investigate the residents of the tent, Pendr only recognized Dosfogal from his squad. The rest of the men were unfamiliar. *Perhaps that means that the rest of my squad are well enough not to be here.* Thinking this way was better than the alternative.

"There he is," Danla said, causing Pendr to face her. Moving abruptly did not hurt—though he felt like he could sleep for several days.

"I didn't mean to wake you," Pendr said.

She smiled, and the familiarity of the expression buoyed his spirits even more. Propping herself up on one arm, she said, "I've been drifting in and out of sleep. I wanted to be awake when you recovered. What do you remember?"

Instinctively, Pendr reached for his side where the lance had impaled him.

"We were attacked—first by footmen, then by cavalry. I was stabbed, here." He lifted his shirt and pointed.

"And after that?" she asked. Her previous cheerful tone became somber.

Pendr turned his head one way, then the other, seeing if anyone else were listening, unsure why he thought it would matter. "I don't recall anything after that—aside from waking up here. Where are the rest of my men? We had to have won the battle, or I wouldn't be here."

"Yes. Your squad won," Danla said softly. She sat up and swung her legs over the edge of the cot. Like Pendr, she too was wearing clothes of a simple fabric and design, though she wore a dress which reached her ankles and a green strip woven into the fabric encircled her wrists. "But the victory was not without cost."

"Tell me," Pendr said. He felt his shoulders tense.

"Of the four of you who survived, you and—"

"Four?" Pender interrupted. *Eight of my squad are dead.* These were men he had come to know over the winter. Men he trusted, men he was responsible for … men he had failed.

Danla seemed to sense his feelings as she reached out to him and placed her hand on his arm. "From what I have been told, which isn't much, if it wasn't for you, *all* of your squad would have been slaughtered. You did all you could."

"Did I?" Pendr said. "How can you say that? There must have been something more I could have done or so many wouldn't have died."

"Pendr, stop that," Danla said sharply. He knew better than to argue with her when she spoke to him that way. "You have to understand there are things you can't fix or could have done better in the moment. This is just like when you first started to work with your father in the smithy. You tried your best to be able to make what your father could create almost effortlessly, but you couldn't. You didn't have the experience or skill yet. Do you remember the night I came to get you from the smithy when you refused to leave because you needed to make a nail as perfect as your father had?"

"I remember," Pendr said. "But this is different."

"Is it?" she asked. "Is it really? Pendr, I was going to wait for you to wake up before getting a full report on what happened. Before resting, however, I overheard Dosfogal give his report to Mistress Halima. From what I gathered, you created a protective ward in the heat of battle, did you not?"

"Yes. I had to do something. But I wasn't strong enough to hold it."

Danla squeezed his arm. "I'm certain you will need to hear this from Mistress Halima to fully believe it, but creating a ward is hard to do even under ideal circumstances. You did all you could do and more than you thought possible. Don't you see? You and three others lived through a battle you should have lost *because* of what you did, not regardless of what you couldn't do."

He thought on what she said. Danla always had insight on aspects of life with which Pendr struggled. Perhaps her wisdom was connected with her ability to wield the green *myelur*. It was something to contemplate.

"I believe you," he said. "Though it isn't easy." He lowered his eyes. "I wish this war had never happened. The things I've seen. The things I've felt. I don't want to remember them."

For the first time since he had woken, Danla did not have an immediate response. He looked back into her eyes. Tears ran down her cheeks and created dark spots on the front of her dress.

"But as my father would say, 'We work with what the metal can do, and not what we wish it could do.' Hoping for something that isn't what it is won't change it into something we want it to be," Pendr said. He realized he needed to be stronger—to be brave for Danla. He needed to do whatever he could to protect her, and the rest of the people of Nothcar, even if he did not like it. "Are we in any danger here? Do you know what we will be doing next?"

Danla wiped the tears from her cheeks and then said, "I heard that Captain Mux is headed to our camp with reinforcements. I can't say why, or even how the overall war is going."

"How soon will he arrive?" Pendr went to stand, but Danla held onto his arm firmly.

"I don't know for certain," she said. "But not for a few days, I believe. And to be any use to him, you need to rest."

Pendr did not like the idea of lying down and doing nothing, but if he was truly honest with himself, he recognized how drained he felt.

"Just lie down," Danla urged. "Rest. We have plenty of guards and scouts around us to warn us of danger."

Fighting the urge to disagree, Pendr reluctantly did as Danla told him to do. "Will you stay close?" he asked her.

"Yes," she said, some of the cheeriness returning to her words. "I need to rest as well. After all, your wound didn't heal itself."

"You?" Pendr asked, pointing to his side.

Danla nodded. "Now, get some rest. Please."

Pendr rested his head on the cot and looked up at the tent. It was thick enough to keep out any moisture, yet thin enough to allow some light to seep in. *I should be dead. Danla is the real reason I'm alive.*

"Danla?" he said quietly.

"Yes?" she whispered in return.

"Thank you for saving my life."

She paused just a moment before responding. "You're welcome. Now, rest so you can help end this war."

"I will." With those words, Pendr understood. There was no going home, no returning to any form of normalcy until the threat was eliminated. To do that, he needed to become stronger—to be able to create tougher, more protective wards. To do that, he needed help and guidance. He would seek out Captain Mux and Mistress Halima once he recovered. For now, he did the best thing he could do. He closed his eyes and let sleep take him.

Chapter 52

Wyjec watched thirty or so of the pups run around the meadow, playing a game only wolves could understand. It was another beautiful day in the mountains which Wyjec had claimed to be his home.

At first, Wyjec thought it was his imagination. But over the last several days, he became clear it was not a trick of his mind, nor his eyesight. The newly born wolves were growing quickly—far faster than Wyjec believed possible.

Alpha's first born son, the pup Wyjec had named as "One," was the same size as his father, if not a bit bigger. If Alpha was disturbed by this, Wyjec could not tell. *Perhaps it is natural for wolves to grow rapidly.* Wyjec had to admit he knew little about the animals, aside from their existence, from his time in the Master's palace. Yet, something felt … strange … about the pups developing into the size of adults in the space of a few days. *Would they get bigger still?* If so, that could only help Wyjec in his quest for revenge.

After his trip north with the adult males to find and kill a bear, Wyjec had felt as powerful as ever. He knew that it was mainly from draining the bear using the yellow *myelur*, yet it was more.

During the days that followed, he contemplated the reason why he felt so strong. Several ideas came to him, but it was not until Alpha brought him a nearly-dead rabbit for one of his meals that he made the connection. *Just as the wolves have complete power over the rabbits, I am in full control of my life.* Spending his youth as a chardi—a slave to the Masters— Wyjec had little to no control over what he would do, nor what he could become.

For a brief time, Wyjec thought he was in control when he had killed the Masters and had Captain Avadi swear allegiance to him. Once again, with that betrayal, Wyjec discovered how truly deceitful men could be, and with it, he had lost control of his life.

That had all changed.

What drove Wyjec now was to exact revenge on Captain Avadi and his men. As he learned from when he killed the Masters, Wyjec wanted to be there, standing over the man who broke his vow of allegiance, when the wolves tore him apart. *Only then will I be satisfied.*

That thought, in combination with watching the younger wolves in action on the meadow floor, caused Wyjec to realize he now had a powerful enough force to take out Avadi—if he planned properly.

The notion of not having to wait several seasons excited Wyjec. *This is what I've been working for.* With more sunlight during the days, traveling south and east would be easier. Also, with so many wolves in one location, hunting became more of a challenge. Yes, moving on would be the right thing to do.

Wyjec whined/growled to Alpha, to which the wolf immediately responded. Though Wyjec had learned to communicate with the wolves on a basic level using various growls and whining sounds, he learned that he could communicate more succinctly through the red *myelur*.

Using the power, Wyjec impressed upon Alpha to gather up the pack—all of them were leaving. Alpha responded without hesitation. By the time the sun was near its zenith, they were on the move.

Two of the older wolves, Acumen and Jittery, scouted ahead while the rest of the wolves stayed close to Wyjec. The females surrounded him, followed by an outer ring of the younger male wolves.

Alpha took the point, guiding them along a stream of clear water which wound through the thick forest floor. It was a good idea, Wyjec thought, as they traveled. The water was cool and refreshing—no doubt because it was run-off fed by the melting snow from the top of the mountains—and gave the pack one less necessity to look for while they traveled.

Food became more plentiful further down the mountain. In all, the wolves seemed in good spirits to be doing something different. Time and again, Wyjec would check on the amber glow of the wolves around him. In each occasion, he found nothing but pure, unwavering devotion.

The first night, they camped by the stream. Alpha assigned scouts to patrol the area as they slept. It was a good plan and one which Wyjec was proud that the wolf had done on his own without having to be prompted.

Traveling the next day went as smoothly as the first, until the early evening. The wolves reacted first, tensing up, though Wyjec could not understand what had them concerned. Before much longer, he smelled it. Smoke.

As the scent became stronger, Wyjec realized the smoke had an almost sweet smell to it. *Something is being cooked.* It had been over a full season since Wyjec had a cooked meal, and he found his mouth salivating habitually.

Acumen and Jittery rushed in from the forest ahead and spoke directly to Alpha. Wyjec reached out with the red *myelur* to gather the meaning of what the beasts communicated. The understanding came less in what words could say, and more in the form of impressions: ahead lay a village.

Wolves were instinctively wary of humans in large groups. Wyjec could sense the uneasiness start to spread through the pack. Using the red *myelur* to touch the amber glow around their hearts, he impressed a feeling of comfort. Wyjec knew that the villagers would most likely be more afraid of a giant pack of wolves than the wolves themselves could understand. There was strength in numbers.

The question next was how to deal with the village. Should they avoid it? With the wolves' tracking skills, it would not be hard to do so. *But how long do we avoid men?* Wyjec knew the general direction of Iredell, but not a specific location. He needed more information.

That meant one thing: he had to go into the village.

Chapter 53

While on the run, the last thing Rheq wanted to do was give any indication of his whereabouts to those pursuing him. One of the most obvious types of beacons was smoke from a campfire—something Rheq was in the process of making.

The sun was still high in the afternoon sky, and the temperature was warm enough that he did not need the fire for light nor warmth. Neither was he cooking a meal—there were berries and roots aplenty to eat which could be consumed raw.

Building a fire was out of pure necessity if he wanted to live, even if it could cause those seeking to kill him to hunt him down. The irony was not lost on Rheq as he continued to stack the small twigs into a triangle shape in an area of the forest floor which he cleared of leaves. Branches, the width of his thumb, were close by to add fuel to the fire once it had caught on. For tinder, the warmer weather had produced dandelions, some already mature enough to create the fluffy white ends, also known as dandelion clocks.

As a child, Rheq loved blowing dandelion clocks into the wind and watching their white, wispy seeds float through the air. Later, he learned they were also a good form of tinder. A small pile of the dandelion clocks lay under the twigs, enough to hopefully start the fire quickly.

Though his luck had mainly been bad that morning, one thing in his favor was that he found a solid piece of yellowish quartz next to a stream bed. That mineral, along with the knife he picked up while escaping, could create the spark needed to start a fire.

Other elements he needed, water, White Oak bark, and Bloodroot leaves, were plentiful.

The only thing missing was a container to boil water. Fortunately, Rheq had a solution for that as well, or at least one that should work in theory.

He would have preferred to have more time to prepare, but as it was, he could feel the poison from the gash in his shoulder starting to spread. The pain was distracting enough that Rheq needed to force himself to focus.

It took less than ten strikes of the quartz against the edge of the knife to create a spark large enough to trigger the dandelion clocks to catch fire. The kindle of the twigs soon followed, which allowed Rheq to then put on larger branches to build a decent sized fire.

Convinced the fire was going to remain ablaze for the time being, Rheq moved to the next step: crushing the Bloodroot leaves into a fine pulp using two fairly flat rocks. With that completed, he tore the White Oak bark into smaller strips.

Deep red embers were now at the base of the fire. Glancing up, Rheq watched the smoke rise. It was not much, and the canopy of leaves dissipated it even more. As long as he kept the fire small, the smoke should not attract attention.

Rheq put several thicker pieces of wood on the fire and stoked the coals with a long branch he had cut off with the knife. He then carefully placed three fist-sized rocks into the heart of the blaze.

The edges of his vision began to dim, a sign he took that he needed to hurry before the poison could do more damage. For the moment, there was nothing he could do but wait. He had built the fire on the banks near a small stream. Before starting to prepare the fire, he had dug a hole in the ground next to the stream, roughly the size of his head, and lined the bottom and sides with rocks. He then diverted enough water from the stream to fill the hole to the brim.

With the strips of bark and the pulp from the Bloodroot leaves in hand, Rheq scooted over to his man-made puddle and placed the elements into the water. The bark floated to the top, while the pulp mixed in fairly easily. *Two more steps to go. I can do this.*

On hands and knees, Rheq went back to the fire. The flames were beginning to die out, but hopefully, it had served its purpose. Wet leaves and fungus covered the forest floor, meaning that at least he did not have to worry about the fire spreading.

Waiting as long as he dared, Rheq then used the long branch to do something else. He reached in and pushed one of the hand-sized rocks out of the fire, down the embankment, and into the puddle.

Right away, the water reacted to such a hot item placed in its midst. *But will it be enough?* To make sure, Rheq pushed another rock from the fire into the water. Faster than he thought possible, the water began to boil. Using the end of his knife, which he had cleaned of any remaining poison before even starting to gather the items he needed for the fire, Rheq pushed the White Oak bark into the roiling water. The liquid was now a brownish color with a green tint. It also started to coagulate into a paste-like texture.

It took all the effort Rheq could muster to wait for the concoction to solidify to the point where it would be useful. Not only was the pain increasing from the poison, but his ability to focus was also drifting.

Finally, Rheq knew he could wait no longer. Using the flat part of the knife, Rheq scooped up a healthy portion of the paste and slathered it onto his shoulder—right where the poisoned knife had cut him. There was a sizzling sound, along with added pain from when the hot paste contacted his skin.

The added agony, instead of causing him to pass out, brought Rheq more to his senses. He picked up a small fallen branch and bit down on it while he applied more of the bubbling paste to his wound.

There was nothing to do now but wait. Carefully, Rheq scooted backward and leaned against a sturdy trunk. He had never tried this remedy before, nor seen it used on someone. Truth was, he had not even been aware of this cure until recently. It was one of the skills the Gymads had taught him, along with how to make poisons.

It seemed fitting to Rheq that those who tried to kill him also gave him the power to cure their damage.

Perhaps it was his imagination, but already he began to feel better. As he watched the fire slowly die out, his mind became clearer. For the first time since his escape, he considered his next step, provided the cure worked.

I can't return to Umstead. It's been burned down. The Gymads are hunting me, and as far as the king's army is concerned, I'm a deserter. With the land in the middle of war, he could not imagine any place safe for him.

Then he considered that perhaps the army did not think him a deserter. Rheq could easily explain how he was separated from his squad and had been trying to return to them, but the winter weather made it difficult. *At least they are not actively trying to kill me.* The thought was far from comforting, but it was all he had at the moment.

Chapter 54

Captain Mux stood on the bed of the wagon—a transport normally used to traffic the wounded from battles to the healers' camp. Today it performed a different function: it acted as a platform from which the commander could address the king's forces.

From her vantage point near the back, Danla saw Pendr stand near the wagon. He was not hard to spot as he was the tallest man in the camp. For nearly two full days, he had slept. He woke only long enough to eat and perform other basic human needs. Just this morning, when Danla inspected him using the green *myelur*, could she tell he had returned to full strength. It was bittersweet. She had missed him and enjoyed having him close, even though he was resting. Now that he was better, once again he would be put in harm's way.

"We have a chance to end this war," Mux stated as an introduction. "And with everyone here performing their best, we *will* succeed."

Applause from the several hundred men and women in the camp answered the declaration. Mux held up a hand, indicating everyone to quiet.

"Our scouts were able to find the root of the problem—the man behind this war. For many winters, Sothcar was ruled by a council of men referred to as 'The Masters.' They were those who controlled everything, including the military. We have been able to piece together a sort of timeline of what caused the war."

The camp was silent, each of them eager to hear more. Danla glanced to her left and right. Even the healers listened intently.

"The Masters ordered Iredell to be captured, which it was. Soon after, all but one of the leaders of Sothcar were killed—though the details of the specific events are unclear. The remaining Master went to Iredell where he was betrayed by his men once we put the town under siege. The soldiers of Sothcar abandoned Iredell. A good number of them were killed, except the one who truly mattered. We've learned his name: Avadi. He is the de facto ruler of Sothcar, and the one orchestrating the attacks. Most importantly, we've learned the location of his camp."

Those in the crowd responded with a buzz of energy. Until now, the enemy consisted of small groups attacking randomly. There was no clear person or area which Nothcar could attack, at least none of which Danla was aware, until now.

"I have a plan for us to take out the leader. For now, I need everyone to prepare to move. Normally we would wait until morning, but we cannot miss out on this chance. We will leave at mid-day. You know your tasks, now, let's prepare quickly so we can end this war!"

Mux ended on a strong, powerful note, lifting a fisted hand in the air as he did. The camp erupted with cheers before dispersing to follow the commander's orders.

"You heard him," Mistress Halima said, standing two strides in front of Danla. "Pack up your things and be ready to move. Eat as you work. I'll not have the camp waiting for us."

Danla turned to head for her tent. She paused and tried to spot Pendr once again. Since he was not normally stationed in the camp, he would not have regularly assigned duties. If he helped the healers prepare, they would be ready that much sooner. Again, he was easy to see amongst the crowd. He followed Captain Mux away from the camp along with what appeared to be a full squad. *Of course, Mux would have plans for Pendr.* A twinge of disappointment made Danla realized that her plan of getting Pendr to help was for more than just completing the task. *I may not get to speak to him again.* Pushing those thoughts away, Danla hurried to catch up with the rest of the healers.

The sun had not reached its midpoint when they were on the move. Precious few details were shared with Danla, or any of the healers aside from Mistress Halima, while they prepared to leave. They started heading east, along a fairly narrow trail between the trees which were now just coming into bloom. Because the path lacked width, the force was strung out far enough that Danla could not see the front of the line. *Pendr has to be up toward the front. Otherwise, I'd have seen him by now.*

When the sun dipped to just above the tree line, the path which had wandered through the forest connected with a much wider road which headed directly south.

"This is the king's road," Yarma said as they arrived. "I traveled this with my family when I was younger. It runs between the capitals of Nothcar and Sothcar. It even goes as far as Virqyna."

"How can you tell?" Danla asked. "I've seen roads this big before. What makes this one special?"

Yarma responded by going to the side of the road and kneeling next to a cube-shaped stone. Danla followed her, also going to a knee to get a better look.

"These are milestones," Yarma said, tracing her finger along a symbol carved into the side of the stone.

"Milestones?" The word felt strange in Danla's mouth.

"It's an ancient word. I'm not sure the meaning," Yarma said. "My father explained that these types of stones were placed along major roads from as far back as anyone can remember. No one knows who placed them."

Danla stood. "So, you are saying we're taking the main road to attack the enemy? Isn't that a bit obvious?"

"Perhaps that's the point," Yarma said. "Sometimes the obvious choice is the one least expected."

"Ladies?" a voice called. It was Eladrel, one of the few male healers camped with Danla. "Is something the matter?" he asked.

Yarma continued kneeling for a heartbeat longer, then stood. "We're fine. Thank you for asking. We're coming."

After rejoining the rest of the healers, Danla asked Yarma, "What do you think awaits us?"

To that, Yarma frowned. "I'm not sure. Certainly, the scouts from Sothcar will see us coming and warn their leader."

"There's something we're missing," Danla said. "Something that Captain Mux didn't tell us."

"Of course, we weren't told everything. All it would take is for one of us to get captured. They'd torture the information out of us."

"Torture? Would they do that?"

"Of course," Yarma said, her voice tightening. "This is *war*, after all."

Danla did not care for the answer. "Just because we are at war doesn't mean all sense of human decency is lost. We wouldn't resort to such tactics."

For a moment, Yarma did not reply. But when she did, the words shook Danla. "Ah, young one. I miss being that naïve. Think about it. How do you suppose we were able to get the information of their leader's location?"

Chapter 55

Magistrate Cason instructed Reginal to open the doors to the throne room. Perhaps it was Nestov's imagination, but the guard seemed to hesitate before complying. Slowly, the large wooden doors were opened.

Unable to fight off his curiosity, Nestov stood on his toes so he could see over Reginal's shoulder in an attempt to get his first look at the king. He could not make himself tall enough to accomplish the task.

To his right, he heard Brother Mey inhale deeply. Whatever he had seen had a profound impact. It was not until Reginal stepped aside that Nestov got his first good view.

The throne room was deep, roughly two hundred paces by his best guess. Large stone columns lined the way, light gray in color, with a hint of greenish veins running through them. They reached up to what appeared to be at least two stories, if not more. Arches, made of the same stone—some type of marble—reached from column to column. The floor was mainly stone, though not the same material as the columns. A long strip of green fabric trimmed with silver fringe ran from the door to where the king sat.

King Viskum sat up straight on his silver throne. Like Reginal, he too had skin as dark as night with a new moon. He was large, without being fat. His tunic was cut to reveal his bare, muscular arms. Though his black hair was just starting to show signs of age at the temples, King Viskum looked powerful.

"Follow me," Magistrate Cason said before striding down the green carpet toward the throne.

Nestov eyed the king as they approached. The ruler of Nothcar said nothing, nor showed any emotion. He simply stared at them.

The man was as physically intimidating as any person Nestov had met. *Is that why Cason warned us that meeting with the king would be unsettling?*

Upon arriving twenty paces or so in front of the throne, the magistrate stopped. "King Viskum, may I present to you Brothers Nestov and Mey from Virqyna."

The king blinked as if seeing them for the first time. "Brothers?" he said in a deep, resonating voice. "They don't look like brothers to me."

Is that a joke? Has the king just made a joke? Unsure, Nestov kept silent hoping that the king would not be offended that he had not laughed.

"Ah. 'Brother' is their title, Your Majesty. They are monks," Cason said. "They have traveled from Virqyna to speak with you."

Viskum tilted his head to one side, then the other. "Virqyna?"

"The land north of ours, Your Majesty."

"Virqyna, Virqyna …" The king leaned forward and addressed Brother Mey. "Didn't I conquer your land?"

"Forgive me, Your Majesty. I am but a servant." Mey turned to Nestov. "Brother Nestov is the envoy."

"Him?" The king sounded incredulous. "If he were any smaller, he'd need a wet-nurse."

Nestov could sense Mey bristle as the statement, though the taller monk said nothing.

"I am young, Your Majesty. It's true," Nestov said. "But Brother Mey speaks the truth. I was sent by Abbot Aydomus himself. I come on urgent business."

"Are we at war?" The king asked. "You!" He pointed to Cason. "Bring me my sword!"

"King Viskum," Cason said slowly and carefully. "You are the king. You are needed here. Your best men are winning the war."

The ruler leaned back in his throne. "We're winning? Of course. We always win." He focused again on Nestov. "And who are you?"

He's gone wrong in the head. The realization explained why Cason had warned them in advance—and most likely the reason they were not allowed to meet him for so long.

"I'm Brother Nestov, from Virqyna. I'm here on urgent business from Abbot Aydomus."

"Why didn't this … this … Abbot come to see me himself? Am I not the king?"

"He is too weak to travel, Your Majesty. I have been authorized to speak on his behalf. May we speak?"

The king frowned. "What have we been doing if not speaking?"

Instead of dancing around the question, Nestov decided to be direct. "King Viskum, there is a darkness coming."

"Already? I feel as if I just woke. I want to spar before retiring for the evening." Again, he pointed at Cason. "Fetch me sparring partners!"

"Not that type of darkness," Nestov said. "Abbott Aydomus is sensitive to the ripples which flow along the *myelur*. He has detected a *shift*, for lack of a better word, if left unchecked will bring ruin to both of our lands."

King Viskum made no response aside from staring at Nestov. After a drawn-out moment, he said, "What?"

"I will handle this concern, Your Majesty, with your permission," Cason said quickly. "May we have your leave?"

"Fetch me sparring partners!" the king bellowed.

Cason bowed his head. "Of course. May we proceed?"

"Yes, yes. Go. Hurry." The king stood and stretched. He then looked up with wonder and completely ignored his guests.

The magistrate motioned for Nestov and Mey to follow him, which they did quickly out of the room. Once beyond the doors, Cason told Reginal, "Send in the trainers. Hurry, before the king—" He cut himself off before he could say anything else.

Chapter 56

Pendr sat on his horse behind the line of oak trees and watched the king's army move southward. From his location, he could see them, but they would not notice him, nor the men with him, unless they knew exactly where to look. Despite the number of non-combatants in the group, it moved at a fairly brisk pace. Their destination was Blythewood—a town not far from the capital of Sothcar. He spotted Danla, traveling next to Yarma and Eladrel. *I wish I could have said good-bye.*

The rest of the men with Pendr, fourteen in all, also watched silently until the last of the army moved on. Only then did Captain Mux speak.

"If we are successful," the captain said, "they, as well as the rest of the kingdom, will come to no harm."

"May I ask a question?" asked a man who Pendr did not know by name. He, like the others who sat on horses around Mux, was a solidly built fighter.

Mux nodded sharply in response.

"With the army so large, and moving directly down the king's road, how do they hope to avoid being detected by enemy scouts?"

Pendr had wondered the same point, along with several other elements of their mission.

"They most certainly *will* be detected," Mux said. "I *want* Sothcar to see them coming."

"Won't that put our forces at a disadvantage?" another man asked. Pendr recognized the man as Sadem, one of those with whom he trained at the castle. "After all, the enemy will be able to choose when to attack."

Mux looked at each man in the group deliberately before speaking. "I know all of you. I've trained you. Each of you can wield the blue *myelur* to various degrees. You were selected to be part of this squad specifically. However, the less you know about the particulars of our mission, the better."

Dosfogal, the only soldier who had been in Pendr's previous squad, frowned before asking, "But how are we to be successful if we don't know what we will be doing."

"You're a soldier," Sadem said brusquely. "Just do as you're told."

Dosfogal bristled at the statement and appeared as if he was going to give a rebuttal. Pendr spoke before the discussion could turn contentious. "We can't risk it."

All of the men faced Pendr upon his odd choice of words. He continued, "I'm certain Captain Mux has a plan. He stated that if we are successful, everyone else will be safe. That means putting an end to this war. If any of us are captured, we can't risk how, specifically, we are going to accomplish that goal. We could fail before we even get the chance."

The men considered his words, and Pendr detected a brief smile on Mux's face.

"Sir Pendr is correct," their captain said. "Now, listen carefully as I give you some general guidance."

Making sure he had each of the soldier's complete attention, Mux said, "All of you can wield the blue *myelur*, at least well enough to shield yourself for a time. We will be traveling quickly. The men in the lead and those in the back will keep themselves shielded. We will rotate amongst the fourteen of us so that no one tires out too quickly. Do not speak unless it is unreservedly essential. I'll give more instructions as needed."

Mux paused to see if anyone else had concerns. They did not.

"Sadem and I will take the lead. Pendr and Dosfogal will be the rearguard," Mux said. Without further instructions, Mux spurred his horse southwest—a path which would parallel the king's road while at the same time put some distance between them and the rest of the army.

Taking a deep breath, Pendr encased his body in the *myelur*. He had learned there were various degrees to which he could let the power flow. Over time, he had discovered the balance between drawing just enough power to protect himself without draining his energy too quickly.

Without speaking verbally, Dosfogal indicated he had done the same. Within a few heartbeats, the rest of the squad was on the move, leaving Pendr and Dosfogal to follow.

Pendr reflected on what he knew as he rode to keep up. The captain had told everyone this morning that they knew the location of Avadi, the leader of Sothcar. He was holed up in the town of Blythewood. The goal was to lay siege to the town, at the very least. The possibility of a full-on attack was a reality depending on the town's defenses.

From what Pendr inferred, if Avadi were defeated then the rest of the army would surrender. The notion was a bit difficult for Pendr to comprehend. *How could one man hold so much power over so many?* Growing up, the only person Pendr met who had any authority was Mayor Lonz. If a group of men came into Logs Pond and killed the mayor, Pendr doubted his father, or many of the rest of the citizens, would cower automatically. While the concept was a curious one, it was also something which Pendr did not want to pursue. *I'm a blacksmith at heart, not a politician.* A pang of longing to return to the forge and work side-by-side with his father hit Pendr. That is what he was fighting for—not control over lands or power over others—he was fighting for the freedom to live a life of peace. Even with his title of knight, that had not changed. It gave him some comfort to think of himself first as a blacksmith, and second as a soldier. Many in the squad, especially Sadem, had embraced becoming soldiers. Pendr did not like what he saw in those who sought out battles and glory. *I don't want to become like them. Right now, I'm doing what is needed.*

The squad had started their travel in the late afternoon. At twilight, Mux stopped the group next to a stream of clear water, too small to be considered a river.

"This is called Sugar Creek," Mux said once the men had gathered around him. "Scaln and Torvo will take the lead from here. Chebur and Wentes will take the rear. We'll travel as far as we can before it is too dark for us to travel safely. Take a quick moment to eat something from your provisions and get a drink from the creek. Feed and water your horses as well. If you need to relieve yourself, do so downstream."

Despite the seriousness of their mission, a few men chuckled at the comment.

Pendr kept his blue *myelur* shielding active during the men's respite.

"You can let it go," Mux said as he approached Pendr.

Swallowing a bit of dried beef before responding, Pendr said, "I will as soon as the other men have set up their shields."

Mux looked around, "How can you tell they haven't done so already?"

The question was odd. *How could I not know?* He could sense it, not with any of the traditional five senses. It was simply something he could detect. And then he realized something. "How did you know I still have my shielding up, Captain?"

Leaning in closer, Mux said, "There are those strong enough in the gift who can sense it in others."

Pendr gleaned the implication. "How many of this group can do that?"

"How many of the others have kept their shielding up?" Mux answered with a question.

"None."

His captain replied with a simple nod.

Chapter 57

The village laid out before Wyjec appeared peaceful. Smoke drifted lazily from stone chimneys and the sound of children playing drifted over the buzz of villagers going about their daily activities. However, Wyjec, himself, was proof that appearances could be misleading. He needed to be cautious.

The wolves had calmed considerably after he touched them with the red *myelur*. Still, the people of the village posed a threat—they would see the wolves as something dangerous, which of course, they were.

Wyjec needed information. He had to find Iredell, and with it, Captain Avadi. That is what the wolves were for; he could not risk anything happening to them until then. Alpha stood next to him as he surveyed the village from a hilltop. The pack was behind them, out of sight.

Through the red *myelur*, Wyjec impressed upon Alpha to remain behind and to keep the rest of the wolves with him. The wolf obeyed without pause.

It had been nearly two seasons since Wyjec had encountered another human being. Anxiousness lanced through him, though at first, he did not know why. He was able to shield himself with the blue *myelur*, and with the use of the red, he could manipulate anyone who posed a threat. *Why, then, am I nervous?*

He contemplated the question as he picked his way down the hill. Spring grass covered the ground and was a bit slippery from a recent rainstorm. Watching where he placed his feet, understanding came. His feet were shod in bear hide—shoes he had created himself, along with the rest of his attire.

A thick, course beard covered his jawline, and his hair hung down to his shoulders. His appearance would mark him as a wildman.

Wyjec conceded that he was, after a fashion, a wildman, though that was not how he felt in his heart. The power of the *myelur* gave him control. *And isn't control the opposite of wildness?* The notion resolved his determination as he approached the dirt road which led to the heart of the settlement.

Two young boys ran from behind a hut made from logs stacked upon each other with the spaces in-between filled with mortar. They stopped, and one of them let out a tiny yelp before turning and running back the way they came.

The small cry must have caught the attention of someone inside the hut as the front door opened quickly. A woman with wide hips and a wider frown stepped into the street.

"You there!" she said. "What are you doing here?"

Immediately, Wyjec embraced the blue *myelur* to shield himself. The woman did not threaten him, but there could be more people in the hut.

Wyjec opened his mouth to speak. He recognized that he had not spoken the human language since the betrayal at Iredell. Instinctively, his mouth recalled how to twist and change shape to form words. "I need directions."

The women eyed him suspiciously. "Do you have any money?"

Wyjec wore a rabbit fur cloak around his shoulders. Bear hide covered his legs, the same material as his moccasins. There simply was no place for him to carry coin, and neither did he have any need until now.

"All I want is information," Wyjec said.

The large woman laughed. "And all I want is to be fed strawberries as I lay by the river. Everything comes with a cost."

He could see it in her eyes: disdain. It was a look with which he was all too familiar. The Masters looked at the chardi the same way, and with that memory came a flood of frustration. He wanted to reach out with the red *myelur*, right then and there, and stop the woman's heart from beating.

Killing her won't get me the information I need. If anything, it would only delay anyone from helping me.

Instead of bickering with the woman, Wyjec turned from her as if she was insignificant—which of course, she was. *Anyone who cannot help me isn't worth my time.*

Making his way deeper into the village, more people noticed him, some staring openly. In an expansive square, near a fountain, parked a wagon. From it, a man called out to people to buy his wares.

Wyjec realized this was a traveling merchant. He had heard about these types of men when the Masters were plotting one night how to tax them. Since they moved from town to town, they held no allegiance to any particular kingdom. The Masters had eventually abandoned the idea of the tax because these merchants brought in goods, as well as information, which the Masters could exploit. The tax could, and probably would, discourage their trade.

A few people, mostly women, looked over the merchant's wares. He had a variety of cooking supplies, as well as fabrics and clothes. Wyjec did not see any items that were extravagant or luxurious in nature. Based on the simple design of the structures in the village, it made more sense that base needs were in demand.

As Wyjec approached, the villagers noticed him and started backing away. The merchant appeared not to appreciate Wyjec scaring away his customers.

"I need information," Wyjec said. "You are a traveler, are you not?"

The merchant's frown deepened. "I travel, yes. But I do not give away anything for free, not even information." He scanned Wyjec from head to toe. "You do not have anything I want in trade."

Once again, Wyjec fought the urge to let anger overtake his actions. He considered his options and decided to pull a tactic he learned from observing the Masters.

"What do you value?" Wyjec asked.

"Coin, items I can sell or trade elsewhere."

"Nothing else?"

The merchant folded his arms across his chest. "Nothing comes to mind."

"How about your life? Do you value that?" Wyjec said the words without menace. The plain-spoken approach often had a more substantial effect.

Quickly, the merchant's right hand went to his side where he wore a long knife in an engraved leather sheath. "I've studied knife play with the Gymads. If you value *your* life, you will walk away. Now!"

Wyjec expected a response of that nature, to which he had a counter plan. Calling upon the red *myelur*, Wyjec studied the man's life force. He could stop the man's heart or close off his windpipe. Then, another idea came to him. He could sense how the man tensed up, ready to pull the knife out. A similar flow of the red *myelur* indicated that his left hand was also preparing, possibly to pull a knife out from behind his back, perhaps tucked into his belt. With a direct and firm nudge with the *myelur*, Wyjec shunted off the commands to the merchant's arms.

"You will give me the information I want," he said calmly, "and in return, I will give you the use of your arms once again."

The merchant looked unimpressed—until he realized that he could not will his arms to move. "How …" His eyes grew wide. "You're him! You're the one who can wield the red *myelur*!"

The statement took Wyjec aback. *This merchant has heard of me?* If it was true, and not just a ruse, this is exactly the type of man who would know how to get to Iredell.

"Ask! Ask me anything!" the merchant pleaded. "I'll tell you. Please, just don't kill me."

Wyjec looked around. None of the villagers were close enough to overhear the conversation. That would make things easier. He did not want the army at Iredell to know he was coming.

"How do I get to Iredell from here?" Wyjec asked.

"Iredell?" the merchant asked. "Why do you want to … oh! That's where it was said that Captain Avadi defeated the last of the Masters. He's not there. Iredell was recaptured by King Viskum's forces."

The news hit Wyjec hard. If Iredell had indeed fallen, then Avadi was already dead. *My revenge has been taken from me!* For days, he had dreamt of standing over Avadi and killing him slowly—with the man knowing the price of his betrayal. That was now gone.

"Wait! I can see this news troubles you," the merchant said. "If it's Avadi you seek, he's still alive. His forces have been invading Nothcar in smaller groups, leaving unspeakable atrocities in their wake. It's been bad for business. If you can stop him, please do so!"

Wyjec inspected the merchant's amber glow. Based on what he could see, the man was sincere. *But I've been fooled by men before.*

"Where is he?" Wyjec asked.

"I can't say for sure. He moves his camp around to avoid being attacked directly. However, from what I have gathered in my travels, he doesn't stray far from a town called Blythewood. I have a map I can give you—free, of course!"

"Let me see this map."

The merchant turned his torso but then stopped. "I can't move my arms. Please, I promise you, I will not attempt to harm you, not that I could."

Seeing the logic in the man's reasoning, Wyjec released the red *myelur* from the man. "Show me the map."

Chapter 58

Rheq awoke to a combination of the sound his stomach made and the discomfort which came with hunger. As unpleasant as the sensation felt, it also meant one thing: he was still alive. He was propped up against the tree near the stream where he had administered the paste to his poisoned shoulder. A brief inspection showed the paste had caked onto the skin, but would flake off if he scraped at it.

The skin underneath was an ugly red, not only from the poison but also from the burning when the hot paste was applied. Gingerly, Rheq rotated his arm. While there was pain, it was less than he had expected.

Beams of morning sunlight bounced off the stream, creating a mosaic of constantly shifting patterns. The fire Rheq created to make the antidote was a pile of blackened wood and cooled off coals.

By fate or some other reason, the Gymads who had been chasing Rheq had not found him in the night, neither had wild animals. *Yes, I made the paste which saved my life, but I'm still lucky to be alive.*

His last thoughts before giving into sleep the day previous were what to do next. He remembered that his conclusion was to find King Viskum's army and convince them he had not deserted. That could be tricky, especially since he had done just that.

There's no use waiting to do something unpleasant which needs to be done. With that thought, Rheq stood up slowly. His head felt light at first, but standing still for a moment resolved that. After taking in several deep drinks from the stream, he was on his way.

While following the stream which led mostly to the east, Rheq foraged more berries and roots.

The knife stuck into his belt was his only weapon. Though he was skilled enough to track and hunt game to eat, that would take time, and what he needed now was the safety of people he could trust, or at the very least, those not actively trying to kill him. Rheq was not entirely sure where he was, though he did know that streams fed larger rivers—and where there were rivers, there were people.

A few times during the day, he was able to spy living creatures using what he had come to discover was some form of the red *myelur*. The idea of him possessing such a gift alarmed him to a degree. He understood little of what it could do, aside from him spotting soft, red glows from living creatures. Yes, it was useful, but it did not explain why the Gymads had reacted in such a hostile manner once they discovered his power. *Perhaps there is more that can be done with the* myelur *than I know.*

It made sense. Just yesterday, Rheq had used wood, dandelion clocks, Bloodroot, and the bark of White Oaks to create something new: a remedy. Each of those items by themselves served other primary purposes, yet they could do more.

In Umstead, his home, talk of the *myelur* was frowned upon, even scoffed. To many, including Rheq, it was no more real than the gnomes said to protect gardens at night from insects. Yes, as a child he believed that night gnomes were real, but as he grew older, and after never seeing one, his doubts became his beliefs. *Maybe it's the same with the* myelur.

By late afternoon, Rheq had yet to come across any sign of civilization even though the stream had indeed merged into a larger creek. The landscape consisted of a thick forest made up of birch and elm. He was now heading mostly southward, which would take him into the heart of Sothcar—the enemy's land.

He paused and, after weighing his options, elected to follow the creek northward—against the flow. It made traveling trickier, and often he had to follow deer paths in the forest to continue heading north.

With the sun setting and the light dimming, it made it easier for Rheq to see glimpses of the red *myelur* through the trees. The animal population was sparser than he would have thought was normal.

However, that was usually an indication of one thing: man was nearby.

To his right, he could see that there was something different with the trees. The fading light made it hard to gauge distances, but it appeared as if the density of the trees was not as thick in that direction.

Moving more carefully, Rheq wound his way towards the oddity. Abruptly, the forest ended. Replacing the wood was a flat path—twenty or so paces wide. Tightly packed dirt made it vastly different than traveling in the forest, and Rheq could see evidence of horses and wagons. It was a road, but one larger than he had ever seen.

He scanned up and down the road. It ran north to south. By the side of the road, just to the north, Rheq spotted a rock which was too cubed in shape to be natural. It reaffirmed that this was a man-made road, and one designed for a lot of traffic. Umstead had roads, but they were little more than two divots which ran side-by-side created by wagons following the same path.

Standing in the middle of the open space made Rheq feel exposed. Yes, he wanted to find people, but it needed to be the *right* people. He went back to the cover of the trees and considered his options. He still had enough light to travel for a bit, though doing so amongst the trees could be treacherous. Holes created by burrowing creatures would be nearly impossible to see, yet they could easily cause him to turn an ankle.

Doing nothing was also not a good option, so he started to pick his way northward through the forest. He stayed within eyesight of the road but far enough away where he doubted he could be spotted.

Finally, the sun dipped too far under the horizon to illuminate his path. A decent sized oak grew not too far from the road, and with a little effort, Rheq climbed into its wide branches. He found a solid place where he could wedge himself between two diverging branches and the trunk. He had slept in trees before, and while it was not the most comfortable of locations, it was safer than sleeping on the ground.

That night he dreamt of being chased through the forest. Several times, he awoke with a start and had to catch himself from slipping out of the tree.

After one particularly vivid dream, one in which he was a rabbit being chased by hunters, he found sleep elusive. In his youth, he had been the hunter, never considering what the prey might have felt. Having experienced being pursued by those who meant him harm made him question whether he would want to hunt ever again.

While his mind wrestled with such thoughts, his body's weariness eventually took over, and he continued in a fitful sleep. When he awoke, it was not to the sound of his stomach growling; it was to something coming down the road from the north. Cautiously, he climbed higher into the tree to see if he could get a better look.

He managed to reach a spot where he could look over many of the trees and see sections of the road. The tree swayed a little under his weight, but it held firmly. With the sun still rising, Rheq used his ability to look for the red glows of living creatures. They were not hard to find.

On the road to the north was a great number of people—that much was clear. And then Rheq saw something else: a banner of green and silver.

He had found King Viskum's army.

Chapter 59

The army came to an abrupt halt, and from Danla's perspective, she could not tell why. They had just set out for the day. From what she was able to glean from those around camp the night previous, it would be several more days until the army would reach its destination: Blythewood.

"I'm not quite ready for battle. Light, when will I be?" Danla heard Eladrel ask to no one in particular.

"We're not under attack," Yarma, who walked next to them, replied. "We'd hear shouting and be given orders."

Mistress Halima traveled several paces ahead. Her short stature prevented her from seeing over anyone, but that did not stop her from pushing forward through the crowd until she was out of Danla's sight.

Traveling close to the healers were the support troops: cooks, armorers, and general laborers who were either too young or too old to be soldiers. Danla noticed many of them shifting around uneasily. Thus far, the trip had been routine—travel, camp for the night, break camp at first light and then travel again until dusk. After five days of traveling, this was the first break in the pattern.

"Maybe our scouts found something," Danla said. "Perhaps that's what's causing the delay."

"Could be ..." Eladrel said, though he did not sound convinced. "Chances are we'll start moving soon and never find out the reason for the delay. We are, after all, just healers."

"*Just* healers?" Yarma said. "We're more than that. We're what keeps this army functioning. Without us, they wouldn't have gotten this far."

Yarma's words reminded Danla of how she recently healed Pendr from a wound which without her skills would have been fatal. Over the last several days, she had asked around about Pendr, hoping to get a chance to talk with him at night. No one had seen him, nor Captain Mux for that matter. The army as it stood now was led by Vice-Captain Becir, Mux's second-in-command.

For the next several moments, those around Danla speculated on the delay. Soon, Mistress Halima returned, a stern look on her face. "Eladrel and Danla, come with me."

Eladrel raised an eyebrow as he glanced at Danla. Calling for healers usually meant the worst—especially if more than one was needed. The soldiers stepped to the side to create a path for them to move forward.

When they reached the front of the line, Danla did not see any wounded. What she did observe was something unexpected—a scenario none of the others had guessed.

In the middle of the road knelt a young man with his hands raised. Several archers had their bows drawn and aimed at him, though to Danla he did not appear to be threatening.

"He said there was a chance that one of the newer healers could verify who he is," Halima said.

"Rheq? What are you doing here?" Eladrel asked.

The young man in the road visibly relaxed. "Thank the Light!" he said. "Eladrel, please tell these men pointing weapons at me that I'm on your side."

Danla thought the name Rheq sounded familiar, but she was not sure from where.

"But *are* you on our side, Rheq?" Eladrel asked. "The last time we were together, you were the point man of our squad. We were ambushed, and you were nowhere to be found."

Several of the archers pulled back on their bowstrings a little more upon hearing the new information.

With his hands still empty and above his head, Rheq said, "I didn't betray you! I promise! I was scouting ahead, looking for shelter in the copse where you were attacked. I spotted the enemy just as the rest of you entered the wood. There was no way to warn you without being caught myself, and there were too many for us to fight off. I didn't have a choice! It was either warn you about something which was already too late or stay hidden and try to find a way to help you later."

Vice-Captain Becir, a seasoned soldier with thinning hair and wrinkles in the corners of his eyes, spoke to Eladrel. "Can you verify this man was once part of the king's army?"

"Yes, as far as I know. If I recall, he was from Umstead. He was one of the few of us that survived the attack which killed Sir Lokan. Pendr was also in the group—in fact, he was our leader. You can ask him."

Becir's eyebrows knotted on his weather-worn forehead. "Pendr's on another assignment. But clearly, you recognize him. You even called him by the name he had shared with us before you arrived at the front of the line." The Vice-Captain shifted his attention back to Rheq. "Stand up, and explain where you have been since the day you went missing."

Lowering his hands, Rheq stood quickly by jumping to his feet. "Once the rest of my squad was captured, I had to find someplace safe. The land was covered with enemy soldiers. I worked my way back to Umstead, my home—but not as a deserter! I went back as a soldier to help my loved ones. I'm sure you have heard what happened to Umstead."

Danla had not heard of anything specific about the town, but rarely was information shared with the healers aside from possible incoming wounded from recent battles. However, the way Rheq spoke of his hometown made her believe something terrible happened there.

"Aye," Becir said. "I've read the reports. But that doesn't explain where you have been during the winter."

"I came across a group of Gymads as I went to return north to find the king's army," Rheq said. "It was mutually beneficial for me to join them until the weather improved—they even clothed me which is why I'm no longer wearing my uniform. When spring arrived, I took my leave of them and continued to search for the king's army so I could rejoin."

"And what of your shoulder?" Mistress Halima said. "You've been hurt. I can see that from here."

Rheq glanced down at the tear in his tunic to the red, swollen skin. "The woods are a dangerous place," he said without elaborating.

"One last question," Becir said. "How did you know where to find us?"

"It's more like you found me," Rheq said. "I've been traveling north. I came across this road. I heard you this morning, and from the top of that tree—" he pointed to a large oak which stood above the other trees on the side of the road, "—I spotted the king's banner."

For a drawn-out moment, Becir remained quiet. He then turned to Eladrel and asked, "Can he be trusted?"

Eladrel seemed to consider the question carefully before responding, "He could have killed us in our sleep when he was on guard for the night while he was traveling with us. He's got a temper, but he followed Pendr's orders. I can't say whether or not his story is true after he left us, but knowing what I know of him, yes, he can be trusted."

"Men, lower your weapons," Becir ordered the archers. "Rheq, come forward so the healers can look you over—from the back of the line. We need to get moving."

Rheq jogged to where Eladrel, Danla, and Halima were standing. "Thank you," he told Eladrel.

Halima placed a hand on Rheq's wounded shoulder. "Don't thank him fully yet," she said. "He's going to be the one to heal you more completely. Now follow us."

The soldiers once again made a path for Mistress Halima and her group, which now included Rheq, to return to the other healers. Along the way, Rheq asked, "Back there, the man said Pendr isn't with this army. Why not?"

Danla perked up her ears at how Mistress Halima would respond. She was disappointed when the leader of the healers answered, "I don't know."

Chapter 60

"I find all of this to be unsettling," Brother Mey said. He paced from one side of the room to the other. "I'm not trained to understand the *myelur*. I'm a protector."

Magistrate Cason had ushered Nestov and Mey out of the king's throne room quickly. Two days had passed since the meeting with the king, and Nestov had yet to speak to Cason about the specifics of his mission. The magistrate said he needed to fetch an expert on such things as the *myelur* before talks could commence. If Cason were true to his word, that meeting would happen today, though Nestov was unsure exactly when.

"And protect me, you have," Nestov said. "I'm still alive, am I not?"

Brother Mey stopped pacing and smiled lightly at Nestov's remark. "I haven't done much," he said.

"Not true," Nestov said. "You've protected me from going crazy while we have had to wait."

"Crazy? Like the king?"

Their meeting with King Viskum was exactly as Cason had warned them—disturbing. The king was suffering from memory loss, possibly due to his advanced age. In Nestov's studies, he had come across a book on human health. One passage suggested that soldiers, especially those who had taken many blows to the head, were more likely to suffer the type of memory loss the king displayed. From what Nestov understood, the king had been quite the formidable fighter in his prime.

"I think it best we not mention the king's condition, even between the two of us," Nestov said.

"You're right," Mey said. He began pacing again. "I just wish we had more to do than just wait."

"Normally we could go to the library," Nestov said, "but Cason said the meeting could happen as soon as this morning. I need the time to collect my thoughts."

The larger brother's response was to nod and continue to walk back and forth in the room.

A knock on the door sounded a little before mid-day. It was Magistrate Cason. He explained the king's expert on the *myelur* had arrived and awaited them in one of the castle's more private rooms.

The magistrate, himself, led Nestov and Mey down a flight of stairs to the second floor. He brought them to a door of unremarkable make and style. Nothing about it suggested the room was any different than any of the others in this part of the castle. *Maybe that's the point—to hide it in plain sight.*

Cason knocked once, paused and then gave three short taps before entering. The room was well lit, despite the lack of any windows. An oval table sat in the middle, surrounded by padded chairs. On the far side of the table sat the room's only occupant: a woman with intelligent eyes.

"May I introduce Mistress Sheric, she who counsels the kingdom in all things concerning the *myelur*," Cason said. "Mistress Sheric, Brothers Nestov and Mey from Virqyna."

Sheric stood. She was of average height, but that was her only trait Nestov considered to be average. Her dark hair rested peacefully on her shoulders, and her olive skin was smooth and wrinkle free. Based on first impressions, Nestov could not guess her age, though her eyes—the feature he first noticed—indicated she was not as young as her physical appearance suggested.

"Please, sit," she said. Even her voice was pleasant.

Cason closed the door before joining the rest of them at the table. Before Nestov could speak, Sheric said, "It appears those as far as Virqyna have detected it."

"You know why I'm here?" Nestov asked, unable to mask the surprise in his voice.

"I believe so, if the magistrate told me true," she said. "But, please tell me in your own words."

Nestov inhaled before responding. He had rehearsed what he would say numerous times, but that was under the assumption that he would have to explain not only the concept of the issue but then the issue itself. Sheric's indication that she might already know much about the *myelur* caused Nestov to reconsider how he would phrase the situation. In the end, he decided to make sure they had a common base of understanding.

"Abbot Aydomus, the leader of our order in Virqyna, has sent me. He is too weak, physically, to travel himself," Nestov began. "He is wise when it comes to the *myelur*. I've been sent because he senses a shift—a change. 'Portents of ill construction' were his exact words."

Sheric folded her hands on the table in front of her. "And what were these portents?"

"Forgive me, Mistress," Nestov said, "I am just beginning to understand them myself. The abbot explained that there are certain … events … for lack of a better term, to indicate changes from the norm."

"Like how certain animals act strangely when a storm approaches?" Mey asked.

"Something similar, yes," Nestov said. "In this case, it is more like the ripples created by dropping a stone in water."

Sheric leaned forward. "That's an apt analogy. My sisters and I have noticed these changes—ripples you might say."

"I don't understand," Magistrate Cason said. "What possible risk could this cause to the kingdom?"

"Nature likes balance," Sheric said. "The *myelur* is the same. In simple terms, there are three main aspects of the *myelur*—they work in harmony. Each one balances the rest. If one aspect becomes powerful or overly used, the other two compensate."

"Compensate? How?" Mey asked.

"From our studies, it is believed the *myelur* is passed down from parents to children," Sheric said. "Most of the time, the *myelur* is so weak that a person could have it and never know. Sometimes a person is born with greater access to one aspect of the *myelur*, which means that they are needed to counter an imbalance. On rare occasions, a person can access more than one characteristic of the *myelur*."

"So, this trouble of which you speak, is it because there is an imbalance in the *myelur*?" Cason asked. "Again, even if that is the case, why is it a threat?"

For the first time since Nestov had met Sheric, he noticed her calm demeanor waver. "Often the parts of the *myelur* are referred to as colors: red, blue, and green. When they work in harmony, they create light. It promotes good in people, though we can't say for sure why that is. But one of the aspects, green, has a fracture in it, of sorts. When exploited, it is what we call the yellow *myelur*. What also makes it different is its potency. It doesn't have to be widely spread to make a big impact."

"But yellow is the color of the sun," Mey pointed out. "How can that be bad?"

"The colors are just a way to help categorize the aspects," Sheric said. "They aren't an exact representation of the powers."

"You are stating that this … yellow is bad?" Cason asked. "How?"

Sheric clenched her hands in front of her tighter. "When yellow is mixed with red and blue, darkness is created. From historical records, it is this same darkness which nearly destroyed the world of man millennia ago."

Cason's face drained of color. "And you sense this happening again?"

"Abbot Aydomus says *he* senses it," Nestov said. "He senses that the yellow *myelur* is again being used, and it is so strong that it is creating an imbalance."

"I'm not sure I would agree that it is that dire, yet," Sheric said. "If it were, my sisters and I would have acted upon it. The yellow *myelur* has been used—that we can sense. The *myelur*, itself, will usually resolve the imbalance on its own."

Nestov stood. The moment had arrived. He needed to make the abbot's directive clear. "The reason I was sent was simple: Abbot Aydomus said that unless we seek out who is using the yellow *myelur* and stop him or her, it is not a matter of if, but *when* the darkness will return. He said the yellow hadn't been used in generations—that, by itself, is cause enough for alarm."

Cason addressed Sheric. "Is this true? The yellow has not been used for such a long period of time?"

"Yes …" Sheric said slowly. "Yes, as I said, we believe, based on our studies, that the *myelur* will naturally resolve this on its own. There is no need to fear."

Though Nestov was much younger and inexperienced, he understood why the abbot sent him. He felt his cause slipping away. *I have to be forceful.* "My abbot disagrees. He claims that the *myelur* has kept the yellow from even being used at *all* until recently. Because it has been used, a point on which we agree, something must have changed to allow it."

"But what could that have been?" Cason asked.

Good. He's still considering what I have to say. "From what I was told," Nestov continued, "those who can use the *myelur*, any aspect of it, usually have an event which triggers it. Healers, those who can use the green, can have it triggered in them by other healers. The blue and the red are often opened to keep the user from danger or something else traumatic."

"But what would cause the yellow to suddenly come back into use?" Mey asked. To his credit, Nestov's protector had been following along.

Sheric spoke up before Nestov could admit he did not know. "First, it couldn't just happen to anyone. Someone would have to be born with the latent talent. Even then, from historical texts, and what we understand, it would take time—many, many seasons—to wear a person down far enough, to have them experience extreme stress, for the yellow to open up to them."

"And that is my task," Nestov said. "To seek your help. We need to find who is using it and stop them. We must hurry."

"I disagree. One person cannot have that much of an impact," Sheric countered. "As I said, the *myelur* will heal itself. Charging through the land on a witch hunt during a war is a terrible idea. People are unnerved enough as it is."

"That's not what Abbot Aydomus believes," Nestov said. "And, it is more than that."

"Oh?" Cason said.

Nestov stood and placed both hands on the table before him. "My leader says that once the yellow *myelur* is active again in the land, those born with the power will be able to access it without experiencing the same pain and trauma as the person who started to use it again."

"We know nothing of that," Sheric said. This revelation appeared to disturb her more than anything else to this point.

Nestov squared his shoulders. "That is why I am here."

Chapter 61

The closer Pendr's squad drew to Blythewood, the more palatable the tension became. If Avadi was there, and he truly was the leader of the forces which had been attacking Nothcar, this could end the war.

What troubled Pendr was not knowing what they would face once they reached their destination. Sothcar's attacks came from smaller groups, not large armies. However, if one were to gather enough small groups together, it *would* form an army.

The king's main forces continued to travel toward Blythewood down the road which connected the two kingdoms. As of yet, they had not encountered the enemy—at least not that Pendr had heard. This was a bit troubling since they were less than a day away. Certainly, Avadi would know of their approach. *Does that mean he is running? Or perhaps, he is leading us into a trap.* Neither of these options was attractive.

Over the last several days, Pendr was able to formulate a guess on Captain Mux's plan, or so he thought. From what he was able to piece together, the original rulers of Sothcar were killed, though how was up to some debate. Avadi took over to fill the void of power. Since the army of Sothcar already answered to Avadi, they followed his directions to attack and pillage. Mux's belief, or so Pendr gathered, is that if Sothcar's current leader were removed, there would not be anyone in Sothcar powerful enough to take over. King Viskum would instead assign someone to rule over Sothcar, thereby ending the war.

The point, then, was to find and remove Avadi. That was the goal of the squad with which Pendr traveled. With their power to wield the blue *myelur*, they could, in essence, ignore everyone else attacking them and go straight at the enemy's leader.

But all of this hinges on many assumptions. There was part of the plan Pendr lacked, something Mux had yet to reveal. Pendr puzzled on that as they traveled.

Not long after their mid-day break, Mux abruptly spurred the men into a gallop. The forest here was thinning, giving way to open meadows of tall, green grass. None of the men in the squad questioned the action—they simply did as instructed.

For most of the afternoon, Mux drove the men hard—cutting more to the west and south than before. In the early twilight, they came upon the king's road. There were not any signs of the king's main army, but Pendr imagined that the throng would be quite the distance behind them due to the heavy riding of his squad.

Captain Mux did not stop at the king's road. Instead, he continued to direct them west towards a rising hill dotted with tall conifer trees. These were different than those from where Pendr grew up. They lacked branches except for the very top of the trees which were higher up than a man could reach on horseback. The floor around the trees consisted of brown, dried pine straw. Traveling through such a wooded area should be easy, which perhaps was precisely what Mux had in mind. Once entering the sparsely spaced trees, Mux continued southwest.

Only when the sun's light dimmed to the point where traveling would be dangerous did Mux motion for them to stop. Gathering the squad around him, he spoke to them for the first time since they had stopped at mid-day.

"Blythewood is just over the ridge to the south," he said, motioning with his hands which held the reins of his horse. "But that isn't our destination."

The shocked reactions of the soldiers matched Pendr's. *If we aren't going to Blythewood, then where?* Mux answered Pendr's unspoken question quickly enough.

"Avadi knows our army is coming. He *wants* them to come," Mux said. "Blythewood is a trap. The town is deserted. He has his forces lying in wait just outside the town and round about."

"How do you know this?" Dosfogal asked. "How can you be sure?"

Mux leaned forward, his stare meeting the other man's eyes. "Lines on maps and names given to towns do not define people as a whole. This is a concept Avadi has seemed to miss."

"Meaning?" Sadem asked.

Clarity came to Pendr in that moment. "Calling a hammer a nail does not make it so," he said. "It's something my father taught me while we were working in the smithy."

"I don't understand," Dosfogal said.

"Things are what they are," Pendr said. "Evil actions, such as those done by Avadi's forces, will be recognized by those who understand what they are—no matter what they are called, or why they are done. Good people cannot stand by and do nothing forever."

Mux nodded. "Pendr is correct. Morally right actions are independent of labels," he said. "There are those in Sothcar who want to see Avadi removed from power."

"Spies!" Dosfogal said. "You've been getting information from someone in Sothcar."

"Spies and others, like those we've captured, as a point of fact," Mux said. "It would be foolish for us to believe only one source. But we received enough information to put together an actionable plan."

"But if there are spies in Sothcar, wouldn't there be spies in Nothcar as well?" Pendr asked.

"That's why no one in our army's main forces knows of our true plan," Mux said. "No one knows where we are going aside from my sources and myself."

"And where is that?" one of the other men in the squad asked.

Mux looked at each of his men before he spoke. "You will see at first light tomorrow."

Chapter 62

Wyjec wished a bear would attack him. Using the power of the blue *myelur*, he could fend off the attack easily enough; using the red *myelur*, he could wound the bear; using the yellow *myelur*, he could drain the animal and replenish his waning strength.

His wolves brought him rabbits and squirrels, but they were too small to satisfy Wyjec fully. The pack was moving along quickly, following the map Wyjec had acquired several days previous which would take them to Blythewood. This path took them away from the mountains, and also the bears. Wyjec would have to find other options.

Thus far, the map had been accurate. If it continued to be so, by Wyjec's best guess, he would arrive at Blythewood tomorrow. What happened then depended on several factors. Would Avadi even be there? If so, how many men were with him? What kind of fight would he put up? The single most important thing for Wyjec was that Avadi was aware who was going to kill him. That moment is one which Wyjec fantasized about. He even picked the words: "Avadi, there is a price for everything, and your betrayal will cost you everything."

The words were poetic, after a fashion. Addressing him with the absence of his title was important. Wyjec would not honor the man—he did not deserve it.

Through the trees, Wyjec and the wolves ran. None of his family gave off even an indication of complaint of how hard Wyjec pushed them. Each of them was strong, quick, and deadly. Their mere appearance would scare most men into inaction—something which Wyjec needed.

That moment of panic would be when his wolves would attack, using surprise to their advantage.

The victory would be ominous and complete. Everyone would know that Wyjec was not to be trifled with. After the battle, he would . . . he would . . . *What will I do?* For the first time, Wyjec realized he had not thought beyond killing Avadi. Revenge had driven his actions for so long he had not considered what he would do once he achieved his goal.

Momentary doubt was replaced with an epiphany: he could do whatever he wanted. Yes, he had grown accustomed to living in the mountains, sleeping in a cave, and eating raw meat, but he also remembered living in the Master's palace. It was a life of luxury. Chardi kept him fed, warm, and comfortable. *Yet, man cannot be controlled as my wolves are, and wolves cannot serve me in the same way as man.* It was a problem. Or was it?

No one would dare challenge him or hurt him with wolves at his side. That was the answer. The men would serve; the wolves would protect. Working together, they would give Wyjec the life he deserved.

Buoyed by the possibility of the future, Wyjec ran on, excited.

He stopped only when the light of the sun disappeared enough from view to make traveling more challenging. The wolves also needed to hunt before the light completely faded. It took more effort to find prey and not kill it—Wyjec needed several of the smaller animals to drain to prepare for the battle which would hopefully take place the following morning.

Within a relatively short period, the moon had just begun to rise. Wyjec had three squirrels and five rabbits placed before him. Each of the smaller animal's legs had been broken—they were alive, but unable to run away.

One-by-one, Wyjec picked up the gifts from his wolves and then reached out with the yellow *myelur* to drain them. After the animals were truly dead, Wyjec offered them back to the wolves for their evening meal—all aside from the last rabbit. He kept that one for himself.

Satiated, Wyjec curled up next to Alpha and let sleep begin to take him. His last waking thoughts were of how he would be standing over Avadi tomorrow. *I will make the man beg before I kill him.*

Chapter 63

At first, Danla did not trust Rheq. The more she learned about his story, the more suspicious she became. Yes, it was believable—to a point. The young man acted like everything that he had experienced was not his fault; he was only doing what he had to do at the time to survive.

As they traveled over the last few days, she got to know him a little better. He had not run away and even proved himself quite helpful when the army stopped to set up camp. *Perhaps he's trying too hard.* If he was working for the forces in Sothcar, would he not try to do all he could to earn their trust? At the same time, if his story was true, and he was trying to show the king's forces that he was no deserter, would he not also try hard to impress them? This quandary bothered her as she traveled along with the healers.

"Tomorrow?" she heard someone ask ahead of her.

"Yes, tomorrow!" came a reply from another person she could hear, but not see, in the crowd of soldiers ahead of her.

Whispers trickled back through the ranks until finally, Mistress Halima spoke loud enough for all the healers to hear her.

"I don't know which is worse," she said. "Trying to feed an army or keeping them from gossiping."

"Then soon our talents will be needed," Eladrel said. He walked to Danla's right.

"You're correct," Halima said. "We will arrive in Blythewood. I know this from meeting with Vice-Captain Becir every night."

"Why wait to tell us?" Danla asked.

Halima gestured around her in response. Danla inspected her fellow healers, as well as the soldiers tasked with protecting them.

Everyone stood a little more rigidly. *They've tensed up now that we are closer to possible attack.*

One of the elements Danla had learned from her training with Mistress Halima was that while tension before battle was a sign of sharper focus, it also drained people of their energy. It required effort to keep a person's muscles tightened, effort which, over time, would be tiring.

"I want you to focus on your breathing," Halima instructed. "Keep it even and steady. Be alert, but relaxed."

"Yes, mistress," each of the healers said.

Danla did as instructed. It was not easy. Her mind reflected on the previous battles she had encountered. They were chaos. In each case, a group was trying to kill another set of people. Her job was to heal those with whom she sided—to heal them enough to be able to kill the others before they could kill her.

While she found new purpose and drive to increase her ability to heal, it bothered her that her skill was used to indirectly hurt others. Back in Logs Pond, people were getting hurt or sick regularly. Her mother had come down with an illness one winter which made her bedridden for nearly half a moon cycle. *It was hard to see her in so much pain.* Had Danla known then what she knew now, she could have eased her mother's suffering. Yes, healers would be valuable to towns like the one in which she grew up.

Though the thought of returning to Logs Pond did not appeal to her—she had seen too much of the world to want to return to her previous life—she could not deny that her new talents would help those for whom she cared.

If this attack works, as Captain Mux insisted it would, then the war between Nothcar and Sothcar would come to an end. Pendr had made it clear that his intention was to return home after the fighting ended. *That's if he is given a choice.* Danla realized she was making the assumption that she, too, would have a say in what she did after the war concluded. There was one way to find out.

She sidled up next to Mistress Halima. Speaking in soft tones, she asked her teacher and leader, "When this war is over, what will I be allowed to do?"

Halima continued to look straight ahead when she answered. "You will be allowed to further your training. You are quite skilled, Danla."

"And if I wanted to return to Logs Pond?"

The question grabbed the mistress's attention enough for her to face Danla. "Why would you want to do such a thing? You've seen what you can do. You've seen how you are needed. Do you honestly believe you could be happy back in that small village?"

"Most likely not," Danla said. "Though, I thought I was happy before."

"Don't mistake ignorance for true, fulfilling happiness," Halima said. "You have a great talent. It needs to be used to help a great number of people, not just a select few in a remote village."

Danla said nothing, though she clutched sides of her cloak and wrapped it around her.

"Don't be troubled by this now, Danla," Halima said. "Focus on your breathing. Focus on the task at hand. We will need you if we are to win tomorrow."

"Yes, Mistress," Danla said. She stepped back and fell in line next to Eladrel.

"Your private conversation with Mistress Halima seems to have disturbed you," he said when she returned.

Danla paused a moment before responding, "It's nothing. We just need to focus on preparing ourselves."

"If your expression is what nothing looks like, I can only imagine what *something* might do to your features," Eladrel said. "Will you be alright?"

No, not in the smallest amount. "Yes," Danla lied.

Chapter 64

The crescent moon reminded Rheq of a man squinting, trying to see beyond his normal abilities. It was somewhat coincidental because that was his task this night—the eve before King Viskum's forces would arrive at the town of Blythewood.

Rheq had worked hard to earn back the trust of the king's men, and he was rewarded—if being assigned to the night watch could be considered a prize.

Unlike the other soldiers who patrolled the perimeter of the camp, Rheq wore studded leather armor and was armed with a bow, arrows, and several throwing knives. The chainmail armor which most soldiers wore, with accompanying swords and shields, were too cumbersome for his smaller frame. He had asked for permission to choose what he would wear for battle and, with some persuasion and stubbornness, had achieved his goal.

The camp normally settled quickly after the evening meal, but this night was different. Rheq sensed the uneasiness among his comrades—a feeling he shared. He did not want to die. However, all it took to regain his courage was to think back on what the men of Sothcar had done to the people of his village of Umstead. His friends, his family, his neighbors—all burned to death as if they were unwanted leaves at the end of autumn.

During the trip since he had rejoined the army, he had been able to gather roots and plants which allowed him to create different types of poisons. This skill learned from the Gymads would be put to use in the battle ahead. Each of his arrow tips and throwing knives, save one, were laced with a poison which acted quickly to paralyze a person's muscles. While an arrow may or may not stop an enemy by itself, the poisoned ones certainly would.

There was one throwing knife which was different. Instead of quick acting poison, its coating glimmered of a slow-acting toxin, the kind which inflicted him when he escaped from the Gymads. If given a chance, that knife would be used on whoever ordered the attacks on his home. It would be a painful way to die without the remedy.

Rheq's watch consisted of the first half of the night. Based on his best guess, the time to change guards would be soon. Normally he relished getting a chance to sleep, but he doubted it would be easy to do tonight.

A glimmer of red caught Rheq's peripheral vision. Whipping his head to the side, he scanned the forest beyond. As quickly as it appeared, it vanished. *Most likely a nocturnal animal looking for an evening meal.* Rheq had not told any of the king's men about his ability to see the red glimmer of living things. The Gymads tried to kill him once they learned, and the skill was not something Rheq wanted to share with anyone for risk of a similar result.

Another glimmer, this one from a different spot. Then another, and yet another. Within a few heartbeats, the forest ahead of Rheq filled with numerous glimmers, each moving slowly, yet steadily towards the camp.

These were no animals. This was an ambush.

Placing two fingers between his lips, Rheq whistled loudly. He then turned and ran back towards camp. He noticed one of his fellow guards across the field turn in confusion—a state which ended quickly when men raced from the wood, each of them screaming battle cries.

"We're under attack!" Rheq heard someone shout. "To arms! To—" the shout turned into a gurgle.

The camp began to stir, too slowly for Rheq, as he reached the outer tents. Kneeling behind a barrel containing grain for the trip, he removed an arrow from his quiver and nocked it. Finding a target would not be hard—hundreds of men emerged from the forest surrounding them, each wielding wicked looking weapons.

Chapter 65

Pendr awoke when someone kicked his foot, hard. He opened his eyes immediately and instinctively reached for the sword at his side.

"It's begun," a deep male voice said. It took Pendr only a moment to attach the voice to Dosfogal.

Distant sounds of screams and metal on metal first confused Pendr; then realization took hold: the main forces were under attack. *That means Danla is at risk.*

"Quickly," Captain Mux's voice said just loud enough for all of the squad to hear. "Saddle up the horses. We need to act now!"

Any remnants of sleep evaporated from Pendr's body and mind as he gathered his saddle and set about preparing his horse. This activity was one of many that Mux had had them practice. In short order, the squad was mounted and ready.

"Hear me now," Mux said. "The latest word from our sources place Avadi in a cabin to the west of Blythewood. He has a small force surrounding him. We race in and kill Avadi first. Be quick—don't hesitate. We dare not let him escape."

"But our army is under attack!" Sadem said. Pendr normally disagreed with the man, but he was glad the soldier echoed his feelings.

"They are doing their part," Mux said tightly, "and now we must do ours. Follow me!"

Without further instructions, the captain spurred his horse into a gallop. Pendr did not need to be told to embrace the blue *myelur*; he did so as soon as they started to move. While following Mux's lead, Pendr noticed that each of the other men in the squad also had covered themselves in the protective shield.

While traveling, sounds of battle continued further into the wood.

Pendr tried to ignore the cries of pain but found it difficult to do so. People he cared about were under attack.

Mux wound his way through the wood, jumping over small streams and fallen logs along the path. With only the light of the stars and the new waxing moon, traveling at such a speed proved challenging, if not treacherous.

And then, without warning, the trees ended. An open field with a cabin, framed in wood but with a stone chimney, stood before them. To either side were large tents. Behind it was a corral of sorts, housing a dozen or so horses.

A cry of surprise, from what had to be an enemy on watch, sounded when Mux's forces emerged from the forest.

Mux did not wait. He aimed his horse straight for the cabin, as did the men who followed him. Before they could arrive, men—armored and wielding weapons of different kinds—emerged from the tents.

Arrows cut through the night air. Pendr worried not for such weapons; they could not pierce the blue *myelur* shield surrounding him. That confidence disappeared when he saw Mux's horse go down, taking the captain with him. Several more of the squad followed a similar fate. *They are shooting at the horses, not us!* It was a smart tactic—one which Pendr had employed himself in battles. He guessed if Mux had not been forced to attack now, the captain would have left the horses behind.

Pendr leaped from his mount just as it crashed into one of the fallen horses he had been following. Remembering his orders, Pendr ignored the men from the tents and headed straight for the front door of the cabin.

In his right hand, he held his sword—a long, broad sword with a good bit of heft. In his left, a tower shield which ran from his shoulder to his knee acted as protection if the blue *myelur* failed and was emblazoned with the emblem of a tree—the kingdom's symbol.

From small windows on either side of the cabin's main door, Pendr saw firelight coming from inside. Without pausing to formulate a plan other than to enter, Pendr crashed into the door, shield side first.

The door had been barred, but the power from Pendr's large body, aided by the blue *myelur*, made it collapse inward.

The light from the fireplace lit the scene. There, sitting up from a large bed, was a middle-aged man who matched the description of Avadi. But he was not alone. Next to him was a woman of similar age, and on a bed to the left were three children—the oldest of whom could have been no more than ten winters.

"Avadi!" the woman cried out. "No! Not us! Not the children!"

Pendr stopped. If the woman had been truthful, she had revealed that this man was indeed the one behind the attacks on Nothcar—the man Pendr was sent to kill. *Did Captain Mux know his family would be with him? I can't kill an unarmed man in front of his family!*

A blow to the back of Pendr's head made him realize he had hesitated long enough for one of the men from the tents to attack. The blue *myelur* prevented the hit from hurting Pendr, though the force was strong enough to knock him forward and to one knee.

Without hesitating this time, Pendr swung his sword around to fend off the man behind him. The strike caught the man in an armored thigh and continued until it sliced all the way through one leg and partially into the next.

The woman and the children were screaming now. Pendr stood, his back to them. He looked out of the cabin, over the man he had just taken down. Those of his squad who had survived the original attack were battling the men from the tents. Another man broke off from the fray and headed toward Pendr.

Quickly, Pendr let a knot build up inside of him—a knot of purple *myelur*—and released it at the man just before he arrived at the cabin. The effect blew the attacker backward thirty or so paces. He landed awkwardly on his head, his neck bending at an abnormal angle.

With that threat eliminated, Pendr turned back to face Avadi.

He wasn't there.

The woman and the children were huddled together on the main bed, but Avadi was gone. In the back corner of the cabin, to Pendr's right, there was a small door, slightly ajar. Pendr raced to it and muscled it open.

There, behind the house, was Avadi climbing on top of one of the horses by the corral. Without looking back, the leader of Sothcar took off to the west, leaving his men, his family, and Pendr behind.

Chapter 66

A nipping at Wyjec's hand brought him to his senses. It did not hurt, but it was forceful enough to wake him. The night was still dark; the shard of the moon was headed westward meaning that dawn was still a ways off.

Through the red *myelur*, Wyjec looked at the wolf's heart which sought his attention. The lines on the animal's heart marked him as Three—one of Alpha's offspring—and one of those who was scouting that night.

A combination of whines and growls came from Three. The sound was one the wolves assigned to a specific thing: man. Wyjec took that to mean men were nearby. *We shouldn't be this close to them yet.* According to the map, Blythewood was a good distance away.

Wyjec asked the wolf for clarification, the best he could with their primitive form of verbal communication. Three made the same sound meaning man.

This could be a problem, or it could be an advantage. Perhaps the men Three had detected would know something of Avadi's exact location, or provide at least some information which he could use. It was too good of a chance to miss.

After giving the command to Three to wake the rest of the pack, Wyjec stood and stretched. He had not slept long, but he had slept deeper than he thought he would. Any traces of drowsiness vanished as he prepared to get the pack on the move.

Just before Wyjec was about to give the order to follow Three to the men, Wyjec heard it: battle cries. Rapidly checking around him, he noted that all of his wolves were with him, aside from the others who were sent out to scout at night. It would not be his other scouts who were fighting; they were in the directions away from the sounds of battle.

Who would be fighting in the middle of the night so close to Blythewood? **Dread** came with understanding: Avadi's enemies. They must have found the leader of Sothcar first.

No! I've come too far to give up now!

Wyjec whined/growled loudly, directing the wolves to head to the fray. Trees whipped by as Wyjec tapped into his inner energy to keep up with the wolves. His family ran silently, as he had taught them. He wanted their prey to have no warning of what was to come.

A ghastly shriek of pain echoed ahead and to the left. The wolves altered their course, panting heavily from the sprint.

Just ahead, Wyjec could see the red glimmers of many men, though some of the lights—those that were stationary—were dimming. *They're dying!* This, in and of itself, was not a bad thing, unless one of those fading lights belonged to Avadi.

Then, the pack broke past the tree line and into a clearing. A cabin, with tents set up by it, sat in the middle. Around it, men fought viciously. They were too distracted to notice the horde racing in their direction, and the wolves refrained from howling until they were on the men. Wyjec called upon the blue *myelur* to protect his body as the wolves began their attack.

It did not matter what kingdom's colors the soldiers wore—the wolves tore into anything which stood on two legs. Then, and only then, did the howling begin.

Wyjec scanned the crowd, looking for Avadi. He did not see him, and none of the men would be in any shape to answer questions once the wolves completed the attack. A scream, different and higher pitched, came from the cabin. Wyjec raced to the front opening. The door lay splintered on the floor, torn from its hinges.

A woman, clutching three children tightly, sat on a bed, her back against the headboard. From the light of the fire in the hearth, he could clearly see the terror on her face.

"Where's Avadi?" Wyjec demanded.

Her mouth worked as if she were trying to form words, but she said nothing.

"Where's Avadi!" Wyjec screamed this time.

With a quivering hand, she pointed to a door in the back corner of the cabin.

He's here! He's close! A rush of anticipation washed over Wyjec as he ran to the back door.

Chapter 67

Danla could not let the screams of the slaughtered distract her. She needed to focus on healing the soldier before her who was bleeding to death. A nasty gash in his left shoulder oozed out the red, life-giving fluid. Her hands pressed down on the wound while she let the power of the green *myelur* flow from her inner reserve to seal up the injury.

Within moments, not only had the blood stopped but underneath the ripped open armor was healthy skin.

"Thank you," he said as he sat up. He reached for his sword and shield by his side.

"You must rest," Danla said.

He heeded not her words. "If I rest, we'll die."

Danla wanted to argue, but she knew he was probably correct. The battle still raged around them. There was no safe harbor here for soldiers to rest after a healing.

Once the attack came, Mistress Halima directed the healers to the center part of the camp. A large tent, big enough for at least twenty people, was pitched with the sole purpose of acting as a healing station.

Cots were set up with sturdy stools next to them. Even though the attack came as a surprise, the army still had a plan. The soldiers would fight. If they were injured, they would be brought to the healers' tent. Once their wounds were mended, they would return to the battle.

As protection for the healers, Mistress Halima sat in the middle of the tent, legs crossed and eyes closed. From what Danla understood, her mentor's sole responsibility was to cast a protective ward around the tent using the blue *myelur*. It would allow friendly forces in, but keep those intent on doing harm away.

Using a bucket of water and a thick cloth, Danla washed the blood from her hands. He had been the third man she had healed since the attack began. The healers—fourteen of them—took turns in an effort to let others recover. If the flow of wounded continued at its current pace, they would all be spent shortly. With the healers drained, the battle would most likely be lost.

Time passed, both quickly and slowly. More men came in with various wounds, and each of them was healed enough so they could return to the battle. Danla began to feel sapped to the point where it became an effort even to stand. Still, more men came.

"Are we going to win?" Danla heard Eladrel ask one of the men he had healed.

To this point in time, no one had spoken the question which loomed over all of them in the healer's tent. It was not that the healers had been told to refrain from asking, rather fear of the answer kept them voicing their main concern.

"I can't say," the soldier said. His right ear was missing, and now smooth skin was in its place from where Eladrel had done his work. "We've pushed them back to the forest, but they keep regrouping and hitting us where we're weakest. So far, we've kept any enemy mages away from this tent. That's one of our main goals." The man stood. "Keep doing what you can in here. It's making a huge difference."

He exited the tent without saying more. Danla looked around at each of those who could use the green *myelur*. Each had their shoulders slumped, and several lay down on the cots reserved for the wounded. *And why not? We are wounded as well, just in a different way.*

"Rest while you can," Halima said, speaking for the first time since she had placed the protective ward.

Needing no more encouragement than that, Danla lay down on the cot next to her. Though spattered in blood, she could not find it in herself to let that bother her. She closed her eyes and tried to ignore the sounds of battle still raging around the tent.

Chapter 68

Avadi kicked his horse in the flanks and headed away from the cabin. He had picked the only saddled horse, meaning it would take time for Pendr to prepare a horse to follow—time he did not have. Once Avadi made it to the trees, Pendr was certain he would not be able to follow him in the dark.

This man, the one abandoning his family, was the sole reason for the war. *He needs to be stopped, now!*

Pendr called upon the purple *myelur*, letting it build inside him. But Avadi was traveling too fast. He would escape before Pendr could form enough power to do any significant harm to the leader of Sothcar's forces. *If only I had my horse!* With that thought came a recent memory— he did not have his horse because it had been shot out from underneath him. *Time to repay that debt.*

Focusing on the right front leg of Avadi's horse, Pendr released what *myelur* he could summon in such a short period. It was sufficient. The horse's right leg buckled enough for it to stumble. The jolt knocked Avadi from his saddle and to the ground, landing hard.

Just then, a new sound entered Pendr's ears. Howling. Lots of guttural, menacing howling came from the other side of the cabin. The effect was chilling and stunned Pendr into a moment of delay. *Why would wolves be here?*

Regaining his wits, Pendr understood that he needed to stay fixated on his primary target: Avadi.

Breaking into a sprint, Pendr raced to where the man was just now beginning to sit up. *I shouldn't have hesitated before.*

While logically Pendr understood the concept, emotionally the idea of killing a man in front of his family, no matter if it was for the greater good, was too hard to conceive.

Still, Pendr doubted it was a coincidence that Avadi had a door in the back of the cabin which led to a horse prepared for travel. *Maybe he wanted his family to be a distraction.* Why these thoughts came to Pendr as he ran to Avadi, he was not sure. One thing of which he was certain: he could not let anything distract him *this* time.

Avadi had gotten to his feet, but stood groggily. His back to Pendr, the man put one hand to his head and then pulled it away, inspecting something on his palm. In the dark, Pendr could not see for certain what Avadi saw, but guessed the captain had hit his head when he fell.

Only a few paces away now, Pendr raised his sword. Behind him from the cabin, a male voice cried out, "Avadi!"

The call was enough for the captain of Sothcar to turn. Avadi's eyes widened when he saw Pendr almost on top of him. He held up a hand in defense, but it was no use. With one complete blow, Pendr's sword went through Avadi's wrist and continued under his chin, decapitating the man.

Pendr spun to see who had called out the warning. Surprisingly, it was not a man dressed like that of a soldier. Instead, the man had long, unkempt hair and wore what appeared to be animal hides. *This doesn't make sense. Who is he?*

For a moment, Pendr and the other man stared at each other across the distance from the cabin to where Pendr had completed his mission. It was at least two hundred paces, if not more. The man in animal skins was not armed, yet something about him made Pendr keep the blue *myelur* shielding around him.

"No!" The man shrieked. "He was *mine* to kill!"

This statement made even less sense. Pendr had never seen this man before, and he was certainly not part of the king's army. *If he wanted Avadi dead, does that make him my ally?*

Pendr's answer came when the odd man made some loud, strange whining and growling noises.

From around the cabin came a pack of wolves—large ones. *There must be nearly thirty of them!* With an emphatic gesture, the man pointed at Pendr. The pack broke into a sprint toward their new prey.

Chapter 69

Wyjec watched his wolves tear their way across the field to the soldier who had just killed Avadi. *It had been him. There was no doubt.* Through the red *myelur*, Wyjec had been able to verify the man was indeed Avadi—the man who betrayed him in Iredell. Each living being's red glimmer was a bit different, and Wyjec had studied Avadi long enough to be able to recognize him.

I was so close! Wyjec gathered that the soldiers attacking Avadi's men were the same who had laid siege to Iredell. Not that it mattered—Wyjec would redirect his revenge on the man who had denied him his vengeance.

He expected the soldier to run for the trees or set himself to fight off the wolves, but he did neither. Instead, the man sheathed his sword and raised one hand in front of him, palm faced outward.

The wolves continued to charge, yet the soldier did not move to run away. *What is he doing?* Then, Wyjec felt a sensation on the back of his neck, as if a warm breeze blew only on that spot. The sensation was familiar, though Wyjec could not say why.

Using his influence through the red *myelur*, Wyjec directed the wolves to attack the man's legs. They were not to kill him; Wyjec wanted that privilege himself. For a moment, he thought about using the red *myelur* to kill the man before the wolves arrived, but that would be too quick. He *wanted* the wolves to attack.

Within ten paces of the soldier, the wolves did something odd. They stopped—not in a way of their choosing. They acted as if they had run into a solid object, yet nothing was there.

The wolves got up and continued to ram themselves into the invisible barrier, still driven by Wyjec's command to attack the man's legs. He sent out the impression for the wolves to stop and return to his side. Most responded, though nearly half of his family lay on the ground, unmoving. A quick inspection with the red *myelur* showed Wyjec that none of the fallen wolves were still breathing.

This isn't possible! How did he do that? Wyjec then realized that it would not be possible for a normal man, but he, himself, could do things others could not. *The soldier can wield the blue* myelur!

This understanding hit Wyjec in a few ways. First, his wolves could not harm the soldier. Second, the man could shield not only himself but an area around him—something Wyjec himself did not know how to do. Lastly, and most disturbingly, if others could wield the *myelur* in such a manner, Wyjec was not as special as Avadi led him to believe.

The soldier now ran off into the trees, but not before picking up something off the ground. Wyjec made no movement to stop him. *Maybe he can enforce his will on me as I can to others—perhaps even better than I can.* But if that was so, why use a sword to kill Avadi? *Too many unknowns!*

The wolves returned now—each of them was injured to some degree, yet they all indicated full devotion to Wyjec. They would fight for him until they died.

What do I do now? Avadi was dead. There were others, or at least one, who could wield the blue *myelur* better than he could himself. For a moment, Wyjec considered gathering the rest of his family and heading back to the mountains. But no . . .

Those who killed Avadi needed to pay. The wolves had been able to attack the men in front of the cabin—at least he thought they had. He had watched just long enough to see the battle joined before he ran into the cabin.

Straining his ears, he listened for any indications that the men were still fighting. He heard movement, but not combat.

Summoning his wolves closer to him, he began to walk around the cabin to get a better look. He was met by five armored men, wearing the same style clothing as the soldier who had killed Avadi. They glared at him, swords in hand.

Once again, Wyjec felt a tingling on the back of his neck. The men were focused on the wolves, though one showed obvious surprise at seeing Wyjec standing among them.

"Kill the wolves. Bring the man to me," one of the men said.

They may also have the power to wield the myelur. *I can't beat them! They're too powerful. They'll kill me!* Wyjec considered his options, which were few. Only one solution came to mind which would allow him to survive—at a steep cost. Trying not to think of anything more than staying alive, Wyjec whined/growled the command for his remaining wolves to attack. They did. Wyjec did not. Instead, he turned and ran away.

Chapter 70

Rheq aimed at an enemy, using the man's red *myelur* as a way to target him, and with a sense of loss, let his last arrow loose. This shot, like his previous attacks, struck his target enough to where the quick acting poison would drop his foe in a matter of heartbeats.

It would not be enough. Sothcar's army had more men, and they kept pouring in from the surrounding trees. From the angle of the incoming arrows, the archers were at ground level.

"They must have their entire forces here," Rheq had overheard one of his comrades say as the battle wore on. "No one expected this many!"

From what Rheq understood from the last several days while traveling with the king's army, Sothcar had used smaller groups to attack areas in Nothcar randomly. Some were larger than others, like the force which decimated his hometown of Umstead. Yet, none of the groups were as large as what they faced tonight.

Sothcar had surprise on their side, better shelter in the forest, and more men. Surprisingly, neither side could gain an advantage over the other. Rheq realized what made the difference: Nothcar had healers, Sothcar did not. *Why doesn't Sothcar have healers?* Rheq did not know, and neither did he have time to consider the reasons.

In essence, Nothcar could replenish its numbers by healing the wounded. *But for how long?* Both sides suffered heavy losses. Both sides were running low on arrows. Both sides were getting tired.

Out of ammunition, Rheq considered his options. Though he had been trained to use a short sword, he was better with knives in close combat. *I'm better at hunting and tracking, not open fighting!* With that clarity came inspiration. From the trees, the enemy continued to fire arrows into the battle.

They had to pick their targets carefully as not to hit friendly soldiers. *If I can reduce the number of archers, we'll stand a better chance.*

Scanning to the east, Rheq spotted an area where no glimmers of the red *myelur* were present. There were tents between him and the spot, enough to offer coverage. Swiftly, Rheq dashed for the trees. His belt held several throwing knives, including one coated with the slow acting poison. Chaos proved to be an ally as Rheq did not attract the attention of the enemy.

Now, within the cover of the forest, Rheq used his hunting skills to move silently toward a glimmer of red to the south. Once close enough, he was able to see that the red *myelur* led him to an enemy archer.

Using one of his throwing knives, he snuck up behind the man and slit his throat. It was quiet and effective.

Rheq repeated the technique at least a dozen times—he lost count—thinning out the enemy's ranged fighters. They were spread out enough, and focused on the battle, that none of them realized what Rheq achieved.

Approaching another man, this one older and larger than most Rheq had come upon, the sky began to lighten. *We've fought through the night.* Darkness proved to be an asset for Rheq's activities, and soon that would be lost.

The pause to notice the light proved to be a mistake. Rheq brushed against a thickly leafed bush, creating enough noise to warn the enemy.

Swiveling, the archer took aim at Rheq and fired. Already in motion from the moment he made the noise, Rheq twisted his upper body while throwing his knife. The arrow missed by a hair length, but his knife found its target: the weapon pierced the meaty part of the enemy's hand and stuck into the wooden bow which it held.

Without pausing, Rheq released another knife, this one embedding in the man's left knee. The older fighter went to stand, but could not do so. Surprisingly, the soldier did not scream out in pain. Instead, he sat down, hard, grunting as he did.

"To be killed by a boy," the man said. "Terrible."

At this, Rheq did hesitate. A scan of the forest indicated no other glimmers of the red *myelur* were close. Even if the wounded man cried out, Rheq could escape easily enough.

To this point of the battle, he had fought faceless men in the dark. *This is different.* It was a chance Rheq could not let pass.

"Tell me," Rheq said, "who ordered the attacks on Umstead?"

"Umstead?" the soldier asked. "That village full of traitors? No one ordered us specifically. We were told to attack randomly. But many of us knew areas we wanted to hit. Umstead was at the forefront." The man barked out a rough laugh. "It was one of the first places we hit."

"You? You were there?" Rheq said.

"Luckily, yes. It was a race to see who would get there first. It turns out several groups arrived at the same time—most of us had the same idea."

The man was overly chatty, most likely to stall for time. Rheq knew no one was close, and the man's hands were in clear view. No help would arrive for him.

"You did more than kill them!" Rheq said, his anger building. "You burned them!"

Lifting his chin, the man said, "And it was glorious. Payment for betraying Sothcar by petitioning to leave. Let me guess. You knew people from that little village."

Rheq's hand moved to his belt where he kept his knives. "More than that," he said. "I am from Umstead."

The man laughed again. "Not anymore! It's not there! We destroyed it! Just as we are destroying your forces here."

With the sky becoming lighter, Rheq could see out to the main battlefield. The fighting was ending, but it was not Sothcar's soldiers who were standing. It was men dressed in green and silver.

"You are mistaken," Rheq said. "We're going to win."

The wounded man looked at the field through the trees. He expertly masked any emotions which would betray if what appeared to be true was in fact so. Turning back to Rheq, he said, "None of this will change what happened at Umstead. Tell me, what was it like living among traitors?"

No more stalling. Rheq heard enough. "You made them suffer," Rheq said.

"What are you going to do? Set me on fire? Go ahead. Gather firewood."

Rheq noticed the man's free hand tense up, an indication of impending action. "I'm not going to burn you. You deserve worse."

"Worse? How?" The man went to reach for something Rheq could not see. Before he could, Rheq let another throwing dagger fly. It caught the man in the forearm of his free hand. Unlike the previous daggers used, this one included something extra: the slow acting poison.

The man cursed, and tried to remove the knife but could not with his other hand still pinned to the bow. "What have you done?"

"I've killed you," Rheq said. "Umstead has been avenged."

Chapter 71

Wyjec had felt pain before, but what he experienced now made the other times seem insignificant. It was not a physical pain, as when the Masters mistreated him as a chardi. Neither was it the hurt which came when Avadi betrayed him. No, this was something worse, something of Wyjec's own doing.

He had selfishly sacrificed his wolves, his family, so that he could live.

At first, Wyjec believed it was the only way he could survive. He had run and found a place to hide among the trees. Instead of seeking safety deeper in, he had paused—his senses returning to him. From where he hid, he had watched his wolves attack. He wanted to help, but the enemy, dressed in silver and green trim and the symbol of a tree on their shields, were able to wield the power to cover themselves in a protective coating—at least for a while. The wolves were relentless and eventually wore the men down. One man with closely cropped hair fled the scene after being commanded to do so—the wolves ignored him as a non-threat.

The battle was gruesome and long. At its conclusion, each of his wolves had been killed but not before they had killed the enemy—save one. From the red *myelur*, Wyjec could see that one of the soldiers still lived, though his glimmer was flickering. *He's wounded.*

These men had prevented Wyjec from getting his revenge on Avadi. They had denied him the right to stand over the man who deceived him and let him know the penalty for such an action.

I will still get revenge, and this time, my victim will know it was me. The sun was rising, illuminating the open field. Dead bodies littered the area, and the harsh stench which accompanied battles filled the air. Wyjec stood from behind his hiding place and approached the cabin from the forest.

He remembered the woman and three children he had seen inside. *They do not matter.* He had almost reached the last of the surviving combatants, a man of some importance by the decorations on his uniform, when Wyjec felt the last of some of his energy drain. The protective coating he had used all night dropped away from him, like leaves falling from trees in autumn.

He tried to resummon the blue *myelur*, but to no avail. There were no signs of danger that Wyjec could sense. Reaching for the red *myelur*, Wyjec was able to grasp it. Again, he recalled how his different abilities were as if they drew liquid from different barrels. With the use of the red, he could kill the remaining survivor any number of ways. The first idea, and the one Wyjec liked immediately, was to stop the man from breathing. It would be a slow death and one of which the man would be aware.

Probing out with the red *myelur*, Wyjec located the section of the man's lungs which received the amber glow from the mind to continue to pump. He did not shunt it yet; the man needed to see his face first.

Stepping over dead men and wolves, Wyjec got into a position where he could see the man's face. It was clenched in pain. His left leg ended at the ankle, and Wyjec could see where one of his wolves had taken a bite out of the soldier's side, just below his chainmail shirt.

"Help me."

Wyjec took a step closer. "Help you? Why would I do that?"

Confusion added to the man's expression. "You're not dressed as a soldier from Sothcar. Why wouldn't you help me?"

"Because you killed my family," Wyjec said.

"These men?"

"No!" Wyjec barked. "The wolves were my family. You killed them!"

Shaking his head, the soldier said, "They attacked us. We were just defending ourselves."

"It's your fault," Wyjec said, taking a step closer. "You shouldn't have been here. Avadi was mine to kill."

"I— I don't understand."

Wyjec knelt in front of the man's face. "Then let me explain. You robbed me of justice. Justice has to be met."

"Listen to me," the man wheezed. "My name is Captain Mux, from Nothcar. If you help me, you will be rewarded."

"What kind of reward can you offer?"

Mux propped himself onto an elbow, though it seemed to take nearly all his strength. "What is it you want?"

"I want you to know that Wyjec, the true Master of Sothcar, was the one who killed you." With that statement, Wyjec reached through the red *myelur* and commanded Mux's body to stop breathing.

Terror filled the captain's eyes as he tried to draw a breath. At last, Wyjec reaped the benefits of revenge. He leaned closer, wanting to see the light in the man's eyes be snuffed out.

Suddenly, the captain did something Wyjec had not expected. In a motion almost swifter than the eye, Mux rammed a short sword into Wyjec's left side, between his ribs.

Immediately, yellow threads of *myelur* appeared to Wyjec's eyes. Never before had there been so many. Instinctively, Wyjec reached out with his right hand and grabbed Mux by the throat. Connecting with the yellow threads, Wyjec pulled on them with all his effort. The healing power from the effect began to reverse the damage, even to the point where the sword began to expel itself from his side.

Abruptly, the yellow threads disappeared. *No! I'm not done! I need more healing!* It was too late. Mux was dead and with it the power for Wyjec to heal himself.

The sword was still half inside his body. The pain came now, and it was nearly crippling. Desperately, Wyjec scanned around the field for any trace of red flickering. No use. Everything was dead. *I will soon join them.*

Then, from the cabin, came the sound of someone crying. *The woman! The children!* Fighting through the pain, Wyjec stood and walked into the cabin.

Chapter 72

The sun rose, red and angry into the sky. It illuminated a battlefield full of carnage with unspeakable indications of what men would do to each other when given a reason.

Danla stood on trembling legs. It was more than exhaustion which caused her body to react in such a way; the horrors of severed limbs and disembowelments covered the landscape before her.

We won, or I wouldn't be here to see this. After laying down last night to regain her strength from healing, the rest of the events were somewhat of a blur. Time and again, she would be jostled awake to heal someone and would do so. The effort of each healing drained her to the point where she would then collapse back onto the cot used for the healing of the injured.

The light of the sun had woken her moments ago. All of the healers, including Mistress Halima, were sleeping in the tent—some on cots, the others on the dirt floor. Why Danla left the tent, she could not say. She felt the urge to see the sun. What she saw instead made her wish she remained asleep.

There were soldiers wearing the king's colors moving about the camp. They went from man to man, checking for what Danla guessed were survivors. At the end of the camp, on the road which led to Sothcar, she could see several men, including Vice-Captain Becir, huddled together.

Picking her way through the fallen, Danla moved toward them. She had regained some of her strength and perhaps one of them needed aid.

Upon getting close enough, she heard the vice-captain ask, "And there is no sign of Avadi among the fallen?"

A shorter man answered, "Not from what he has told us." Danla then recognized it was Rheq speaking, the one who they had found on the road a few days previous. *But who is Rheq referring to?*

Danla moved closer. In doing so, she saw there was a man, bound hand and foot, on the ground in front of them. He wore the colors of Sothcar, blue and black with a crescent moon emblazoned on his tunic. Laid out on the road beyond were several men, all dead from what she could tell. Closer inspection revealed that each of the men had similar facial features.

"I promise you," the bound man said. "None of them are Captain Avadi. As I said before, he wasn't with us on this attack."

"Where was he then?" Vice-Captain Becir asked.

"I don't know," the prisoner answered. "I'm just a foot soldier. Rumors had it that he had holed up someplace out of the way for safety. But where, I can't say."

One of the king's men noticed Danla approaching. "Healer? Do you need something?" he asked, his brow creased.

"That's Danla," Rheq said. He stepped toward her. "Is something the matter?"

The question hit her as ridiculous. Here they were, standing among the fallen in a battle which had claimed hundreds of lives, and from what she understood, they had failed their mission to find and kill the leader.

"I … I came to see if you needed help," Danla said.

Becir looked her over. "You should rest. You need to regain your strength."

She could see that each of the men had wounds, though none were life-threatening. "Are you certain?"

The vice-captain glanced down at his arm where blood had stained through the broken links of chainmail. "It's nothing. A graze. We may need you later. Please, rest."

Numbly, Danla made her way back to the tent. She tried to avoid looking at the faces of the fallen, but with the bodies strewn about so, care had to be taken where she stepped. Two of the dead she recognized as men she had healed during the battle. *I made them whole again, just to have them die gruesome deaths.*

This understanding shook her more than any of the actual wounds on display. *This is madness. I shouldn't be here.*

Shouts of surprise jerked her out of the stupor. Quickly, she faced toward where the sounds originated. It was Vice-Captain Becir and his men. One of them was pointing to the west. *Are we under attack again?*

Squinting, Danla's eyes followed to where the man pointed. From out of the forest came a singular figure. Even from this distance, Danla recognized him. It was Pendr. *He's alive!* The large man strode out from the tree line. He was on foot and appeared out of breath. However, it was what Pendr held in one hand which made Danla's blood turn cold.

Chapter 73

Trying not to stumble as he walked, Pendr concentrated on placing one foot in front of the other. He had run until he could no more, then even walking became a challenge. He had not heard the wolves in a while—a good sign.

After running away from the strange man and the wolves which accompanied him, Pendr skirted to the north, then the east in an effort to find the king's main forces. *Who is the odd man? And why do the wolves obey his commands?* Pendr had seen dogs and horses be trained, but not wolves. Never wolves. They were too wild to bend to man's will.

While running, Pendr had heard the wolves howl and then the sounds of fighting. He assumed the animals attacked Captain Mux and the rest of his squad. That was a concern. Most of the men who had traveled with Pendr had only a simplistic ability with the blue *myelur*—they could not hold it for long. Chances were that they were spent during the original battle when they attacked the men protecting the cabin.

Going back to help them fight was not his priority. Captain Mux had made that clear before the battle. The main goal, and the one that truly mattered, was killing Avadi. But killing him was not enough, a report of the death of Sothcar's leader was needed, or the fighting could continue for no good reason.

Pendr knew that if he traveled east, he would eventually find the king's road. From there, he could find the rest of the army—the ones headed to Blythewood. *I hope there is someone left to report to.* The attack happened last night. The king's forces were large in number, and well trained. It also had healers—something which Sothcar lacked if Pendr believed the word around camp.

Danla. I pray to the Light she lives. That, more than anything, drove Pendr forward until now, when he stepped out of the forest and into the light. The sun was red, a strange sight indeed, and not one which Pendr had ever recalled seeing.

It was not the sound of battle which helped Pendr adjust his course to arrive where the army resided. It was the smell—the stench of newly butchered men. The dead lay in heaps on the battlefield. At the southernmost part of the road, Pendr noticed a group of men wearing the king's colors of green and silver, washed in the red light of the sun. One of them saw him and pointed.

Pendr noticed someone that raised his spirits to a level he had not felt since the march south began. Danla stood among the fallen, halfway between a large tent and where the group of men stood. *She's alive!*

He saw her recognize him as well, but her expression tightened. *Why isn't she happy to see me?* Her gaze was not upon his face, but rather what he held at his side: Avadi's severed head. Even with all the bloodshed around her, Pendr understood that seeing him holding a bodiless head would be unsettling. *Duty first, then I'll comfort her.*

Watching his step, Pendr headed to the men who had spotted him. One of them was Vice-Captain Becir. What Pendr found most curious was one of the men standing next to him. It appeared to be Rheq, the smaller man who had abandoned him and his group. *Why is he here?*

That question would have to await an answer. Sitting on the ground was a man in Sothcar's colors. He was bound, and in front of him lay bodies of his comrades. It only took a moment for Pendr to piece together the situation. *Becir is looking for confirmation that we succeeded.*

Without saying a word to the rest of the men, Pendr strode up to the captive and held up Avadi's head. "Is this Avadi?"

The enemy's face betrayed the truth before his words could. "Yes. That's him. How did you find—?"

Pendr cut the man off by tossing Avadi's head by the other slain soldiers. Addressing Becir, he said, "The mission was a success, Vice-Captain."

Chapter 74

Nestov woke to red light flowing through his window. It was morning, at least from what his body told him from the amount of sleep he had experienced. Brother Mey was already up and dressed, as was the case each day.

"Ah, good," the muscular monk said, "you're awake."

"What is that light?" Nestov asked, propping himself up on two elbows.

Mey slid the green and silver curtains to the side, allowing even more light in. "It's the sun."

"The sun?" Nestov lifted the quilted blanket off him and swung his legs to the side of the bed. "Have you ever seen it that red before?"

"No." Mey frowned. "I don't care for it, either."

Nestov stood and went to the window. In the past, when the sun was different colors, it was due to clouds or smoke in the air. Not today. The sky was clear aside from the red sun.

"I think we need to seek out Mistress Sheric, *now*," Nestov said.

Mey displayed his agreement by helping Nestov put on his formal robe.

The guard at the door, one Nestov had yet to meet, agreed easily enough to escort Nestov and Mey to see Sheric. They found her in the same room where they first met. She sat behind the table, shoulders slumping. "You've seen it, I take it?" she asked tiredly.

"The red sun?" Nestov answered. "Yes. Do you know what it means?"

Sheric's eyes hardened around the edges. "It's a portent—a dire one."

"Portent?" Mey asked.

"It means a warning, an indication of something foul or possibly malevolent," Nestov said.

"An apt explanation," Sheric said. "The red sun is one of the signs we look for when there is a dangerous unbalance in the *myelur*. It appears you were right to warn us."

Nestov felt his body tense. "What would have caused the sun to change color?"

"The yellow *myelur*. It was used recently, and significantly." Mistress Sheric slumped even more as if a great burden rested on her back.

"What do you mean by significantly?" Mey asked. "Does it make a difference how it is used?"

"Most certainly," Sheric said. "I did more reading since our last meeting. I learned something I hadn't fully understood before. Let me explain. The blue *myelur* is used for protection. It is the most common and has the least impact on the balance. Many people can use the blue, some without realizing it, and it does little to offset things.

"The red *myelur* is the least common, aside from the yellow. At its most basic, the red allows a person to see the life force in individuals—often as red glimmers, hence the name. More powerful users of the red can manifest the red outwardly to affect others, causing their bodies to act differently. However, accounts of such actions are so old and vague; we don't know much more than that.

"The green *myelur* is restorative by nature. It allows someone to draw from their life force and give it to another. The result is healing. It is considered a selfless act, therefore, by its nature, is considered benevolent. Use of the green *myelur* often counters use of the red and blue effectively."

"And the yellow? What have you not told us before?" Nestov asked, a sense of dread lurking within him as he posed the question.

"The yellow is the opposite of the green. I did explain that it is extremely rare if you recall," Sheric said. "The yellow *myelur* is selfish. It takes the life force from another and draws it to the user. From what we

296

have gathered over time, it is also addictive. Unlike the other aspects of the *myelur*, once a person uses the yellow, they become dependent upon it."

Nestov understood. "Someone, someone very powerful, is using the yellow *myelur*. Because it is so potent, whatever they did recently was enough to cause a noticeable change—like with the red sun."

"Exactly," Sheric said. "The *myelur* is now ominously out of balance, and will continue to get worse with each use of the yellow *myelur*."

"What can we do to stop it?" Mey asked, his voice tight.

"As you noted in our previous meeting, we need to find this person and stop them," Sheric said.

Nestov noticed that her words seemed to lack conviction. "Will that be enough?"

She looked up, tears in the corners of her eyes. "I hope so. What scares me the most is what you told me when we first met. If your abbot was correct, then anyone who is now born with the ability to use the yellow will be able to do so easily."

"If the balance is off now, with only one person using it, then—" Nestov began before Sheric interrupted him.

"Then, we are indeed headed for dark times which could destroy us all."

Chapter 75

Wyjec felt as strong as he ever had, at least physically. Draining five people using the yellow *myelur* was exactly what he needed. Not only did it heal the sword wound in his side, but it also helped him regain his physical strength.

Walking away to the west of the cabin, he considered what to do next. All of the wolves he brought with him, including Alpha, were dead. He tried to push away the grief, but it was too fresh. They had all died to save him. *Wait, that's not true. Not all of them are dead!*

Each night, Wyjec would send wolves out to scout—one in each direction. Three of them had yet to return. Reaching out with the red *myelur*, he could sense them. It was akin to feeling which way the wind was blowing by moving around in a circle. His remaining wolves were moving closer to him. In a matter of time, they would rejoin him.

All is not lost. Or is it? The vision of him sitting in a palace no longer held the same attraction. Men could never be trusted. That point was driven home, literally, when Mux had stabbed him. *I will never truly be safe around men.*

That singular thought expanded into a greater realization. *No one is truly safe around men. They are, at their center, treacherous beings. I must stop them.* To do so would take more than just a handful of wolves, no matter how loyal. More than that, Wyjec needed to learn more about his gifts and how to make them even stronger. *Others may be able to use the myelur, but I can be better. I will be better!*

That would take time. He would need to find and breed more wolves. He would have to find information about the *myelur* and how to increase his power. He would need to practice and train. Even considering all these barriers in his way, he would grow stronger. This he vowed.

ABOUT THE AUTHOR

J. Lloyd Morgan is a best-selling author and English Professor. He graduated from Brigham Young University with a degree in Communications and a minor in English. Morgan earned a Master's degree in Creative Writing in 2014. He has lived all over the United States, but now resides in North Carolina with his wife and four daughters. Aside from writing, Morgan is an avid reader. He's also a huge fan of baseball and enjoys listening to music.

Aside from *Darker the Shadow*, Morgan's other published novels include *The Bariwon Chronicles* (*The Hidden Sun, The Waxing Moon, The Zealous Star*), *Wall of Faith, Bring Down the Rain,* and *The Mirror of the Soul* written in conjunction with musician Chris de Burgh.

His published short stories include "Howler King," "I Heard the Bells on Christmas Day," "With Bells On" and award-winning "The Doughnut."

An anthology of short stories, observations and insights called *The Night the Port-A-Potty Burned Down and Other Stories* was released at the end of 2012.

www.ingramcontent.com/pod-product-compliance
Lightning Source LLC
Chambersburg PA
CBHW070653180626
46817CB00006B/2348